His to Claim

ALSO BY SHELLY BELL

At His Mercy

His to Claim

A Forbidden Lovers Novel

SHELLY BELL

FOREVER

New York   Boston

Copyright © 2018 by Shelly Bell

Cover design by Elizabeth Turner. Cover image © Shutterstock. Cover copyright © 2018 by Hachette Book Group, Inc.

Forever
Hachette Book Group
1290 Avenue of the Americas
New York, NY 10104
forever-romance.com
twitter.com/foreverromance

First Edition: April 2018

Forever is an imprint of Grand Central Publishing.
The Forever name and logo are trademarks of Hachette Book Group, Inc.

The publisher is not responsible for websites (or their content) that are not owned by the publisher.

The Hachette Speakers Bureau provides a wide range of authors for speaking events. To find out more, go to www.hachettespeakersbureau.com or call (866) 376-6591.

LCCN: 2017963493

ISBNs: 978-1-4555-9599-0 (pbk.), 978-1-4555-9598-3 (ebook)

Printed in the United States of America

LSC-C

10 9 8 7 6 5 4 3 2 1

To Spencer—for giving me one of my favorite lines in this book and for making me laugh. I'm so proud of you.

Acknowledgments

I never knew how many people went into making a book until I visited the Grand Central Forever office in New York! Thank you to my editors, Madeleine Colavita and Amy Pierpont, for your patience and guidance. Working with both of you has been a dream come true. Also, a huge thank you to everyone at Forever who worked behind the scenes to get *At His Mercy* and *His to Claim* into readers' hands.

Writing is a solitary profession, but knowing that my author friends are only a click of a button away helps me through those tough days. Thank you to Aliza Mann, MK Schiller, Heather Novak, Sage Spelling, Dana Nussio, Isabella Drake, Sienna Snow, Codi Gary, and T. J. Kline for always bringing a smile to my face.

Thank you to Jodi Ellen Malpas and Alessandra Torre for your support and all your kind words. I can't tell you how much it has meant to me.

Thank you to Neda Amini, publicist extraordinaire, for keeping me organized and for being a champion of my books. I can't wait until I finally get to meet you!

A huge thank you to Jessica Alvarez for helping me through one of the roughest years of my life. I'm thankful to have you in my corner.

To my husband and kids, thank you for peeling me off the ceiling when I get a little crazy. I hope you know how much I love you.

Last but never least, to my readers. I know there are thousands of books out there, and I'm honored that you choose to read mine. A special shout-out to Melanie G., Miriam L., Rachel B., Crystal B., Jennifer R., Kathleen R., Carolina L., Christi L., Amy B., Ralou, Tamara B., Jennifer A., Jennifer S., Misty P., Nicole K., Rebecca W., Susan M., Cara R., Crystal C. B., Bridget W., and the Shelly Bell Insider's Facebook group. Thank you for going above and beyond for me. I love each and every one of you.

His to Claim

PROLOGUE

Twenty-four years ago

Ryder McKay woke up in his race car bed, sweaty and damp underneath his new Star Wars comforter.

The room was pitch-black.

He didn't like pitch-black.

That's why he had his R2-D2 night-light. But it wasn't working, because if it was, he'd be able to see something other than black.

His dad didn't think he needed a night-light. He'd said it was only for babies.

Ryder wasn't no baby.

His brother, Finn, had told him he sometimes got scared of the dark, too, and Finn was *fifteen*, ten years older than him. Then Finn had bought Ryder the night-light from his *own allowance*.

Ryder missed Finn a lot. He'd gone to visit his mother in a whole 'nother state for the summer.

Ryder didn't have no mother.

She'd died giving birth to him. That's what Dad had said when his eyes had gotten shiny.

Ryder had killed her.

Dad hadn't said *that*, but Ryder was smart, so he'd figured it out.

Ryder had never even seen a picture of her because Dad didn't have none. It must make him too sad. Ryder got sad about it too sometimes because all his friends had mommies.

But he had Finn and that was better than a mommy. When Ryder got scared, Finn would make him feel safe.

Dad and Nanny Spector didn't do the kinds of things Finn did to make him feel safe. No hugs. No smiles. No funny jokes. Dad just patted him on the back and told Nanny to take care of him. Nanny pretended she liked Ryder, but she liked his daddy more. He knew this because he'd seen them hugging and kissing in Daddy's bed once. Naked! It was yucky and it made him feel weird to see, so he'd left before they knew he was there. He didn't know why she had to sleep in Daddy's bed when she had her own room in the house.

He didn't like Nanny. Her breath smelled funny after she drank from the square bottle she kept hidden in her purse. Sometimes she fell asleep with the bottle in her arms like it was her baby. On those nights, Ryder couldn't wake her up even when he jumped on her bed.

A loud bang came from downstairs, shattering the silence.

His body twitched before he lay perfectly still.

It sounded like a firecracker had exploded *inside* the house.

That would be so cool.

He hopped out of his bed and put his arms out in front of him to find the door.

He heard angry voices. His daddy and a lady. It wasn't Nanny. This lady was talking in another language, but he understood one word very clear.

Ryder.

Ryder slid his hands along the smooth wall until he found the door. Not wanting to make any noise, he slowly turned the knob and cracked open the door. The shouts grew louder.

Careful as to not make a sound, he tiptoed along the carpeted hallway, passing by all the fancy artwork on the walls that Daddy always warned him not to touch.

"You're not taking him, you crazy bitch!" Daddy shouted.

Daddy said a bad word.

He must really be mad.

Ryder got on his knees and looked down through the white wooden railing. Yep, there was his daddy, and he was wearing his shiny pajamas, so the lady must have woken Daddy out of bed.

The lady kept yelling at his daddy in that funny language while waving something gray in her hand. Every time she moved, her long, straight black hair swayed. He'd never seen hair so long. It was like that stupid princess stuck in the tower, only this lady's hair was black instead of yellow. Black as his room without his night-light.

And she was just as scary.

"Give me the gun before you hurt someone," his daddy said. He spoke to her like Ryder talked to his friend's dog when he wanted to pet him.

But maybe the lady didn't understand or maybe it was because his daddy didn't say *please*, because she started screaming for Ryder. Then she said another word he recognized.

Mama.

Ryder must have made a noise because both the lady and his daddy turned their heads toward the stairs.

Was the lady his mama?

He touched the top of his head. He had black hair too.

But his mother was dead.

Wasn't she?

The lady started running toward the stairs and Daddy grabbed her arm, swinging her around and stopping her from going anywhere. She growled like a wild animal and then they were wrestling over that gray thing in her hand. For a moment, they looked like they were dancing, and he giggled.

There was a loud bang, so loud it hurt Ryder's ears and made him shake. Warm pee trickled down his legs and turned the white carpet yellow.

The lady slumped to the floor in front of the stairs and Daddy stood over her with the gray thing in his hand. There was bright red blood all over both of them and it was pouring out of her stomach onto the tiled floor.

Ryder wanted to run and hide, but he was too scared, so he curled into a ball, hoping he could make himself small enough to disappear.

The lady's eyes rolled upward, and she stared at him. "Ryder," she said between coughs. Blood was dripping from her mouth now as she whispered his name over and over.

Then she stopped whispering. Stopped coughing. Just... stopped.

That's when he knew that the lady with the long black hair was dead.

Daddy had killed her.

Daddy spoke on the phone. "Got a situation. I need the crew here for cleanup." He hung up without saying good-bye and looked upstairs.

Ryder's heart was beating really fast. Would Daddy kill him next?

His eyes filled with tears. He didn't want to die.

He crawled backward until he could no longer see downstairs. After jumping to his feet, he grabbed a towel from the closet and tried to get the pee out from the carpet. Maybe if he cleaned it up good enough, Daddy wouldn't notice. As he worked, he heard doors slamming, lots of footsteps, and a bunch of different men's voices.

A few minutes later, he ran to his room and stripped out of his wet clothes. He threw them and the towel into the back of his closet and changed into dry pajamas. Things began to get quieter downstairs as he fell back into bed and drew the covers over his head.

It was pitch-black again.

But this time, he didn't mind.

Because it was much scarier out there in the light.

His door creaked and someone walked across the carpet toward him.

He held his breath, wishing that Finn were here to save him.

"I know you're up, champ," Daddy said, dragging the blanket off his head.

Light beamed into his room from the hallway. Ryder blinked, his eyes focusing.

Wearing different pajamas than earlier, Daddy stood over him and rubbed his eyes with his hands like he'd just woken up.

He didn't look mad anymore.

Just tired.

"Was she my mama?" Ryder whispered.

Daddy's eyebrows crinkled. "Who?"

Ryder sat up. "The lady you killed downstairs."

Daddy grabbed his shoulders. "Nothing happened."

"But I saw—"

"Nothing." Daddy sat on the bed and leaned in close, his breath blowing on Ryder's face. It smelled like Nanny Spector. "You saw nothing. You had a bad dream. But Daddy's here now. He'll always be here. You know why?"

"Why?"

"Because you're mine." Daddy put his hands on both of Ryder's cheeks. "As my son, you belong to me. And that means, no matter what happens, Ryder, I'll never let you go. Now go to sleep and don't let me ever hear you talking about the bad dream again. Because if you do...well, let's just say, I would hate for anyone to get hurt."

Ryder didn't want to belong to Daddy.

Not if it meant being trapped in this big, scary house like a hamster in its cage.

But if he told on Daddy, Finn could get hurt. And he didn't want nothing bad to happen to Finn.

He'd have to keep it a secret.

Even if it killed him.

ONE

Present day

Ryder McKay knocked back a shot of Jameson, slammed the glass down on the bar, and grabbed the next one, relishing the smooth burn sliding down his throat. It wasn't every day your brother was about to marry the daughter of the country's most powerful man.

The press was calling the union a "marriage made in heaven."

More like a deal with the devil.

Only in this case, it had been a deal between *two* devils. Two criminals posing as legitimate businessmen who were likely using their offspring to solidify some kind of pact between the two families. If Keane McKay and Ian Sinclair joined forces instead of working against each other, they'd have the potential to be largest crime syndicate in North America.

It had been years since Ryder had turned his back on Keane and that life. After he'd graduated high school, he'd made good on his lifelong promise to himself. He'd moved out and never returned.

Any conversation with Keane over the past decade had been limited to Ryder's insistence that his father not contact him again. It had taken several years, but he had eventually gotten the hint and stopped calling.

To maintain his distance from Keane, Ryder hadn't planned on attending his brother Finn's wedding.

Then last week, he'd come across a photograph that had changed his mind.

A photo of Jane.

Recalling the vixen he'd spent one wild night with almost a year ago, he licked remnants of the whiskey from his lips and swirled his finger along the rim of the glass. Before falling asleep that night, he'd realized one time inside of Jane hadn't been enough for him.

He'd wanted more.

Not just sex, but the chance to get to know her.

Crazy thoughts for a man who'd spent his adult life never having sex with the same woman twice.

But she'd pulled a Cinderella on him, fleeing his hotel room in the middle of the night. Other than her first name, he'd known nothing about her.

Obsessed with finding the woman he couldn't forget, he'd wasted months searching for her. He'd checked with the organization that had sponsored the conference where they'd met. Called other attendees. Combed through photos of the conference. Hell, at one point, he'd been so desperate, he'd hired a private detective.

And what had he found?

Nothing.

It was as if she'd never existed.

His fingers tightened around his glass.

He'd been a fool.

Because now he knew the truth.

Shortly after their night together, he'd realized someone had copied design and software files from his computer. He hadn't wanted to believe that Jane had been the one to do it—the time stamp didn't match—but last week, Ryder stumbled upon a recent article online about his father's foray into the automated commercial kitchen business, the same business as Ryder's company, Novateur.

Then the photo accompanying the article caught his attention.

It was a photo of the company's vice president of innovation standing beside Keane.

Jane.

A muscle popped in his jaw as he acknowledged once again what an idiot he'd been that night.

He'd played right into her hands, lowering his guard when he brought her to his hotel room, not suspecting she would stab him in the back while he slept.

Novateur was one of the first in the world to bring "smart kitchen" technology to restaurants and bakeries. Already in business together providing productivity consultations to restaurants, Ryder and his best friend Tristan had formed the company shortly after their discussion that automation was an effective way to cut costs and increase efficiency in restaurant kitchens. Voice-activated appliances, robotic arms, and conveyor belts for restaurants and bakeries—even the smaller, family-owned ones—were now an affordable reality.

Novateur was the only restaurant automation company to custom design and install the technology per the customer's specific needs—until McKay Industries.

The evidence was indisputable. Jane had been the one to steal the designs for his father.

Had she thought Ryder wouldn't find out? Or had she thought that changing the time stamp would save her?

In the end, the joke was on her. Because anything she copied was worthless without key pieces of code. That alone should have given him the satisfaction to move on.

And yet he couldn't. Something about her didn't add up. He couldn't equate the woman he'd met that night with the woman he now knew her to be. She'd acted so innocent in his bed, her eyes widening in something that looked like awe as he'd removed his clothes and given her the first glimpse of his cock.

Not that it wasn't awe-worthy. He didn't bother with false modesty.

But Jane's response had seemed . . . honest. She'd actually flinched when he'd first entered her. Even now, he could hear her husky voice in his head and the way she whispered his name as he brought her to climax. He remembered the sensation of her silky thighs against his cheeks and how tight her pussy had clamped around him when she came.

He rubbed the stubble on his chin with his knuckles.

Since that night, every time it came down to sealing the
deal with a woman, thoughts of Jane popped into his head.

And while he could admit he was bit of an asshole when
it came to the opposite sex, he wouldn't fuck one woman
while thinking of another.

She hadn't only stolen his technology.

She'd stolen his *fucking mojo*.

He should hate her, and yet there were nights he'd roll
over in bed and reach for her, only to find the sheets cold.

According to Finn, all of McKay's essential employees
had been invited to the wedding.

Which was why Ryder was here.

Tonight, he was on a mission.

Find Jane.

Confront her.

And get her out of his system, once and for all.

Whatever it took.

Even if whatever it took meant him having to dress in
a monkey suit, smile at people he detested, and kiss up to
his father. If he'd shown up at McKay Industries, no doubt
Keane would have had security toss Ryder out of the building.

But he couldn't keep Ryder from the wedding.

And Jane wouldn't be expecting him.

Ryder gulped down his next shot, not even bothering to
enjoy it, and returned it bottom side up to the white-satin-
covered bar top. Thank fuck his brother and his fiancée had
chosen to get married in the city's only five-star hotel instead of having the traditional church wedding. He'd never

make it through the next couple of hours if he had to do it sober.

"Make the next one a double and keep 'em coming," he told the bartender.

A hard slap on his tuxedo-clad back had his teeth rattling. He didn't need to turn around to know who had smacked the shit out of him. Finn may be ten years older but he'd never gone easy on him.

"Save some of the good shit for the other guests," his brother said.

Ryder turned around, relieved that Finn was alone. He definitely needed more whiskey before dealing with the rest of the family. "Thought you'd be getting ready with Keane and all the other groomsmen."

Although they shared a father, they looked nothing alike. The only thing they had in common was their gray eyes, a trait shared by all the McKay men. Otherwise, Ryder took after his Mexican mother with his dark brown hair and tanned skin while Finn was a younger version of their Irish father with reddish-blond hair. Not to mention, Ryder towered over Finn by a good five inches, something he never let his older brother forget.

Smooth shaven and with his hair cut short, Ryder barely recognized his brother. Where was the beard? His trademark long hair? This guy was a carbon copy of their father. Of course, it had been a couple years since Ryder had last seen Finn. It had killed Ryder to do it, but once his brother had chosen to take a position at McKay Industries, Ryder had been forced to put some space between them.

Finn gave him a wink. "Wanted to make sure my best man hadn't taken off with some random chick to get his pre–wedding ceremony blow job."

More like Finn was worried Ryder had again changed his mind about attending the wedding and wouldn't show. Understandable, since Ryder had questioned his brother more than once as to why Finn was marrying Ciara.

Bad enough Finn had left the attorney general's office to work at McKay Industries, but to marry into a family possibly even more corrupt than theirs? Finn must have lost his damned mind.

Ryder scratched his head. He had to try one last time to convince Finn he was making the wrong decision. "Listen, I'm sure you don't want to hear this, but—"

"I'm marrying Ciara." Finn held up his hand, effectively stopping Ryder from continuing. "I appreciate that you're concerned for me, but I assure you, I know what I'm doing."

Folding his arms across his chest, Ryder snorted and leaned his back against the bar. "Yeah, because after all, your first marriage went so well."

His brother shifted his weight from one foot to the other. "Marriage is complicated."

Complicated was something Ryder didn't need in his life. That's why he was never getting married. "Especially when your wife tries to kill you."

"She wasn't trying to kill me," Finn mumbled, rubbing the back of his neck. "Greta was an expert marksman. Got me exactly where she wanted to."

Ryder would never forget the night he'd gotten the

phone call that his brother had been shot. Nearly ran off the road trying to get to the hospital, only to arrive and find his brother resting comfortably on his stomach as he watched the Tigers' game on his iPhone.

Asshole.

"What does your new woman think of the scar on your ass?" Ryder asked Finn.

Finn grinned. "She thinks it's sexy."

"Only the daughter of a criminal would find a bullet to the ass sexy."

His brother shushed him and stepped closer, looking around the empty room in a move that hinted at paranoia. "Keep your voice down, would you?"

Ryder tamped down his urge to chuckle. Fucking with his brother rated high on his list of favorite things to do. "What are you worried about? Someone finding out that your future father-in-law is a criminal or that your ex shot you in the ass when you asked for a divorce?" he asked loud enough for anyone close by to overhear, including the bartender, who stopped his cleaning at Ryder's words and let out a snort.

Finn only shook his head. "You're an asshole. Do you know that?" He clamped a hand on Ryder's shoulder and squeezed. *Hard.* "But you're also the best brother any guy could ask for. I'm thankful every day that Dad boinked the maid and fathered you. Which is why I'm going to tell you that when it comes to Ciara and her family, I know what I'm getting into."

"I thought we agreed we were both getting out of the

family business. Me with Novateur and you by becoming some hotshot lawyer. We don't need Dad's money and we certainly don't need his connections."

His brother clenched his jaw and looked away, almost guiltily. "As long as Dad is still in charge of McKay Industries, we'll never be free of him. Don't you get it by now?"

"So you just gave up and figured you'd make him even more powerful by marrying a rival's daughter?"

Pinching the bridge of his nose, Finn sighed. "I told you. I love—"

"You love Ciara." He rolled his eyes. Childish, but appropriate. "I heard you the first twenty times. But I still don't believe you."

Ryder wasn't completely dead inside. He had the ability to love. He loved his brother, Tristan, and an ice-cold beer at a ball game, but as for the so-called everlasting romantic kind of love?

Not in his genetic makeup.

His father was on marriage number four—*no, five*—and his brother's first marriage had ended in gunplay.

The odds were definitely not in Ryder's favor...or his brother's.

Long ago, Ryder had made the decision never to get married or have children. Both a wife and a kid would be a vulnerability he couldn't afford. Look at what Keane had done by stealing Ryder's designs and competing against him. No, Ryder could never give Keane that kind of power over him.

Finn shot him a look of disappointment. "I know you

don't, but I wish you had at least a little faith that I know what I'm doing." He puffed out his chest and straightened his bow tie, cutting the awkward tension with his smirk. "After all, I'm the big brother. You're supposed to look up to me."

"And I would if you weren't such a midget," Ryder deadpanned.

His brother grabbed his crotch. "Yeah, well, unlike you, I'm large where it counts."

Ryder was about to challenge that comment when his brother's smirk slid off his face and all the joy was sucked out of the room. He didn't have to turn around to know the source of the sucking.

"Pop," Ryder said in greeting.

A firm hand clasped his shoulder and a raspy voice, created by a two-pack-a-day cigarette habit, came from behind him. "Ryder. Good to see you, son."

Too bad he couldn't say the same.

He waited for the scent of cigarettes to assault his nose and was surprised when it didn't happen. Had the old man finally quit?

His father moved to his side, giving Ryder a glimpse of the man he hadn't seen in years.

Always robust and thick around the waist, his father had shrunk to half his old size. Still not skinny, but to Ryder, the difference was jarring. His white hair had thinned on top, showing off the reddened scalp underneath it, and his wrinkled skin seemed especially pronounced because of his weight loss.

He looked...tired. Old. Too old for seventy-one.

For a moment, Ryder experienced a rush of compassion for his father, until he remembered that his father had never once had any compassion for anyone else.

He expected a lecture. A snide remark. Something.

But his father simply gave him a nod of regard and focused his attention on Finn. "There's been a slight delay with the wedding ceremony. Apparently, Jane has had an incident with her bridesmaid dress and had to run to the bridal shop to have it repaired. She's on her way now."

Ryder froze mid-breath. Although he tried to keep his voice disinterested, he was anything but. "Jane?"

His father's eyes twinkled with something resembling pride. "My step-granddaughter. Or soon-to-be step-granddaughter."

No.

It had to be a different Jane.

"Ciara has a child?" he asked his brother, surprised that fact hadn't come up before.

"Jane's an adult now. Ciara had her at fifteen," Finn said quietly. "Jane was raised by Ciara's aunt and uncle down in Florida. Even now, not a lot of people in our circle know Ciara has a daughter, so I'd appreciate it if you kept the information to yourself."

Whoever this Jane was, anger flared hot in his gut on her behalf.

They wanted to keep the girl a secret as if she had a reason to be ashamed. Why even bother inviting her to the wedding?

Mumbled curses and frantic footsteps echoed from down the hall, growing louder as someone approached.

Ryder's mouth went dry.

Even mumbled, he'd recognize that silken voice anywhere.

Like a tornado, she whirled into the room, every part of her in disarray, from her long, dark brown curls to the thick black-framed glasses tilted on her nose.

She was as beautiful as he'd remembered.

It made it difficult to remember she was the enemy.

"I'm so sorry," she said, gripping the sides of her dress in her hands to keep it off the floor and looking down at her feet as if worried she'd trip. "As I was leaving my apartment, the hem of my dress got caught in the"—she looked up and her eyes widened as she caught sight of Ryder—"door."

This wasn't the plan. He'd wanted to surprise her.

But he hadn't expected to be just as shocked.

If Ciara was Jane's mother, that made Jane his . . .

He couldn't even finish the thought.

Finn kissed her warmly on the cheek. "Jane. This is my brother, Ryder. Ryder, this is—"

"Jane," she said, smiling tightly while her swanlike throat worked over a swallow. "Your soon-to-be stepniece."

TWO

One year ago...

Joining the hundreds of other conference attendees for evening cocktails, Jane stepped into the ballroom of Mackinac Island's Grand Hotel. The dichotomy of having the state's biggest business innovation conference on an island that didn't even allow for automobiles on its roads wasn't lost on her.

She smoothed her fingertips over her head to tame any frizzy wisps of hair before remembering that she'd had it professionally straightened a couple days ago.

How long would it take before she wouldn't feel like a little girl playing dress-up? Thanks to McKay Industries' generous clothing allowance, she'd be able to purchase a red Armani power suit for the day's activities and a dressier outfit for tonight's cocktail party. Conservative yet a tad provocative, the Carolina Herrera white button-down silk blouse wrapped around her like a second skin, and the black

A-line faille party skirt flared out at the knees, showing off her newly waxed legs.

When she'd looked in the mirror a few minutes ago, she'd barely recognized herself.

It was amazing what a trip to the spa and a pair of contacts could do.

And she owed it all to Keane McKay.

She fiddled with the diamonds dangling from her earlobes. Her jewelry alone cost more than she could earn in a year as an intern at McKay Industries.

But when your boss gave you an opportunity to represent a billion-dollar corporation, you accepted it and all the gifts he gave you. She didn't understand why he'd taken such an interest in her. He had nothing to gain by winning her favor. Yet the spring before Jane had graduated from the prestigious Edison University's Lancaster Business School, Keane had called Isaac Lancaster, the dean of the business department, to offer Jane a paid internship at McKay Industries. It had only been after she'd accepted and moved to the city that she'd learned her mother was dating Keane's son Finn.

And that her mother hadn't even known that Keane had offered Jane the job.

Jane hadn't been disappointed. *Really.* After all, Ciara had never wanted anything to do with her before. Why should now be any different?

While McKay Industries was known for its controversial and often hostile mergers and acquisitions, Keane had placed her in its much smaller innovation division, teaching her about start-ups and emerging technologies. Still, she was shocked when he'd not only insisted she attend this conference, but also paid for her to have a day at a spa, where she'd been treated to the works, including a manicure, a haircut and style, and makeup.

For the first time in her twenty-two years, she could pretend she was someone different than Plain Jane, the virgin who gave modern meaning to the word *wallflower*. She looked as lush and regal as the Victorian hotel she was standing in, but inside, she knew the truth.

She didn't belong here.

But what else was new?

She didn't belong anywhere.

She owed it to Keane to network this weekend. He wouldn't have sent her if he didn't believe in her, and she didn't want to disappoint him after he'd been so kind to her.

She'd pretend she belonged here until she actually believed it herself. She'd smile at people. Meet their eyes. Engage in conversation. Live a little.

Be the opposite of Plain Jane.

No one had to know she wasn't actually an executive at McKay. Tonight she would forget that the only thing she had less experience in than business was in the bedroom.

She scanned the room for a semifriendly face. For some reason, she'd expected a younger, geekier crowd, but the average age was probably around forty and there didn't appear to be a geek in the crowd. Everyone was polished, suave, and experienced. These were the corporate executives. Not the brilliant minds behind the innovations. Maybe a little liquid courage would help loosen her tongue.

Waiters walked through the room offering glasses of wine, but she'd never been much of a wine drinker. If anything, hard lemonade was more her speed, but somehow she didn't think they stocked it behind the bar.

Leaving her spot by the entrance, she made her way toward the bar, stopping only momentarily to snag a cheese puff off a tray of passing hors d'oeuvres. Remembering she hadn't eaten since noon, she popped it in her mouth as she stood in line for a drink and surveyed the limited selection of premium booze.

After only a minute, she got to the front. "I'll have an Absolut and plain water, please," she said, choosing her uncle's standard drink. She'd accidentally tried it once, thinking it was a glass of water. When she finally stopped choking, she'd sworn off vodka for the rest of her life. Of course, she had been twelve at the time.

"You strike me as more of a Sex on the Beach type of girl," said a low male voice from behind her.

She spun around, expecting a gray-haired executive in a three-piece suit.

She'd never been more wrong.

Sex.

That was the first thing—the *only* thing—that came to mind. Hot, sweaty, messy sex on every conceivable surface. It radiated off him like heat radiated off the sun. Her tongue stuck to the roof of her dry mouth as every bit of moisture in her body flew south.

His dark brown hair had that tousled look, giving the impression he'd just rolled out of bed and run his fingers through it. Unlike the other men there tonight, he wore dark jeans and an azure V-neck sweater that clung to his torso and hinted at the muscles underneath.

But it was his eyes that drew her in. At first glance, she'd thought they were blue, but close up, she realized they had picked up the color of his sweater. In actuality, it was like looking into a piece of glass, the irises an unusual light gray. She blinked, realizing she was staring. "Excuse me?" she finally said, not sure if seconds or minutes had passed since he'd first spoken.

"Sex. On. The. Beach," he said, punctuating every word so that she could almost imagine the feel of the cool, wet sand beneath her and his weight on top. "The mixed drink."

He ordered himself a scotch on the rocks and reached around her, his forearm brushing the side of her breast. She sucked in a breath at the contact, heat shooting between her thighs and her nipples hardening underneath her blouse. His gaze dropped to her chest as he passed her the vodka and he made a noise in his throat, something between a grunt and a hiss, making her wonder what he'd sound like if she dropped to her knees and took him to the back of her throat.

Okay, that was random.

"And why is that, Mr....?" Willing her nipples to behave, she knocked back the entire glass in three large gulps. Although she enjoyed the burn as it made its way down her throat, the alcohol tasted just as awful as it had ten years ago.

He snatched his own drink off the bar and the ice clinked in the glass as he lifted it in salute. "Ryder. Just Ryder."

Figures he has an original name. Unlike…

"Jane."

Warmth spread throughout her belly from the vodka… and Ryder.

He took a sip of his scotch. "Well, *Jane*," he said as if he didn't believe it was her real name, "women usually fall into three different categories at these things. You've got those who are the traditional wine drinkers. If you look around, you'll see most of the women here drinking wine. They're conformists. Followers. Afraid to take a risk and drink something different."

She shrugged. "Maybe they just like wine."

Splaying his hand on her lower back, he led her to a vacant area beside the bar. The action felt intimate, as if he were staking a claim to her.

"Then you have the hard liquor drinkers," he continued. "These are the women who have something to prove. The ball-busters. They're the ones who rise through the corporate ranks and crash through the glass ceiling only to replace the glass once they're at the top, keeping other women from accomplishing what they have. They're basically men with vaginas."

He plucked the empty glass from her hand and set it on a tray beside the bar. "Despite your drink of choice this evening, you don't fit."

"Exactly." She inhaled his dizzying scent, a mix of cologne, soap, and something… unfamiliar. Unfamiliar but not unwelcome. "Did it ever occur to you that categorizing women by their drink order isn't only obnoxious, but also outrageously flawed?"

He paused, finishing his drink before shaking his head. "No. Now where was I?" He rested his glass next to hers. "Right, the third and final category. The mixed drink. These are your average girl-next-door kind of women. They like to have a good time and get a little buzzed, but they despise the taste of alcohol. They're hard workers, but they'd never step on anyone's toes to get to the top, and if they do manage to get there, they do whatever it takes to help other women get to the top as well."

"And you think I'm one of those women?"

A smile played at his lips as he moved closer. "Oh, I know so. No woman who dresses like you enjoys wine or hard liquor."

She took a step back, putting her flush against a pillar. "There are plenty of women here dressed like me." While he'd nailed his assessment of her, what was wrong with the way she was dressed? It wasn't as if she was wearing her favorite jeans and Florida State sweatshirt. Thanks to Keane, she fit in with everyone else there tonight. At least on the outside.

"No." He leaned forward, placing a hand on the pillar next to her head while he settled the other on her hip. His touch seared through the silk of her skirt as he swept his thumb back and forth over her hip bone.

She shivered even as a fever began to rage within her. "No?"

He smiled, the skin crinkling around his eyes. Then his gaze dipped to her chest. "As much as I appreciate the peek-aboo view of your nipples, your blouse is misbuttoned."

Horrified, she slapped her arms over her chest. "What?" She looked down and confirmed he wasn't joking. Somehow she'd missed a button, allowing for a huge gap in the fabric, and since she barely filled a B-cup, she hadn't bothered with a bra. How many others had she inadvertently flashed?

She closed her eyes and sighed. So much for making a good impression. Everyone was probably laughing behind her back. "Fuck me."

Ryder grabbed her hand and pulled her from the pillar. "Usually I prefer a bit more banter, but I'm game."

Her eyes flew open as she stumbled forward, slamming into a hard wall of muscle. His arm encircled her waist, helping her regain her balance. She clutched his sweater in her hands. God, he smelled good. "I'm sorry?"

He looked perplexed, one of his eyebrows shooting up while the other remained in place. "You asked me to fuck you."

"I didn't," she said, her protest coming out much weaker than she'd intended.

Damn him. He confused her with that quick-witted tongue of his.

She clenched her thighs together, picturing him putting that tongue to better use. *Crap, I shouldn't be thinking that. What's wrong with me?* "That was me...I mean, I—"

He pressed a finger to her lips, silencing her stammering. "Tell me the truth. Do you or do you not want me to fuck you?"

Was that a trick question? She didn't think there was a woman in the room who wouldn't want Ryder in their bed.

He removed his finger, giving her the chance to reply. "I . . . I don't even know you."

"What better way to get to know someone than by fucking them?"

The way he said *fucking* made her hot and needy. "Um . . . a conversation?"

He chuckled, the sound of it like a caress between her legs. "You want a conversation? How about this?" His arms tightened around her waist and he pulled her closer, letting her feel the full effect of his desire for her against her hip. "If I don't get my mouth on your pussy within the next five minutes, I'm going to stand on top of the bar and tell everyone you crashed the conference without paying."

The aforementioned pussy clenched, completely on board with Ryder's blackmail. *The traitor.*

Her brain and body warred with one another. It would be embarrassing enough if anyone discovered she was an intern, but if Ryder actually did what he threatened, she'd be mortified.

"You wouldn't." She waited for him to admit it was a joke, but his grin said otherwise. "You would."

His fingers brushed a path down her arm, eliciting goose bumps in their wake. "Unless you tell me you really don't want me to fuck you five ways to Sunday. But that would be a lie, wouldn't it?"

She laughed. "You're insane. Has anyone told you that?"

"Several times." He held out his hand. "Jane?"

What would Plain Jane do?

The answer was obvious. She'd politely decline and walk away.

But Plain Jane wasn't here tonight.

He didn't need to blackmail her into sleeping with him, because her body had already won the war.

She wanted him.

He didn't need to ask her again. She slid her palm against his, shivering at the feel of his warm skin against hers. "I'm coming."

Tonight she'd be bold. Reckless. Pretend she was the type of woman who had one-night stands. Tomorrow she could go back to being Plain Jane. But for the next few hours...

She was his to claim.

THREE

One year ago...

Ryder held on to Jane's hand a little tighter, hoping she wouldn't change her mind and bolt.

She wasn't his typical conquest. Everything about her screamed innocence and yet he couldn't walk away. He'd spotted her earlier in the day, nibbling on her lips during a session as she took notes on last year's award-winning innovations by Michigan inventors, and his response had been so strong, it was like a punch to the gut. For a moment, he could barely breathe and it took everything in his power to remain in his seat.

Without even knowing it, she'd enraptured him and for the next hour, his attention had been focused solely on her. The way the sides of her eyes crinkled when the speaker told a bad joke. The way she pursed her lips when someone's cell phone went off. The way she absentmindedly played with the ends of her hair.

Her face had displayed a million expressions and he wanted to know what each one meant.

Beautiful didn't even come close to describing her. She reminded him of Snow White with her dark hair, fair skin, and thick lashes, only better because she was fucking *real*.

And when the speech had ended and she'd stood up to clap, his cock had stood up as well, his only thought that he had to taste her. Fuck his lunch appointment. He would rather have her.

He'd taken a step in her direction when his lunch date commandeered him, moving between him and Snow White and impeding his view of her.

"Ready for lunch? I made us reservations at the nearby steak house. We can take my car."

The ginger-bearded guy worked for Sinclair Corp, a company Ryder had no desire to do business with. Not even if they offered him a billion dollars. Ryder would never sell his software to a company that specialized in weapons engineering and arms production. He'd been willing to hear the guy out, if for no other reason than for curiosity's sake, but right then, his curiosity had been otherwise engaged.

"I'm sorry. I'm going to have to cancel."

The guy—his name had already slipped Ryder's mind—had turned red-faced. "What? Why?"

Ryder had patted his stomach. "Stomach issues."

"Then we don't have to make it lunch. Dinner. Or drinks even. I won't take up much of your time if you're not interested in the opportunity I have for you. How 'bout a drink at the bar at three?"

The guy had looked so panicked, his pupils huge, nostrils

flared, his throat incessantly swallowing, that Ryder had felt a little bad for him.

"Yeah, sure," Ryder had said, throwing him a bone. "Excuse me." He'd left the guy standing there and hurried toward where Snow White had been sitting, but she'd disappeared.

Like a lovesick asshole, he'd spent the next twenty minutes looking for her around the hotel, hoping maybe to find her in the bar or in one of the restaurants. But she'd vanished.

He never did meet that guy in the bar. Instead, he'd eaten lunch in his room and taken a long shower, jerking off twice to fantasies about his mystery woman sitting on his face.

But tonight he'd found her and he planned on turning that fantasy into a reality.

When he saw her walk into the ballroom, he'd known she wouldn't be walking out alone. All the men in the room had turned to ogle her, and it had nothing to do with the fact that her tit was practically visible. (Okay, that wasn't the only reason.) The way she held herself told him that she had no idea how beautiful she was. Her gaze had darted around the room and she'd kept tugging on her dress, both signs that she was nervous. But at the same time, she'd thrown back her shoulders as if she'd been ready to take on the world. He wanted to be the one to show her, to prove to her that she was beautiful. He'd teach her to own her beauty and never make any apologies for it.

He just hadn't expected her to be so sharp or witty.

He was tired of the giggly submissives who practically

fell to their feet at the sight of him. Unlike them, Jane made him work for it, volleying back everything he'd lobbed at her. He'd felt like a million bucks when she'd agreed to come to his room.

God, he couldn't wait to have her long legs wrapped around him.

He didn't care that tangling with this woman might threaten his one-and-done policy.

Because he couldn't imagine ever growing tired of her.

Ryder tugged Jane toward the exit of the ballroom. From the corner of his eye, he saw the guy he was supposed meet at the bar heading toward him. Shit, he really didn't want to stop and give her a reason to change her mind. He had the guy's card somewhere in his room. He'd just call him tomorrow and tell him he wasn't interested in anything he had to offer.

His arm curled around Jane's waist as they left the event. Luckily his room wasn't far. He led her down the long hall and had just taken out his key when he realized the door was already open a crack. He remembered pulling the door closed before he left for the banquet, but it was possible he walked away before noticing it hadn't fully shut. A quick scan of the room confirmed nothing was out of place or missing.

The walls were covered in pink and green floral wallpaper and the carpet was red and pink striped. It should have been ugly as hell and yet it somehow worked. Along the far wall under the window sat two green chairs with a round white table between them, his laptop open upon it. The bedding matched the wallpaper and behind the headboard was a pink striped curtain as if the bed were on a stage. It was perfect because tonight he was going to give Jane a performance she'd never forget.

Fidgeting, Jane stared at the bed as she nibbled on her lower lip.

The sight of it punched him in the chest. He wanted her so much he physically ached, but he wouldn't pressure her into something she didn't want.

He strode to her and took her hand, lifting it to his chest. "If you've changed your mind, we don't have to do this. You can leave now, go back to the party. I won't stop you."

Her gaze fell to their joined hands, and she flattened her palm over his heart. Could she feel how it raced for her?

"I want you to...f-fuck me," she whispered.

He knew that admission didn't come easy for her. That's why he hadn't given her much of a choice back in the ballroom.

He tipped up her chin. "You're a very bad girl underneath that good-girl persona, aren't you?"

A bright smile spread across her face. "I am tonight."

"Bad girls deserve to be punished," he said, needing to gauge her reaction.

He was a perverted bastard, but he didn't need kink to enjoy sex. If Jane wasn't into it, he'd be fine with some old-fashioned, sweaty, vanilla fucking. But he had to admit, the thought of bringing her to the highest heights of pleasure made his dick hard. He'd love to see her bound to that bed, helpless and writhing, her legs spread for him.

Something about Jane brought out the Dom in him.

She giggled, passing his statement off as a joke. "You're not going to break out the whips and chains, are you?"

"No."

"Thank good—"

"I didn't bring any with me."

Her breathing hitched and her pupils dilated. "I'm not into that."

He dragged his fingers down her neck, over her throbbing pulse point, and cupped his hand over her breast, confirming her nipple was hard under her dress. "Your body is saying otherwise, but like I said, I don't have any toys with me." He lightly squeezed her breast. "You'll just have to make do with my hand. Ever been spanked, Jane?"

She swallowed hard. "No."

He rubbed his palm over her nipple. "Ever want to be? Aren't you the least bit curious what all the fuss is about?"

"I . . ." She blew out a breath. "What do I do?"

He knew it. There was an instinct that had originally drawn him to her and it was much more than physical attraction. There was a connection between them. Like a magnet to steel. Or a Dom to a sub. Hiding beneath that innocent exterior was a wanton woman dying to get out.

But his gut said she needed some help to do it.

He reclined on one of the chairs. "Take off your clothes for me."

Her hands shook as she worked the buttons of her blouse. Maybe it made him a sick fuck, but he liked that he made her nervous.

After what felt like forever, she undid the last button and

slid the blouse off her shoulders. He licked his lips as he soaked in the beauty standing before him. Her breasts were small and firm, the perfect size for him to take the entire flesh into his mouth. He kept his gaze trained on her, not even blinking, for fear of losing a single moment of her shy striptease.

She nibbled on her bottom lip as she hooked her fingers underneath the waistband of her skirt. Inch by inch, she lowered it over her thighs, bending over and giving him a glance of her luscious round ass and smooth, shapely legs that would soon rest on his shoulders.

Fuck, she was wearing a thong.

His dick twitched in his pants, and he crossed his legs to relieve the throbbing.

She sashayed over to him, her hips swaying back and forth.

His gaze locked on to the tiny scrap of lace covering her pussy. "Bad girl. You didn't follow my directions."

A challenge twinkled in her eyes. She snapped the waist-band of her panties against her skin, the sound reverber-ating in the room. "I thought you might want to do the honors."

Fuck yeah, he'd do the honors. He slipped his fingers under the flimsy waistband and within seconds ripped the panties away from her body. He leaned forward and inhaled her scent before looking up at her shocked face. "You're beautiful. If Botticelli were alive, he'd create a statue of you."

She smiled. "Botticelli didn't do sculptures."

"That's only because he died before he got to sculpt you."

"I bet you say that to all the girls."

Other than tossing out the occasional "good girl" or "fuck, you're good at that," he didn't bother with compliments, and the women he fucked didn't expect them. Jane was different. He could tell she didn't have a lot of experience with men and required some extra coddling. But it didn't make the words any less true.

"I can honestly say that not only have I never said that, but I also mean every word." He patted his thighs. "Lie across my lap."

"Aren't you going to get undressed?"

Remaining clothed while she was completely naked gave him just one more pretense of power.

She stood stock-still, realizing he had no intention of taking off his clothes. He could almost hear her thinking. He held his breath as he waited for her to accept that she wanted this as much as he did. Pretending to have patience, he drummed his fingers on his thigh. Truthfully, he was about thirty seconds from tossing her onto the bed.

A small sigh of acquiescence puffed from her lips. After removing her earrings and setting them down by his computer, she awkwardly lay facedown across his lap. Because of her height and the level of the chair, her palms and toes rested on the carpet. He swore he felt the heat of her pussy through his pants and he clenched his hands to keep himself from finding out. Instead, he caressed the globes of her delectable ass, tempted to do more than just spank it.

"Ready?" he asked, although he didn't give her a chance to respond. Immediately, he swatted her rear, barely using any force.

Her reaction wasn't typical. She started laughing uncontrollably, her body convulsing on his lap and the vibration of it going straight to his dick. He didn't stop her, knowing it was probably a nervous reaction. Besides, it was honest. Real. So unlike the practiced moans of the usual subs he played with. She laughed with her entire being, holding nothing back. He could only imagine what it would be like if she fucked like she laughed.

Her laughter tapered off after a minute and she sighed. "Sorry," she said, then hiccupped.

He ran his finger down her spine. "Don't be. It's adorable."

She looked up at him. "This just strikes me as a little ridiculous."

Ridiculous, huh? He'd assumed he'd need to ease her into it, but obviously she required a heavier hand. And he'd be happy to provide it.

"Let's see if we can't help you take it a bit more seriously." He raised his hand high in the air and swung, palm meeting flesh with a resounding smack.

Her body bucked, tensing and releasing on a loud gasp.

"How about that? Was that ridiculous?" he said with a smirk.

She groaned as she arched her torso, lifting up her ass in invitation. "Not ridiculous. Do it again, please?"

Hearing her ask for his hand sent a jolt of heat surging through his veins. He spanked her again, barely giving her any recovery time as he peppered her ass five more times. He didn't use as much force as he would if she was one of the subs at a play party, but it was enough to turn her ass a dark shade of pink. Each time she whispered a quiet "yes" and squirmed on his lap, leaving what he'd guess was a huge wet spot on his pants.

He squeezed her cheeks together, digging his fingers into her hot flesh. "You have a biteable ass. Just want to sink my teeth into it." And he would. *Soon.* He dragged his fingers down her crack, eliciting a shiver out of her. Testing, he dipped his pinky between her cheeks and pressed against her tightness but didn't enter. "Or maybe my cock," he said, his voice hoarse as his cock throbbed at the thought of pushing inside that tight heat. She stiffened, and he let out a chuckle, gently patting her backside. "Don't worry, baby. No back-door play until you put up the welcome sign. Besides, I haven't even kissed you yet, baby doll." He lifted her up and maneuvered her so she straddled him.

"Jane," she said emphatically, her eyes flashing with defiance. "Not baby. Not baby doll. Jane."

God, he loved her fire.

"Jane," he repeated just before he captured her mouth with his own. His head buzzed as her taste exploded on his tongue. Vodka. Sugar. And something undefinable, except to say it was uniquely Jane. Tart, sweet, and mysterious.

She wrapped her arms around his shoulders. Her hands sank into his hair and her soft fingertips massaged his scalp. He shivered, her touch sending chills through him. Her petal-soft lips surrendered under his, parting, silently asking for more.

Lucky for her. He was in the mood to give it.

He held on to Jane as he stood up from the chair and walked them to the bed. He dropped her onto the mattress, enjoying the image of her small tits bouncing as she fell back.

How far was she willing to go? Allowing someone to spank her was one thing, but what he had in mind would require quite a bit more trust.

"How do you feel about restraints?" he asked her, eyeballing the sashes hanging from the curtains behind the headboard.

"In general?" she quipped, followed by a nervous giggle.

He didn't blame her. She should be nervous. Bondage wasn't just about adding a layer of kink to the bedroom. It was also about trust. If she gave her consent to be bound, she'd be giving him power over her. "I want to tie you to the bed."

She lifted her head off the mattress. "I'm not sure. I don't know you." Her voice shook, but at least she wasn't running out of there, disgusted at the thought.

He untied the long strips of fabric and dragged them lightly down the length of her body. She undulated underneath it, her lips parting as she let out a quiet moan.

"I won't tie it tightly," he promised. "You'll be able to get away if necessary. It will just *feel* like you're bound and helpless."

She paused, considering his words, then bravely raised her arms above her head. "Then yes."

He would make sure she'd never regret her decision.

At home, his bed had a built-in restraint system, complete with rope and pulleys that could lift his lover into the air, if he wanted. He licked his lips as he imagined what Jane would look like suspended above his bed, cradled by rope, all her secret places exposed for him. She'd tremble, wondering what filthy, incredible thing he'd do to her first.

But unfortunately, this upscale hotel didn't exactly cater to the kinky.

Good thing Ryder had a creative mind. Like the Mac-Gyver of kink, he could pervert almost any object.

The headboard wasn't slatted, but it did have knobs on each side that would work perfectly for this particular purpose. First on one side and then on the other, he wrapped the end of the sash around the knob and tied it with a knot. Then he tied the other ends around her wrists, giving her almost no slack.

He slipped his finger between the fabric and her skin, making sure it wasn't too tight. "How does that feel?"

She looked at him, her eyes slightly glazed as she tried to move her hands but couldn't. "Good," she whispered.

They'd barely started and he'd wager anything that she'd already begun slipping into subspace, that trancelike state that subs sometimes achieved. "If it starts to get too uncomfortable or you get pins and needles in your arm or hands, you have to let me know, okay? I don't want to cut off your circulation." He'd never topped anyone who'd gone under that quickly. That Jane was already floating, coupled with the fact that she was probably inexperienced meant he had to take extra care of her. "We didn't talk about safe words." He didn't think they'd need one. "Say 'no,' 'stop,' or anything remotely negative and I'll stop. You understand, Jane?"

She smiled dreamily. "I get you."

That smile would be the death of him.

He grabbed a condom from his wallet and quickly undressed, loving the sight of Jane's eyes widening as she perused his naked form. His knees hit the foot of the bed and on all fours, he stalked his way up the mattress until he caged her in with his body, his hands bracketed beside her face. Her lips parted, her breath coming out in little puffs and beneath him, she trembled. "I won't hurt you. I promise."

"I'm not scared."

"Such a pretty, little liar."

She looked like a goddess splayed out before him, her long hair spread out on the pillow beneath her. Her small breasts were tipped with pale pink nipples that begged to be licked and sucked and bitten. His mouth literally watered as he imagined his tongue on them. His gaze lowered to the creamy skin stretched tight over her rib cage and down past her adorable outie belly button to the thatch of brown curls covering her pussy. She was soaked, the hair glistening with her arousal. With a shy smile, she slowly parted her legs, giving him his first glimpse of the pink flesh between her thighs. It was one of the most erotic moments of his life.

He kissed her then, her lips like a magnet he was helpless to resist. If he could figure out a way to kiss her mouth and pussy at the same time, he'd die a happy man.

He had a million and one things he wanted to do to her lips alone. They were plump, wet, and soft. He wanted to slide the tip of his dick over them, back and forth, and get them glossy with his precum and then watch them stretch around his girth as he shot his load down her throat.

Her mouth grew pliant under his, allowing him to direct the kiss. He licked into her mouth, teasing her with soft caresses before a rush of adrenaline had him craving more and the kiss turned carnal.

He hovered over her, not a single part of him touching a single part of her, but it didn't matter because he felt her *everywhere*. She arched her spine upward, but his ties held her prisoner. Sweat dripped down his back as he lowered himself on top of her. She groaned and wrapped her legs around his waist. Her skin was hot, soft, and moist with perspiration. He had to feel her wet heat surround his dick before he embarrassed himself and came all over her tits.

Hmm...maybe he'd do that later after he ate her pussy.

He rolled the condom down his length, leaving a space at the tip, and noticed the spermicidal lubricant had dried out. He shrugged it off, figuring Jane was already plenty wet to take him.

She trembled slightly as he aligned his cock to her entrance and pushed himself into her. A wince flashed across her face and her body tensed, but she didn't complain. He could understand her discomfort. He was on the bigger side and she was tight as hell. But it wouldn't be long before she was screaming his name in ecstasy. If there was one thing Ryder did well, it was fucking.

"Are you okay?" he asked, concern for her pleasure at the forefront of his mind even though his dick was screaming at him to just thrust all the way inside her.

Pressing her lips together, she nodded, relaxing her muscles.

He didn't give her another chance to tense up. He slammed his way forward, driving himself all the way home inside of the tightest, hottest pussy he'd ever experienced. For the next hour, he pulled her body into dozens of positions, throwing her into climax after climax. And she'd eagerly met him thrust for thrust, vocal and uninhibited, writhing beneath him as he took her to the heights of ecstasy again and again with his cock, fingers, and tongue.

Her pussy tasted like a rare fine wine, complex and earthy, and hearing her moan his name was like hearing the heavens sing for him. Finally, he couldn't hold back any longer. His balls drew up tight as an electric current ran down his spine and wrapped around them. With the force of a speeding train, he shot his load, his dick pumping into her until every bit of his climax had been wrung out of him.

That was, hands down, the best fuck of his life.

He kissed her softly, caressing her and cuddling her, something he'd never bothered with before but now couldn't imagine going without. She sighed, lazily kissing him back, her eyes closed.

Holding on to the base of the condom, he reluctantly withdrew from her body. Immediately, his eyes went to the head of his dick, which should have been covered by latex...but wasn't.

"Fuck. The condom broke."

Her eyes fluttered open and fixed on him.

"I promise I'm clean," he swore to her. "Just got my physical last month. You good?"

Since losing his virginity in high school, not once had he not gloved up during sex. But condoms weren't just to prevent disease, and he silently prayed she was on the pill.

She nodded sleepily. "I'm good." Sighing, she closed her eyes again.

Thank fuck.

Because the very last thing he ever wanted to do was bring an innocent child into the world.

FOUR

Jane stood frozen, staring at Ryder, wondering if this was really happening.

It just wasn't possible.

Ryder, *her Ryder*, couldn't be Keane's son.

This man had seen parts of her even *she'd* never viewed. He'd spanked her. Tied her to the bed. She'd given him her virginity.

And he'd given her something precious in return.

Oh my God.

Ryder was her soon-to-be-stepfather's brother.

In less than an hour, he'd be her *stepuncle*.

They'd be related.

Her head was spinning with the ramifications.

Most people had no idea that she was Ciara's daughter, and even if they did, Jane didn't care about their opinions. But she did care about Keane's and Ian's. What would they think when they learned the truth?

What would Ryder do?

She didn't know whether to laugh or cry.

Maybe she'd fallen asleep and this was a nightmare. *Yeah. That has to be it.* After all, she hadn't had a good night's sleep in months.

She looked at the three men at the bar—really looked—and her heart stuttered.

How had she missed it?

They all shared the same unusual-color eyes. The same clear gray eyes she saw every day for the past year.

Her stomach dropped as though she were on an amusement park ride. The thought that Ryder was the pigheaded son that Keane had mentioned a couple of times had never crossed her mind.

And Finn had never spoken about him at all around her. Not that she'd spent much time with him.

How many times had she thought about Ryder since that night they'd shared together? Too many to count. In fact, he never strayed far from her mind. After failing to unearth his name from the conference organizers, she'd given up hope that she'd ever see him again. And he'd been only one connection away from her this whole time.

Would he call her out and admit they spent the night together? She wasn't prepared for the fallout when Keane, her mother, and Finn connected the dots; Ryder deserved to hear the truth from her lips. But now, twenty minutes before the wedding, wasn't the time to get into any of it.

When Finn coughed, she realized that she was just standing there, gawking at Ryder, who held his hand out for her.

Just as he had that night. "Nice to meet you, Ryder," she said, tentatively accepting it.

Heat zinged through her chest at the strength in his grip and the calloused pads of his fingers. Fingers that had brought her both pleasure and pain. They'd caressed her. Spanked her. Been deep inside her. The spark between them was still there. Still as strong as it had been that night. Maybe stronger.

"Likewise." He quirked a brow. "Jane, was it?" he asked, playing along.

She let out a breath, relieved she had a little more time before her life imploded. "Yes. That's right."

His eyes burned into her as his grip tightened. Flecks of desire danced in his gaze, but there was something else there. Something that looked like...anger?

She tried to break away, but he refused to let go. "Can I have my hand back?" she asked on a forced laugh.

The last thing she needed was for Keane to pick up on her discomfort and start questioning her about it. He'd been her rock for the past year. She would never lie to him.

Ryder blinked hard and looked down at their joined hands before releasing her. His eyes narrowed on her. "There's something familiar about you. Have we met before?"

His tone gave her pause. There wasn't a hint of teasing to it.

It was hard to believe, but maybe he didn't recognize her.

Tonight, instead of the stunning Carolina Herrera blouse and skirt, she was wearing a floor-length, beige satin bridesmaid dress that did nothing to flatter her figure. With its empire waist that fitted her just below her bust, the dress had obviously been designed for women who actually had breasts and hips.

Tonight, she'd worn her curly hair down. When they'd met, it had been up and pin straight.

Tonight, she was wearing her glasses rather than contacts and more natural makeup. Contacts made her eyes itch and drugstore makeup was more affordable than the pricy kind she'd gotten at the spa.

So, she guessed it was possible he didn't recognize her.

Or maybe he'd simply forgotten her.

But no…looking at him, she couldn't miss the tension in his jaw or the animosity in his gaze.

He *was* angry with her.

Why? Because she'd run off in the middle of the night? If anyone had the right to be angry, it was her. After all, he hadn't bothered to tell Jane he was in a relationship with another woman. She'd figured out that piece of information when she'd overheard him talking on the phone while she'd been in the bathroom.

"No." *Lie, lie, lie.* She pasted on a fake smile. "I'm sure I would've remembered."

Keane lifted her freed hand and kissed the top of it. "You look beautiful as always, Jane."

Hardly. These days, it was hard leaving her apartment without a stained blouse or in today's case, a ripped dress. If it weren't for her roommate Dreama, she wouldn't even have time for a shower before work. "That's kind of you to say, Keane, but I know I look a mess."

"My father's right," Ryder said, raking his gaze over her form before staring at her mouth as if he remembered what she'd done with it during their night together. Confusing her, the hostility in his gaze had all but disappeared. "You look...lovely."

Finn gave her a fond smile. "Listen to them, Jane. The last time those two have agreed on something..." He scratched his head. "Well, I don't think it's ever happened."

"Thank you." She grew uncomfortably warm as Ryder continued to stare at her. "Well, um, I should probably go find my mother before the ceremony starts." Without pausing, she twirled around as well as she could in her monstrosity of a bridesmaid's dress and fled out of the room.

Her heart was racing so fast she could barely catch her breath. She'd always hoped she'd find him, but not this way. Not tonight. Not when she had to deal with the family she barely knew and the work associates who'd just love to gossip about her personal life.

There was already talk circulating about how quickly she'd climbed the corporate ladder within Keane's company. It would have been easier to deal with if they'd believed it was just a clear case of nepotism since Finn was marrying her mother. But honoring her mother's wishes, she and Keane had kept that fact private.

Although she'd worked her butt off for the promotion to vice president, a part of her wondered if she really deserved it or whether he'd only given her it because of their familial connection. Regardless, she would've been stupid to turn it down. The job afforded her flexibility to work at home when necessary and came with great medical insurance, both of which she'd needed this past year.

Jane came to the door marked BRIDAL ROOM and squared her shoulders, determined not to let on to her mother that anything was wrong. Even though they weren't close, Jane wouldn't do anything to ruin her big day.

She pushed open the door and stepped inside.

Straightening her veil, her mother sat in front of a dressing table and mirror while her three other bridesmaids—friends from high school who were among the few people who were aware of Jane's biological connection to her mother—stood around her drinking champagne and chatting. As soon as they caught sight of Jane, the room went quiet.

Her mother was beautiful and polished and everything Jane wasn't. Petite, but curvy in all the right places. Straight, glossy blond hair. Wide blue eyes and a button nose. She never stumbled or misbuttoned her blouse or ripped her skirt. She was the epitome of class in every way that counted while Jane felt like a bumbling idiot half the time. It wasn't that she was ugly. Taller than average with dark, curly hair, plain brown eyes, and a nose with a slight bump to it, she obviously took after her birth father. Not that she'd ever met him or even seen a picture of him. Her mother refused to talk about him. Sometimes Jane wondered if her mother simply disliked her because of the way she looked.

"Good of you to finally join us," her mother said with a tight smile.

Jane flinched. No matter how hard she tried to please the woman who gave birth to her, she never seemed to get it right. She had a feeling Finn or Keane had talked her mother into having Jane as one of the bridesmaids. Even now, more than two years after Jane had moved back to the area, her mother had kept her distance emotionally. It would make sense to Jane if her mother were a cold and insensitive person to everyone. But she wasn't. Only to her.

"We'll just give you two some privacy," said one of the bridesmaids, ushering the other two out of the room.

As soon as they left, Jane went over to her mother, passing a couch she'd give anything to nap on, a full-length mirror, and a bottle of champagne resting in a bucket of ice. "I'm sorry I was late, Mother." Jane gave her an air-kiss over her cheek, not wanting to ruin her makeup.

Her mother peered over her shoulder at Jane, frowning. "That reminds me. Why don't you just call me Ciara today? I don't want to have to answer any questions about you at my wedding." She returned to the mirror, her face a passive mask. "You understand."

Jane clenched her teeth, trying not to be hurt. Of course she didn't want to cause her mother any distress on the most important day of her life. But Jane hadn't asked to be born. So why should Ciara make her feel as though she should be ashamed for it? "Right. I understand."

Ciara paused, her lips briefly mashed together before blossoming into a fake smile. "Did you see Finn out there?"

She nodded. "Yes, he was with—" She couldn't manage to say Ryder's name. "His brother."

Her mother's mouth dropped open. "Ryder actually showed? I'm shocked. Finn said they were close but I've never met him."

"That's odd, don't you think?" she asked.

"You of all people know how complicated family dynamics can get. He and Keane haven't spoken in years. From what Finn told me, Ryder cut all ties to Keane when he left for college."

Ryder was the one who cut ties? Why would he do that with such a wonderful father and brother? Jane would've given anything to be a welcome member of her family. Not that her aunt and uncle didn't love her or make her feel like she was their daughter. They did. Only they were much older and out of touch with modern society. Between their arthritis and health issues, they didn't leave the house much, which was why they couldn't make the wedding. "That's sad."

Ciara applied another layer of lip gloss to her already shiny lips. "I'm happy he's here because I know Finn wanted him to be, but he better not do anything to ruin this day for Finn. The last thing he needs is to play referee between his father and brother."

There was a knock on the door. It opened and the wedding planner stuck her head in. "Ciara, darling! It's time. You don't want to keep the groom waiting."

Jane took her mother's hand and helped her out of the chair. Practically glowing, her mother looked like a fairy-tale princess in her Oscar de la Renta strapless wedding gown.

"You look beautiful, Moth—Ciara," Jane said.

Her mother's eyes clouded with tears before she blinked them away. "Thank you, Jane. For being here today. For being a bridesmaid. For"—she hugged her—"everything."

Jane didn't know what had come over her mother, but it was the first time she could ever remember her mother hugging her.

Ciara whispered in her ear. "Don't forget, if anyone asks who you are, tell them you're my cousin."

Moment over.

"Right. How could I forget?" Jane muttered as she pulled away and grabbed her flower bouquet on the way out the door.

She'd given up on the belief that her mother secretly loved her. She didn't. If Keane hadn't invited Jane to work for McKay, she probably wouldn't have been in attendance today. To Ciara, Jane was simply a reminder of her mistake. Jane had thought things might change now that she was living in the same area as her mother and working for Keane, but Ciara had shown no indication she wanted anything to do with Jane.

Jane shook off her melancholy and followed her mother to the double doors that separated them from nearly five hundred guests, one in particular she both dreaded and anticipated seeing.

Ian waited by the doors. He wore the same tuxedo as the others in the wedding party, but for some reason, it made him look even more formidable. When she'd decided to major in business, she'd dreamed of someday working for

Sinclair Corp, but now she couldn't imagine ever leaving McKay. He gathered Ciara in his arms and chastely kissed her lips. When he stepped out of the hug, his gaze fell on Jane.

"Jane." He walked forward and took both her hands in his. "You look lovely."

She gave him a smile of gratitude. The fact was the color of the dress made her appear pale and the cut did nothing to flatter her figure. But it was her mother's big day. Not hers. As one of the bridesmaids, she'd wear a paper bag if her mother wanted her to. "Thank you, Ian."

Although he'd privately told her he didn't agree with Ciara's decision to keep Jane's true identity a secret, she didn't dare refer to him as Grandfather in public. But she couldn't help holding on to the hope that someday he'd introduce her to the world as his granddaughter.

Someone tapped her shoulder. "Jane, can I talk to you for a moment?"

She turned around at the sound of the familiar voice. Evan Donaldson, McKay's innovation department's software engineer, pulled on his tie as his gaze darted wildly between her and the wedding party. Several people who worked for McKay had been invited, but most of them were from management. She wouldn't have expected to see him here, but maybe he was friends with Finn.

"Sure," she said, distracted by the wedding planner's orders for the wedding party to line up.

Glancing at Ciara and Ian, he lowered his voice. "Somewhere private."

Sweat dripped down the side of his face and his pupils were dilated. He looked uncomfortable, almost...scared. If he yanked on his tie any harder, he'd strangle himself.

She'd never seen him like this, but then again, she'd never seen him outside of work. Perhaps he suffered from some sort of social anxiety. "It's probably not a good idea for me to leave right now. The wedding is about to start. Is it about work?"

"Yes. No. It's complicated." He moved closer to her as the wedding ceremony music drifted through the doors. "It's about that program I've been working on. I finished it and—"

"Places, everyone," said the wedding planner. "I'm opening the doors."

"Can it wait until Monday?" she asked. Between Ryder and her mother, there was no way she'd be able to concentrate on work tonight. "I can meet you first thing in the morning. I promise to give you my full, undivided attention."

Evan's face fell, disappointment written all over it, even as he nodded. "S-sure."

For a moment, she almost reconsidered, but Evan turned and walked away in the opposite direction from where the guests had gathered for the ceremony.

That was strange.

Frowning, she took the arm of her assigned groomsman, a friend of Finn's from college. The wedding planner opened the double doors and all thoughts of Evan disappeared. Ryder was in there. Her pulse quickened as she stepped into the packed room and strolled down the long aisle.

She told herself to keep her eyes forward. To concentrate on Finn standing at the front of the room or the reverend up on the platform. But she couldn't keep herself from searching the guests for Ryder.

And it didn't take long.

Like a beacon, he called to her, her gaze landing on him almost immediately since he was sitting on the aisle at the front of the room. For a moment, she could almost imagine herself walking down the aisle toward him on their own wedding day.

His eyes fixed on her as she moved closer and closer to him, heating her. When she passed him, she inhaled, and she swore she smelled him, a mix of whiskey and musk that made her head spin and brought memories of their night together to the forefront of her mind.

She stumbled in her heels, and he smiled as if he knew exactly what had set her off-kilter.

On the platform, she took her place and concentrated her efforts into not looking at Ryder again. The ceremony was short and sweet, Finn and Ciara using their own vows in lieu of the traditional ones. It was clear that they were in love, and even though her mother wanted little to do with her, Jane was happy for her.

But a selfish part of her, the part she wouldn't want to acknowledge out loud, resented her mother. Not for her happiness or even for getting married, but for complicating an already complicated situation.

She couldn't worry about the repercussions of all this tonight. She looked down at her bouquet and counted the rose petals. She didn't need to see him to know he was watching her. She could feel the heat of his gaze burning into her.

Her heart pounded, dizzying her. It had been so long since she'd felt desirable. Not since that night with Ryder. Hell, she hadn't even had an orgasm in months. And the ones she'd had, all by her own hand, never came close to what she'd experienced with Ryder. If she wasn't careful, she'd fall under his spell as easily as she had that night. Only this time it would prove much more devastating.

It wasn't until the reverend declared Finn and Ciara husband and wife that Jane lifted her gaze from the flowers. Like she had practiced in rehearsal, she allowed herself to be led back down the aisle by the groomsman and out of the room. Unlike when she'd entered, she kept her gaze forward, refusing to turn her head and look at Ryder even once.

Okay, so *maybe* she peeked at him from the corner of her eye and *maybe* she found him still staring at her as if she were as naked as when she'd been tied to his bed, and *maybe* it might have caused her to stumble a bit, but she quickly recovered.

For the next two hours, she put Ryder out of her mind (well, as much as she possibly could) and performed her duties as a bridesmaid while she took hundreds of wedding photos. She tried not to be hurt when she was left out of the majority of the family pictures. After all, she was only supposed to be Ciara's *cousin*.

By the time the band announced the wedding party, she was hungry and tired, and her feet hurt. She'd only had four hours of solid sleep last night. At this point, she just wanted to eat dinner and watch Finn and Ciara cut the cake so that she could slip out of the wedding reception and go home.

No one would even miss her.

Nope, not a one.

Following the rest of the bridal party, she was about to go into the grand ballroom when someone grabbed her by the arm, preventing her from making her entrance. For a brief moment, she thought it might be Evan, too impatient to wait until Monday to speak with her, but almost immediately she registered the familiarity of the fingertips and the heat at her back.

The door slammed shut, leaving her behind as the guests clapped loudly in the other room.

"We need to talk," Ryder said, firmly spinning her around to face him.

Talking was the last thing she wanted to do with him.

Just having him this close to her, breathing his scent into her lungs, feeling the weight of his hand on her arm, made her mind go blank and her body come alive. She forgot all about her hunger, her aching toes, and her exhaustion as a rush of lust hit her. The same thing had happened to her that night. It was as if when it came to him, she lost all control.

Which was why being alone with him here at the wedding was dangerous. But he was right. They did need to talk. He needed to learn the truth before he figured it out for himself. At least that's what she told herself. It wasn't because she hadn't had sex in over a year and during that time, she had been fantasizing about all the dirty things he could do to her body. No, this was about something more important than her poor, neglected vagina.

Even knowing it was a terrible idea, she went with him anyway, not fighting him as he led her to the vacant bridal room.

With her mind and body at war with one another, one thing was clear.

No matter what happened in there tonight, she knew when they came out, neither of their lives would ever be same.

FIVE

Jane walked into the room where her mother had gotten ready earlier and didn't stop walking until she was as far as she could get from Ryder. Keeping her distance was the only way to remember why they were in here.

She wasn't normally this weak. She was a successful businesswoman who managed several employees. In negotiations, she went toe-to-toe with powerful people who had years of experience on her. But with Ryder, she was a different woman. Someone motivated by primal urges rather than reason. He wielded a power over her, one crafted out of Domination and her need to submit. Only he had ever brought that side out in her, and once again she felt helpless to resist him.

Once the door closed, Ryder rested his back against it and folded his arms across his chest. Instead of tearing her clothes off or engaging her in sexual banter, he simply glared at her.

Waiting for him to start the conversation and uncomfortable by the long silence, she fidgeted with the top of her dress. There were so many feelings swirling through her—confusion, longing, desire, fear—she didn't know which one to focus on.

When he continued to stare at her, she decided to take the initiative and said the first thing that came to mind. "So . . . you're Keane's son?"

His lip curled in disdain. "Like you didn't know."

What? She was taken aback by his accusation and the fury behind it. Why would he think she knew? "I didn't. Not until I saw you tonight."

His body shook in laughter. "You honestly want me to believe that it's all a big coincidence?"

In not one of her imaginary scenarios in which she saw him again had she anticipated this kind of behavior from him. He was so different from the flirtatious and playful man she'd met a year ago.

At first glance, he looked the same. His hair was a touch shorter, and he was dressed more conservatively, but it was the hostile way he spoke to her and the way he held himself that was different. He was completely closed off. Accusatory. And damn it, she didn't deserve to be treated that way.

She hadn't done anything wrong.

"Yes," she responded, crossing her arms as well. "Because that's the truth."

He ground his jaw, his gaze dropping to her chest.

He stalked toward her and used his body to propel her back against the wall. Her heart was thumping wildly, but she wasn't scared. Not even when he slammed his hands beside her ears and pinned her between his warm body and the cool wall.

No, she wasn't nervous.

She was *aroused*.

They were so close their chests were touching. Her nipples tightened and her lower belly clenched.

Breathing heavily, she looked into Ryder's eyes, searching for the playful and passionate man she'd met on that one magical night. Within seconds, his pupils grew from tiny dark dots to huge circles that ate up the gray of his irises.

He softly traced the shell of her ear. "I can't tell if you're lying to me."

She shivered. "I'm not." Her voice came out as a raspy whisper.

"Right now, I'm not sure I care if you are."

She knew she should push him away, and yet all she wanted to do was get closer. "Well, even if you don't, *I* care. I swear to you that I had no idea who you were that night."

His hardness nudged her belly. Thank the Lord she wasn't the only one affected. "For the past year, I've been consumed by the need to see you again. And here you are..."

"Here I am." She squeezed her thighs together to quell the mounting achiness, but as her folds pressed into her clitoris, the action only managed to increase it.

He let out a shuddered breath. "You're my fucking stepniece and possibly a liar to boot. I should walk out that door. I shouldn't want you like this. So much that I feel as if I'll suffocate if I don't get another taste of you." He lowered his head and began to kiss the sensitive skin between her neck and shoulder.

Both confused and turned on, she moaned from the onslaught of sensations racking her body. Her pulse was roaring in her ears and her limbs trembled.

Her overwhelming need for him defeated all reason.

Was it the same for him?

Is that why he'd gone from angry to passionate within the blink of an eye? His swift change in mood would've given her whiplash if she wasn't going through her own battle of emotions.

She licked her lips, moistening them. "We can't..." She fisted the fabric of her dress in her hands to keep from wrapping her arms around him like she craved. "You said it yourself, we're related now. It wouldn't be right."

On top of that, she should be furious. She *was* furious. He'd just accused her of lying. And only moments before, he'd been just as angry with her for some unknown reason. Not to mention, there were still things hanging over them, unspoken words that would likely stop Ryder right in his tracks once they were uttered.

Again, she was torn between her body and her mind. After overhearing his end of the phone call with his girlfriend that night, she'd been angry, but she'd also been devastated. In only a few hours, she'd fallen hard for Ryder.

She should stop this before she fell even harder for him.

But underneath her dress, her nipples hardened and poked out of her ugly bridesmaid dress. Her neglected vagina clenched and dampened in celebration. Everything she promised herself suddenly disappeared until the only thing she could concentrate on was how good it was to have Ryder's body pressed against hers and how much she desired to be filled with him.

He kissed and licked his way up the side of her neck, stopping to nibble on her earlobe. Heat blasted through her core.

"Love the glasses, but they're gonna get in the way soon," he said huskily, removing the frames and tossing them onto the nearby table. "I want to hear you moan my name one last time."

One last time.

What would it hurt?

He might hate her when she told him the truth, but at least she'd have one more incredible memory of him to keep her warm on cold winter nights.

"I need you to be honest." She drew back and stared into his eyes. "Do you have a wife or girlfriend I should know about?"

A notch formed above his nose and his brows dipped. He looked genuinely confused by her question.

Had she been wrong about what she'd overheard that night?

He grabbed her face between his hands and put his forehead against hers. "I don't know where you got the idea that I have a wife or girlfriend, but I swear, there's no one else. Not now...and not the last time we were together."

Call her naïve, but she believed him.

"Then fuck me, Ryder," she said shyly, the words coming out like a plea.

And maybe it was.

He didn't hesitate. Like a man possessed, he growled as he covered her mouth with his, stealing her breath from her lungs. He tasted the same as he had that night, the whiskey he'd drunk earlier still on his tongue. She could become intoxicated on his mouth alone. Not from the alcohol, but in the way his lips slanted over hers, caressing and claiming at the same time. His tongue danced with hers, teasing her before darting away.

Her body was on fire and her heart raced.

The fabric of her dress rubbed almost painfully against her fevered skin, a barrier she no longer wanted between her and Ryder.

"Need to see you," he mumbled between kisses. With deft precision, he unzipped the back of her dress, the sound of it mingling with their mutual groans of want. Her sleeveless dress slid down her chest and fluttered to the floor, leaving her completely bare.

And she did mean completely.

The color and material of the dress weren't conducive to undergarments.

He stopped kissing her and took a step backward. His gaze raked a languid path over her breasts, down her belly, to the patch of hair between her thighs. She trembled, wondering if he noticed the changes—her slightly larger breasts and the extra ten pounds she carried on her lower abdomen.

If so, he didn't seem to mind.

He reached out for her and cupped her breasts in his hands. His fingers strummed her nipples, lighting up every nerve in her body. It was as if Ryder had awoken her from a deep slumber, reminding her she was a sexual creature who deserved to be touched.

His expression turned fierce, and in one swift motion, he scooped her up into his arms. He carried her over to the couch, snagging the half-filled bottle of champagne along the way, and settled her upon the cool leather. Lying down, she spread her thighs apart in expectation of him settling between them.

Instead he fell to his knees and drew a nipple into his warm mouth. Her head lolled to the side as each pull of his mouth sent tendrils of hot embers to her clit, almost as if he were sucking on them at the same time. Her nipples were much more sensitive since the last time he'd done this to her.

It had been so long.

The tension inside her wound too quickly, too tightly, but she couldn't hold back. Crying out his name, she broke apart, shattering, trembling, as wave after wave of hot bliss poured through her core and outward.

When she came back to herself, her gaze met his.

"Did you just come?" he asked with a smile.

She looked away. "Yes. It's embarrassing."

His fingers gently turned her chin back toward him. The irises of his eyes had changed to a darker gray. "Hey. Don't be embarrassed. It was fucking sexy as hell to witness. In fact, I want to see it again."

Again? She tried to sit up, but he pushed her down with a hand to her belly.

Okay, then.

He maneuvered her body so that her legs dangled over the couch cushion and he had full access to her sex. Moving between her thighs, he leaned up and took her mouth in a blistering kiss that made her lips tingle. A cool splash of fizzy liquid hit her neck and chest.

Ryder licked a trail down her neck to her breastbone, lapping up the champagne with his hot tongue. He alternately sucked and bit her nipples, playing with them until she was sure she'd go crazy from want. Returning to her mouth, he shared the champagne pooled on his tongue.

Whatever this crazy chemistry was between them, it played havoc with her common sense. He slipped lower, spilling champagne over her belly...her pelvis...the V between her legs...his tongue lapping up the alcohol along the way. Her thighs quivered, spreading wider on their own volition, anticipation building with every inch of skin he covered. He leaned back and stared at her, a glimmer in his eyes that she didn't recognize, and slowly brought the champagne bottle to her entrance.

Would he...?

Her head rolled back as he carefully slid the first couple inches of the bottle into her slickness. Oh God. This wasn't right. Wasn't proper.

Bubbly liquid dripped out of her. He pulled the bottle from her and covered her champagne-drenched flesh with his hot mouth, devouring her as if she were a rare delicacy. He fucked her with his tongue, plunging and retreating it, giving her only a small taste of what it would feel like to have him fill her with his cock.

His mouth glossy with her arousal, he inserted the bottle again, this time a little farther. Her muscles clenched around the smooth glass, the sensation odd but exciting. He pulled back, making her think he was going to take it out, before gliding it back in. Over and over, he fucked her with the glass, building her arousal but not giving her enough to push her into climax.

It was wicked and decadent.

She barely recognized the woman who was allowing this man to defile her with a glass bottle.

The sound of people talking right outside the door caused her to tense. "Ryder," she whispered in warning.

"What's wrong, Jane?" he said, smirking up at her. "Are you worried someone will come in here? Or does it excite you? Knowing that all they have to do is turn that knob and they'll see you naked, thighs spread, your pussy pink and swollen as I fuck you with a three-hundred-dollar bottle of champagne?"

She shut her eyes, not wanting him to witness the truth in them. That every word he uttered just drove her arousal higher and higher. That the idea of someone catching them turned her on more than she'd ever care to admit.

Ryder's thumb pressed on her clit, rubbing and making tiny circles. "No hiding. Open your eyes and give it to me, Jane. I want to drink your come directly from the bottle."

She was helpless against his command.

Her lids flew wide as the orgasm built deep inside her core, the strength of it liable to rip her apart. Every cell in her body buzzed. Her arms and thighs shook. Her fingers curled into the couch cushions. She sucked in a large breath just as she reached the pinnacle of her pleasure. And then she was free-falling.

She covered her mouth with her hand to keep from crying out. Her sex contracted around the hard, smooth glass, and liquid heat expanded outward, bathing her limbs in exquisite rapture.

Either the people standing outside the door had left or they were at the door listening, but she didn't hear any voices in the hallway anymore. Not that she cared. Ryder had a way of making the rest of the world disappear when she was with him.

His gaze was locked on hers, his eyes darker now. Ryder removed the bottle and brought it to his mouth, his lips wrapping around the rim. He threw his head back and tipped the bottle, drinking it down with a groan that she felt like a graze between her legs. Mesmerized by the sight and jealous of the bottle, she watched the way his Adam's apple worked as he swallowed.

He slipped the bottle out of his mouth and lifted it to her lips. "Delicious. Taste yourself," he ordered.

She curled her lips around the same rim where his had been only moments ago, tasting her arousal still on the glass along with the flavor of Ryder's mouth. Champagne splashed onto her tongue and she drank it down greedily. Eagerly.

The room spun.

She was intoxicated but not on alcohol.

On sex.

On desire.

On Ryder.

Before she finished swallowing, his mouth crashed into hers.

He covered her with his clothed body, every part of him touching every part of her.

She laughed softly. "You're going to stain your tuxedo."

He dragged a single finger down her cheekbone. "I don't care."

She wanted to feel him. Skin to skin.

But there wasn't enough time.

Even though she'd already come twice, she'd go mad if she didn't have his cock inside her soon.

Her hands clumsily worked the button of his dress pants. He lifted himself off her just enough so she could pull down the zipper and tug his shirt out.

But just as she slipped her fingers below his waistband, he stilled her seeking hands.

He sucked in a breath. "Don't." His eyes and mouth were pinched as if he was in pain. "We shouldn't go any further. Not until we have that talk and you tell me the truth."

The truth. Right. She had to tell him everything. Not tomorrow, but tonight. He deserved to know. Making love with secrets between them would be wrong. But why, then, did it feel so right?

Keeping her eyes on his, she slid her hands from underneath his and continued to move them on their original path until she got to their target. His hard penis jerked as she wrapped her hand around it.

He hissed. "Jane," he said in warning.

She waited for him to order her to stop, but instead he thrust his pelvis up in a silent demand for more.

Feeling victorious, she yanked down his underwear enough to reveal him. Their first night together, she'd been shy and hesitant. Worried about doing everything right. She hadn't given herself permission to look closely at his...cock.

Long, cut, and with a thick crown, it was a bit of a mystery as to how she'd ever taken all of that inside her. She traced the bulging vein that ran up the length, feeling it pulsate under her fingertips. The skin itself was soft—much softer than the rest of his skin—and reddish around the corona.

She wanted to make him feel good, as good as he'd made her feel. Mouth open, she leaned forward to take him inside.

"No. I'm not going to last long and I don't want to come in your mouth." He tossed his wallet onto the carpet and flipped it open, grabbing a condom packet. "I want your pussy. Put this on me."

Her hands shook as she rolled the latex down over his cock. He gestured for her to get on his lap. "Ride me, Jane. I need to feel you."

She sucked in a breath at the terrifying yet exciting idea of being on top of him, of having the control. Would she know what to do?

Climbing on his lap, she shivered at the feel of his clothes against her naked flesh. It reminded her that although she was on top, he retained the power. For some reason, that thought gave her comfort.

Gripping the top of his cock, she lifted herself above it and notched it to her slick opening. She lowered herself onto him, watching as he slowly disappeared inside her. Although she was no longer a virgin, there was still a slight burn as he stretched the sensitive tissues.

He hissed, his hands firmly gripping both her hips. "Even dripping for me, you're so fucking tight. Take it all. I don't want a single inch of my dick to be left out of your pussy."

Sweat dripped between the valley of her breasts. She was already feeling stretched to capacity and she still had a few inches to go. But along with the intense fullness came a sense of rightness, as if they were two pieces that were meant to fit together.

If he wanted it all, she'd give him all because she wanted to please him.

Biting the inside of her cheek, she sank all the way down until her ass rested on his thighs.

Within seconds, the pressure building behind her clit compelled her to move. Slowly, she slid upward, testing how far she could go. On the way, his cock rubbed a couple of spots that brought stars to her eyes and electric sparks shooting through her core.

She let out a very unladylike groan as she tossed her head back and shamelessly rode his cock, clenching her internal muscles along the way up and releasing them on the way back down. He thrust his pelvis up, hitting her clitoris on every downstroke. His fingers dug into her hips as he helped her to move faster and faster, relentlessly pounding into her without a single reprieve.

"Get there, Jane," he said hoarsely, reaching between them to pinch her clit. "I'm not gonna last much longer. It's been too long."

She didn't know what he'd meant by it being "too long," but the urgency in his voice coupled with the extra stimulation to her clit sent her to the very edge. "I'm there, Ryder. I'm coming." Her body thrashed as deep pulsations rocked her core and her walls clamped down over and over again on Ryder's cock.

With a guttural shout, Ryder stilled, his eyes shut so tight, he looked as if he was in pain rather than orgasmic pleasure.

She collapsed on top of him, her arms flung over his shoulders and her head on his chest. His heart hammered underneath her ear as they both attempted to catch their breath.

Nothing had ever felt so good. At least nothing since that first night. Neither her own hand nor her plastic vibrator could ever re-create the sensation of having Ryder deep inside of her.

Unfortunately, she might have to be content with her memories.

Because it was time to tell Ryder the truth.

And once she did, he may never want her again.

SIX

If it was possible to sink his dick even farther inside of Jane, he would. Ryder wanted to thrust his entire being into her, fuck himself so far into her, she'd feel him there for the rest of her life.

One last time.

Who had he been trying to kid?

How many nights had he fantasized about being inside of her again?

When he'd nabbed her before she went into the reception, he'd only planned on confronting her about her theft of Novateur's designs. He didn't know what had come over him. One minute he'd wanted to take her over his knee and punish her with fifty whacks to her bare ass and the next minute all his fury had morphed into a raging lust.

Slumped against him, drenched with sweat and her curly hair sticking to his chest, she was oblivious to how much power she held over him.

He shouldn't have touched her. Because now that he'd gotten another taste, he only wanted more.

Which was a problem.

He needed to confront her about the theft of his designs.

But once she confirmed that she was responsible, would he still want her?

His gut said short of her being a serial murderer, and possibly even then, he'd always want Jane.

That didn't mean he'd allow himself to have her.

Since seeing her photo in the trade magazine, he'd been under the belief that her innocence on Mackinac Island had all been an act in order to get him to lower his guard so that she could gain access to his laptop.

Yet tonight she radiated that same innocence. The more he thought about it, the more he realized it was possible he had jumped to conclusions.

After all, *Ryder* had been the one to approach *Jane* at the conference. If his father had sent her, wouldn't he have chosen someone who fit Ryder's...typical conquest? The women he slept with were experienced and obvious about that fact. Jane was the exact opposite.

She had no idea how beautiful she really was.

He caressed her back, drifting his fingers back and forth, and she shivered, goose bumps popping up on her skin. Maybe sensing the time to talk had finally come now that they'd temporarily satiated their lust, she pulled back from him.

He held the base of the condom as she lifted herself off his lap and stood, putting her glistening, swollen pussy at eye level. And just like that, his cock twitched, apparently not quite as satiated as it should be considering he'd come harder than he had in...well, ever. Guess that's what happened when you didn't have sex for more than a year.

After disposing of the condom in the wastebasket, he got back into his penguin suit, leaving his jacket and tie off while he cooled down, and Jane quickly dressed and perched those "sexy librarian" glasses on her nose.

Considering they'd just fucked like bunnies, things shouldn't have been as awkward as they were between them. Ryder sat on the couch and patted the cushion in invitation for Jane to sit beside him.

Nibbling on her bottom lip and wringing her hands, she looked anxious as she joined him.

He wanted to hold her, soothe her nerves, put her head against his chest again, but as soon as he touched her, he'd lose control.

"Ryder—"

"How is it that you were able to disappear without a trace?" he asked at the same time she spoke.

Her brows crinkled in confusion. "I don't know what you're talking about."

"I searched for you after our night together," he explained. *Searched* was an understatement. More like obsessively hunted for her. "No one who worked for the conference knew who you were or what company you worked for."

"That's because at the time, I technically didn't work for McKay." She squirmed and dropped her gaze to her lap. "I was an intern."

"An intern," he said, unable to keep the skepticism from his voice.

"Yes."

She wouldn't meet his eyes.

Was she lying? If so, why lie about *that*?

He rubbed his hand down his cheek, catching the scent of Jane's pussy on his fingers. His cock swelled beneath his zipper. "My father sent an intern to the conference? He would never do that." Sure, Ciara had been dating Finn at the time, but Keane wasn't the type of person to do anyone—even his own kids—any favors.

Unless he got something in return.

So, what the hell would he get out of sending Jane to the conference?

Ryder couldn't stop himself from thinking the worst.

She lifted her gaze. "Well, he did," she said tightly. "In fact, he's the one who offered me the internship in the first place. *He* took the initiative of calling Dean Lancaster—"

"Dean Lancaster? You mean Isaac Lancaster?" Not only was Isaac a friend of Ryder's, but he was also his business partner in Novateur. "You went to Edison University?"

"Yes, I graduated from their business administration program. First in my class," she said with pride. As well as she should. It was one of the top business schools in the country. "Do you know of him?"

What the hell? It was like he was playing "six degrees of Kevin Bacon," only swapping out the movie star with Jane.

While he'd been looking for her, she'd been only one degree away from him the entire time. She was the daughter of Finn's now-wife. Worked for Keane. And had graduated from the business school where both his business partners worked.

If only Jane had a name like Desdemona, he would've found her within days.

He shifted on the couch to give his hard-on some relief and inadvertently bumped his leg into hers. Heat shot to his groin, making his move for relief irrelevant. "You can say that. He's one of my business partners."

She gave him a little smile. "Oh. Weird. Small world."

Why would his father call Isaac to hire an intern? And more importantly, why hadn't Isaac mentioned that Keane had called him?

"Did Keane hire you before or after your mother started dating Finn?" he asked, resting his arm on the top of the couch, his hand only inches from the back of her neck. His fingers itched to play with her hair and feel her skin beneath his fingers again.

Her gaze darted away from his and then back again. "After. But I didn't know they were dating when he hired me."

"Your mother hadn't told you?"

She smoothed her fingers over her dress. "We're...not close."

He didn't know why he was surprised by that information. He'd already known that Ciara refused to publicly acknowledge Jane as her daughter. "I see."

She tapped her foot on the floor. "I'm sure you do."

"What's that supposed to mean?"

"It's my understanding you don't want anything to do with your family," she said accusingly.

"And you have a problem with that?" He bristled.

She pressed her lips together, pausing before responding. "Your father is one of the most compassionate, decent men

I know. I don't understand why you'd willingly choose to abandon him and your brother."

Jane was either naïve or had a different definition of *decency* if she believed Keane was a decent man.

He didn't want to fight with her, but hell if she thought she could judge Ryder for getting away from his father and McKay Industries. "You don't know the first thing about Keane or my relationship with him."

She jumped up from the couch. "I know he's taken me under his wing and given me an opportunity I'd never have gotten anywhere else."

He harrumphed, knowing exactly what opportunity his father could provide a beautiful young woman like Jane. He just didn't know Keane's end game. *Yet.* "As an intern?"

Her jaw tightened. "I'm no longer an intern. I'm now VP of innovation."

Of course she was. All she had to do was steal Novateur's designs to get there.

"Vice president, huh? That's quite the leap in such a short time."

She folded her arms, her eyes narrowing. "What are you implying?"

"You must have done something to deserve such a swift promotion."

Her jaw dropped. "Oh my God. You think I'm sleeping with him."

What? He shuddered in revulsion. "Hell no."

The thought of anyone—especially his father—touching her turned his mouth sour.

Jane softened a bit, dropping her arms to her side. "Then what? Because it's clear to me that you don't believe I got the position because of my work ethic."

He let out a snort. "Ethics. That's rich coming from you."

She crossed her arms over her chest as all signs of her softening instantly disappeared. "Excuse me?"

"My father doesn't believe in work ethic. He believes in doing everything he can to get what he wants, even if it means committing a crime along the way."

Okay, now she was pissed. Standing rigid, it was as if her spine had elongated and she'd grown a couple inches taller right before him. Her eyes blazed with fire, and suddenly she looked every bit the businesswoman she purported herself to be.

If her ire wasn't directed at him, he'd totally be turned on by her right now.

Oh hell, who was he kidding? It didn't matter that she was mad at him.

She was sexy as fuck like this.

"First of all," she said, pacing back and forth, "I've never once observed anyone at McKay acting outside of the professional boundaries. Even your father. And secondly, I would never work for anyone who believed the way to get ahead was through a criminal act."

He had to give it to her. She was very convincing. Either she was innocent or a seasoned liar. His gut was telling him it was the former. Well, maybe it wasn't his gut so much as his cock.

But still. He had to get to the truth.

He stood up from the couch and stalked toward her. "So you're denying it."

She stopped pacing and frowned. "Denying what?"

"My computer showed that someone made copies of my restaurant automation design files the night I met you. And then suddenly you're VP of the division of McKay that's implementing those designs? Come on, surely you've done your research. How many companies in this country design smart kitchens for restaurants that utilize mechanical arms and conveyor belts in lieu of people?"

Less than a handful and none of them as successful as Novateur.

At the wrinkle of her brows, he continued. "Tell me, Jane, why should I believe that you weren't the one who stole them?"

She threw her arms up in the air. "Because I'm telling you the truth, damn it! I didn't steal your designs. Up until now, I had no idea you even owned a restaurant automation business."

Standing in front of her, he searched her face for the evidence she was lying. "You went from intern to VP in a year. How? What reason would Keane have to give you such a high position at his company?"

She glanced at the door and took a breath, her shoulders rising and falling. "I worked hard to get the promotion, but that's not the only reason he gave it to me." She bit her lip as she twisted her fingers together. "I needed money. Security. He didn't want me to worry."

"Worry about what?"

A long silence followed as Jane seemed to grapple with something. She walked away from him, moving closer to the door. Every second seemed like a minute as he waited for her to speak. Once she reached the door, she hung her head, and for a moment, he thought she was going to leave without answering.

She swirled around and faced him. "Taking care of my son. Maddox." She looked him straight in the eyes. "Ryder . . . he's yours."

SEVEN

Ryder had prepared himself for Jane to admit she had only slept with him in order to steal Novateur's designs.

He'd been prepared for her to deny all the accusations against her.

Prepared to hear that she hadn't given him another thought since that night.

In the eventuality of seeing Jane again, he'd prepared himself to hear many things.

Hearing that he was a father was not one of them.

In all these months, the possibility hadn't even occurred to him once.

Displaying a calm he didn't feel inside, he asked, "You had a baby?"

Less angry than she'd been a minute ago, she moved away from the door and stepped closer to him. "Yes. Maddox. He's three months old now. His birthday was on August fourteenth."

Three months.

Three months ago his son had been born and he hadn't even known.

Ryder might not have wanted a child, but rather than panicking at Jane's proclamation, he swelled with pride.

He had a *son*.

Unless...

Ryder hated that it had to be asked, but he'd be a fool if he didn't. "Don't take this the wrong way, but you're sure he's mine?"

He had to give her credit. Jane didn't so much as flinch.

Instead, she held his gaze, head-on. "I was a virgin before that night," she said quietly. "And I haven't been with anyone since."

A virgin?

He recalled all the ways he'd debauched her in Mackinac—and *tonight*—and his stomach bottomed out as if he'd just dropped from a ten-story building. Although he'd known she didn't have much experience, he had dismissed the possibility that she was a virgin. For some reason, the fact that she had been one hit him almost as hard as learning about Maddox.

When she'd fallen asleep that night, he'd gone into the bathroom and brought back a towel to dry the sweat off her skin and a warm, wet washcloth to clean the stickiness between her thighs. Because he had taken her hard and long, it hadn't surprised him to see a little blood. "A...virgin? Why didn't you say anything?"

Knowing that he'd been her first gave him some sort of sick satisfaction. But fuck...at the same time, he was filled with guilt. If he'd been aware she was a virgin, he would've used extra care.

"I didn't want you to treat me differently," she insisted. "I didn't want you to change your mind."

The only way he would've walked away from her that night would have been if she had asked him to.

He strode to her, gathering her into his arms, then stroked the soft skin of her neck. "You deserved better than what I gave you."

Loving caresses instead of spankings. Candles instead of the harsh hotel lighting. Champagne instead of vodka. Whispered murmurings instead of crude dirty talk. Rose petals instead of restraints. He would've ensured her comfort rather than ramming himself into her like an animal.

Her hand went to his chest. "You gave me my first real orgasm. You made me feel desirable for the first time in my life. And most importantly, you gave me my son. I don't regret one thing from that night."

He wished he could say the same. While he'd never regret their night or that Maddox had been conceived, he regretted not having been more responsible. It was his fault she'd gotten pregnant. Blame it on his eagerness, but he shouldn't have used that condom knowing it was possibly dried out.

"Except...," she added, her hand now rubbing circles over his heart, "I wish I'd had the guts to stay the night."

Jane amazed him. Rather than railing against him for his actions, she was apologizing for hers.

"If you really didn't steal the designs, why did you leave?" he asked.

"I couldn't sleep. There were too many thoughts racing through my mind. I wasn't sure what the etiquette was or whether you expected me to stay the night. I went into the bathroom to get dressed when I heard you answer your cell phone. It was a woman you called Isabella. I figured..." She looked down and shrugged. "I left while you were still on the call."

He'd been sleeping soundly when his cell had awakened him. It wasn't until after he hung up that he realized Jane wasn't sleeping beside him. "Isabella is my friend Tristan's fiancée." Had Jane honestly believed he'd been cheating on someone with her? No wonder she'd asked him earlier if he had a girlfriend or a wife. "You thought she was my—"

"I didn't know," she said. "But I didn't want to stick around and find out. So I left."

As disappointed as he'd been to discover she'd left, he couldn't blame her for her actions. He hadn't asked her to stay the night before he'd fallen asleep or made any promises for the future. Coupled with him answering a call from a woman in the middle of the night, her decision to leave made sense.

He played with the ends of her curls, loving how they sprang back when he tugged on them. "Is that why you didn't tell me you were pregnant?"

She shook her head vehemently. "No. I wouldn't do that. As soon as the doctor confirmed my pregnancy, I tried to find you. I called the conference association but they didn't have any record of you."

What a mess.

If only he'd known before he'd gotten on the last boat leaving Mackinac Island that night that there would be no way to find Jane, he would've asked for her phone number before he took her to his bed.

"Tristan was the one who originally registered for the conference," he explained. "I went in his place."

"So do you believe me?" she asked.

"Believe you didn't steal my designs or believe that I'm Maddox's father?"

She shrugged. "Either. Both."

He didn't know who had accessed his computer to steal his designs.

But he knew in his heart it wasn't Jane.

As for Maddox's parentage, nothing about this woman suggested she was lying to him.

"I believe you," he said, pressing his lips to hers.

So much had happened tonight, first finding out Jane was Ciara's daughter and then that she had his child.

He'd had a baby with his *stepniece*.

Not exactly forbidden, but it would definitely raise some eyebrows.

Maddox was the descendent of two of the wealthiest men in the state. Most would think it a blessing, but Ryder knew otherwise.

At least for now Jane seemed to have a limited relationship with her grandfather, Ian Sinclair, but she was already close to Keane.

Was that why he'd given her the promotion? Had he somehow figured out Maddox was his grandson?

He stepped back and gripped her shoulders. "Is it possible Keane knows I'm Maddox's father?"

"I never mentioned your name." Excitement lit up her expression as she processed the implication. "Oh my God. Keane is Maddox's grandfather. He's going to be thrilled."

"You can't tell him," he said a bit too harshly.

Her brows wrinkled in confusion. "What? Why not?"

Why not, indeed?

Maddox was Ryder's son. The child deserved his birthright.

And yet...

There were ramifications to being a McKay. Ryder had grown up knowing bloodstained money bought the clothes on his back and the food in his mouth. There was nothing Keane wouldn't do to get what he wanted.

Bribe political officials, blackmail opposition, intimidate business owners in the form of broken bones...

Even murder.

If Keane found out that Maddox was his heir, he'd do everything in his power to exert his influence over Maddox's life. And Jane would allow it. Because it was apparent that she had no idea what kind of evil Keane was capable of.

Keane could turn Maddox into what Ryder himself had feared becoming.

A monster just like Keane.

"I meant to say not yet." He cupped her face in his hands. "Just give me some time before you tell anyone."

Soft Jane melted away and ballbuster Jane returned with a vengeance. With both hands, she pushed him backward and folded her arms, her eyes narrowed into slits again. "Right, you need time," she said, her tone positively glacial. "If you don't want anything to do with us, I can make it on my own."

Not want anything to do with them? He was already having flashes of moving her and Maddox into his house.

"I don't doubt that you can make it on your own," he said. "But you don't have to. Please, just give me a few days before you tell Keane that I'm Maddox's father."

Jane pressed her lips together and nodded. She retrieved her clutch and opened it before pulling out a card and handing it to him. "This has my cell number on it. If you'd like to meet Maddox, let me know." She strode to the door and with her back turned to him added, "There's nothing I wouldn't do for Maddox. Right now, he's only three months. Too young to know what it's like to have a father. I don't want him to know you—to trust that you'll be there for him—only to have you change your mind and leave. If you think there's any chance of that happening, I'll have an attorney draw up the relinquishment of parental rights paperwork for you."

"I get it," he said, swallowing the lump in his throat.

"That's the thing," she said quietly, not turning around to look at him. "You don't. Until you're a parent, you can't understand."

She's wrong.

He did understand. More than he could say. Ryder's stomach churned as it occurred to him it was possible the best thing he could do for Maddox and Jane was to stay out of their lives.

A good parent would sacrifice anything to keep their child safe.

Even give them up.

Which was why when Jane walked through that door and out of his life again . . .

He let her go.

EIGHT

Lying on the couch and staring at the ceiling, Ryder was still in the dressing room five minutes later when the door swung open. For a moment, he thought it might be Jane, coming back to...well, he didn't know why she'd come back, but that didn't stop him from hoping.

Instead, Finn stormed inside, his bow tie and the two top buttons of his dress shirt undone. "Where've you been, man? I've been looking all over for you."

Good thing Finn hadn't found him ten minutes earlier.

"Where's the wife?" Ryder sat up and locked his hands behind his head. "Trouble in paradise already?"

Finn removed his tie and tossed it on the same table where Jane's glasses had been. "No, asshole. She's in the ballroom." He gazed at his feet and sighed. "I just wanted to...to thank you for coming tonight. I know you didn't want to and it meant a lot to have you here."

Okay. They were going to have one of *those* moments.

Ryder stood, went over to his brother, and punched him

lightly on the arm. "I can't say I'm thrilled to have Ian Sinclair in the family, but if Ciara makes you happy, then who the fuck am I to judge?"

Yeah, that was a bald-faced lie. Other than Ciara's beauty and her money, Ryder didn't understand what his brother saw in her. She hadn't even shed a tear during the wedding ceremony. What sort of woman didn't cry at her own wedding?

Oh yeah. The same sort who didn't publicly acknowledge her daughter.

Finn nodded once. "I know you and I haven't been as close these past couple of years, but maybe we could hang out when Ciara and I get back from our honeymoon next month. Go for a drink. Catch up on things."

Honestly, there was almost nothing he wanted more. He missed the older brother he'd always looked up to. But there were a fuck ton of questions Finn refused to answer. Until he did, Ryder couldn't completely trust him.

"Any of the things include the truth about why you broke our agreement and came back to work for Keane?"

"Ryder," Finn said in a tone that warned him he'd crossed some invisible line that had been drawn.

"Right. I didn't think so." He took a step back from his brother. "All those times we talked about challenging Keane's expectations for our future was what exactly? Did you mean any of it?"

"I meant every word."

Then what the hell changed? And why was he so damned secretive about it?

"And yet here you are," Ryder said, spreading his arms. "McKay Industries' head legal counsel, responsible for protecting him from the law. What was it that brought you back into the family fold? Money? Power? The salary in the attorney general's office not afford you the lifestyle you'd grown accustomed to?"

Finn pointed a finger in Ryder's face. "You of all people should know me better than that. I don't give a rat's ass about those things. It's just a job. It's not like I'm signing away my life to it."

No, just his soul.

Ryder shook his head in disappointment. "Well, as McKay's attorney, I'm here to inform you that your client stole Novateur's intellectual property and committed corporate espionage."

Finn jerked backward. "The fuck you say?"

"Oh, come on. You can't tell me it escaped your attention Keane started a restaurant automation business to compete with my company?"

His brother's gaze dropped to his shoes. "Of course it didn't."

Ryder had suspected his brother had been aware, but it still hit him straight in the gut to hear it confirmed. "And you were okay with that?"

"Hell no," Finn growled. "As soon as I heard about it, I confronted him. He swore he did it for you—for when you come to work for McKay." He rubbed the back of his neck. "I don't know...he still has it in his head that you two will reconcile eventually. But he didn't say anything about stealing."

"Plausible deniability. That way you don't have to lie to me or the court when I sue McKay." Even though they were alone, he still lowered his voice. "Last year, I was at a conference up on Mackinac Island. Someone accessed my laptop and downloaded my design files."

"And you have proof that it was Keane?" he asked quietly.

Ryder searched his brother's expression. He almost looked... eager.

But why?

"No," Ryder admitted. "I don't have proof. Not yet."

Finn's mouth opened and closed a couple times, as if he was about speak but changed his mind. He glanced at the door and moved in closer to Ryder. "Listen, I'll check into it when I get back from my honeymoon, and we'll have that drink." He paused. "You're right. You deserve an explanation as to why I came back to work for Keane. Just give me—"

"Finn?" Ciara strolled into the room, still picture-perfect, unlike her rumpled husband. She wrapped her manicured hand around Finn's biceps and gave Finn what Ryder could only describe as a practiced pout. "I was wondering where you had disappeared to. I turn around to talk to some guests and the next thing I know, I can't find you or our fathers anywhere. I don't suppose you've seen them? I need you and them for the toasts, and we're already running ten minutes behind schedule."

Finn's eyes darted between Ciara and Ryder. "Sorry. Do you want me to go look for them?"

She sighed. "No. We'll just have to do a little rearranging, that's all." She pasted on a smile and turned to Ryder. "It's very nice to meet you, Ryder. Thank you for coming." On those words, she spun on her heels and walked toward the door. "Coming?" she asked Finn from over her shoulder.

Ryder slapped Finn's back. "Go. Call me when you get back into town." He was curious as to what Finn had been about to say before Ciara interrupted. But it could wait a month. It wasn't as if anything would change between now and then.

Having already talked (and more) with Jane, Ryder had no reason to stay for the wedding reception. As he walked down the hallway to the coatroom, laughter and clapping floated in from the ballroom.

He shook his head. Based on family history—namely, Finn's and Keane's previous marriages—Ryder gave Finn and Ciara no more than a year before they called it quits.

He just hoped this marriage ended up less violently than Finn's last one.

As he turned the corner, hushed conversation caught his attention. He moved over to the wall and quietly inched closer to the open door of the coatroom.

Families. Business. Pact.

Most of the words were too muffled for Ryder to decipher. But then after a beat of silence by the speakers, he recognized Keane's voice as he spoke clearly and loudly. "It's a deal, Sinclair. Shall we shake on it?"

What the hell had those two agreed to?

He didn't know.

But whatever it was . . . it couldn't be good.

* * *

Tonight marked Jane's second walk of shame.

Only this time, there was a witness to it.

Luckily, the witness happened to be her best friend.

Jane opened the door of her apartment, careful not to wake Maddox. Wearing SpongeBob pajamas and a nicotine patch on her arm, her roommate Dreama bopped out of the kitchen, a glass of water in her hand. Her brown- and pink-streaked hair was up in a high ponytail. "Hey, Chickie. How was the wedding? Did your mom do her usual impression of Maleficent?"

Dreama was not a fan of Ciara's and never had a problem saying so. It was her opinion that Jane was better off without her, especially because she hadn't come to see Maddox once since visiting him and Jane in the hospital the day he was born.

Jane sighed as she slipped off her heels by the door. "How was Maddox tonight? Did he take his reflux medicine? Did he have his bath? How many ounces of formula did he drink?"

Dreama ticked off the fingers of her right hand. "Happy. Yes. Yes. No formula, but he did finish off a bottle of vodka."

"Ha. Funny." She stuck out her tongue. "Do we have any ice cream?"

"Uh-oh. That sounds ominous." Dreama twirled on the balls of her feet and strode back into the kitchen as if on a mission. "Of course we do. What kind of roommate would

I be if I didn't keep us stocked in frozen sugary goodness?" She opened the freezer and pulled out five quarts of ice cream.

Neither of them believed in buying the pint-sized crap. That might be good for an after-dinner snack, but for talks like these, they had to bring out the big guns.

Between dealing with the usual rejection by her mother, the strange interaction with Evan, and seeing Ryder again, she'd reached her limit of stress. Tonight required chocolate. Lots and lots of chocolate.

"I'm taking the fudge brownie," Jane said, grabbing it off the counter and getting two giant spoons from the utensil drawer. She handed a spoon to Dreama. "What kind do you want?"

Dreama ran her finger along each of the remaining icy containers. "Hmm. Judging by your mood, I think I'm going to require the salted caramel ripple. Oh, and grab the chips." She pointed to the pantry. "The ones with the ridges. The others tend to crumble under the weight of the ice cream."

Jane stuck out her tongue. "Ugh. That's disgusting." But she snatched the chips anyway and brought them with her to the table.

"Says the girl who ate tuna and ketchup sandwiches all through her pregnancy."

Jane chuckled. Even now, she had to admit to craving that bizarre concoction every once in a while. It was like Maddox had permanently altered her taste buds. "Hey, don't knock it 'til you try it." She plopped down on a kitchen chair and took the lid off the ice cream. No bowls for them. "How was Maddox tonight?"

Dreama returned the currently unwanted flavors of ice cream back into the freezer. "Slept like a baby." She clutched her caramel swirl container against her chest as she joined Jane at the table. "Oh, right. He is a baby." She laughed, taking a chip and dipping it in the ice cream. "Like clock-work, he got up for his eleven o'clock feeding and went back to sleep. If you go to bed now, you could get a solid three hours until he's up again."

Sleep? What was that? She was so used to being ex-hausted, she wasn't sure if she remembered what it was like to have energy. Or spare time.

Not that she'd change a thing.

In some ways, she'd never been happier. She had her dream career, a best friend as her roommate and part-time babysitter, and a healthy baby boy. What more could she ask for?

"I had sex tonight," she blurted out, her cheeks heating. *Oh yeah. That.*

Dreama stilled with an ice-cream-covered chip halfway to her mouth. She nodded enthusiastically. "I thought you had a certain glow I'd never seen before. Go on."

"With Maddox's father."

Dreama's hazel eyes widened and her jaw dropped. "Shut the front door. No wonder you need the ice cream. He was a guest at the wedding?"

A guest? She shifted uncomfortably in her chair. "He's Finn's brother."

Dreama took a handful of chips and dumped them into the container of ice cream. "Finn. Your *stepfather*, Finn?"

"Of course I'm talking about Finn, my step..." *Okay, that just creeped her out.* "Ciara's husband. How many other Finns do you know?"

Dreama pushed Jane's container of fudge brownie closer to her. "Just trying to lighten the mood, Chickie."

She shouldn't be taking her frustrations out on Dreama. That's what the ice cream was for.

"I'm sorry. I shouldn't snap at you." She took a big spoonful of brownie chunk and shoved it in her mouth. Not surprisingly, a glob of it ended up on her dress. *Oh well.* She was never going to wear it again anyway. "You're not the one who accused me of corporate espionage and stealing to get ahead in business."

"Wow. He did that?" Dreama made circles with her spoon in the air. "Does he not know you at all? Wait, stupid question. Other than the one night together where you barely exchanged any information outside of your first names, he doesn't know the first thing about you," she pointed out. "But still, corporate espionage? Why did he think that?"

Jane frowned, trying to recall his exact words. "Something about stolen designs taken off his computer that night. Honestly, I'm not sure." And it didn't matter because she had not done it, and neither had McKay Industries. The Keane she'd come to know would never engage in theft of corporate secrets. Not even his son's. "All I know is he doesn't speak to Keane at all and he rarely talks to Finn. He assumes anyone who works closely with his father must be unethical, which is ridiculous because in the time I've worked for Keane, I've never observed him do anything remotely unethical."

Not only that, but also Keane had never even asked her to do something that would compromise her principles. Yes, she had to admit, it was odd that Keane had started a restaurant automation business that competed with Ryder's, but he must have had his reasons. The fact that they were building designs similar to Novateur's was likely a coincidence and Ryder was just assuming the worst because of his prejudice against his father.

Dreama poked her tongue against her cheek, considering Jane. "I believe you haven't, but one thing I've learned as a parole officer is that people aren't always the way they appear. One client of mine has the sweetest face you could imagine. Big innocent blue eyes and chubby cheeks. He's shorter than me and weighs probably twenty pounds less. Not a muscle on the guy. Girl meets him in a bar? She wouldn't even think to be afraid of him." She paused, pursing her lips. "Just got out after twenty years for raping his mother."

"Dear God."

"I'm not trying to say that Keane's a rapist or anything," Dreama continued. "But he's not going to show you all sides of himself. You see the best part of him. Your baby daddy, on the other hand, may have witnessed something different while growing up. Doesn't mean you have to believe him, but you also shouldn't completely discount his life experiences either."

She nibbled on her bottom lip, Dreama's words sinking in. Was she right?

Jane supposed it wasn't much different than her experiences with her own mother. Anyone who knew Ciara would never guess how cold and aloof she could be.

"What did he say about Maddox?" Dreama asked. "You did tell him, right?"

"Yes. After we..." Her cheeks warmed.

Dreama's brows rose. "Hmm. After, huh?"

"It just happened," Jane mumbled.

"I get it." Dreama waved her hand in front of her face. "My vagina falls on random cocks all the time. You don't need to be embarrassed. I'm all for you getting some. No one should suffer through a drought as long as yours. You deserved a night of good, kinky sex."

Knowing Dreama was into the BDSM lifestyle, Jane had confided in her about the spanking and bondage that had taken place the night she'd lost her virginity. She hadn't been sure if what she had experienced that night with Ryder was typical in sex.

According to Dreama, it wasn't. She confirmed that both were practices of BDSM.

At this point, Jane wasn't sure whether she was truly a sexual submissive.

All she knew was she wouldn't mind doing them again.

"How do you know it was good?" Jane asked, unable to prevent the small smile from forming.

"Other than the glow? Your hair's a mess, your lips are swollen, and you smell as if you took a bath in champagne." Dreama sighed loudly. "I love creative men."

"Yeah, he is that," Jane said, thinking about the champagne bottle. "I guess it's good it happened before we talked because right now, I'm not sure where we stand. On one hand, it seemed as if he wanted to be a part of Maddox's life. But on the other, he doesn't want me to tell anyone that he's the father just yet. Apparently, he needs time. Whatever that means."

Her friend's smile disappeared and her expression turned deadly. "Excuse me? I hope you told him what he'd be missing before you twisted his balls and shoved them where the sun don't shine."

"No." She choked down the lump in her throat. "I told him I could raise Maddox without him, and I gave him my card. I'm not going to force him to be a part of Maddox's life."

"Aw, Chickie." Dreama reached over the table and squeezed her hand. "I know you were hoping if you ever found him that he'd come through for you. But you told me he was a player. Didn't you say he took a call from another woman right before you vamoosed your way out of there?"

"Yeah." Jane used her spoon to dig out a chunk of brownie, then popped it in her mouth. "I might have jumped to conclusions. Ryder explained it. Turns out it was his friend's girlfriend."

Dreama coughed on her ice cream/chip combination and beat her chest with her fist. "Ryder?" she finally spit out.

"Yeah, Ryder. Maddox's father," Jane clarified.

Once her coughing fit had ceased, her roomie had a big smile on her face. "Where did you meet him again?"

"At a business conference at the Grand Hotel." Jane

frowned when Dreama shook her head and laughed. "What's so funny?"

The moment Dreama parted her lips, a loud cry came from the bedroom.

Dreama stopped laughing, but her smile remained. "Guess Maddox missed you. Go get some snuggles with your son. I have a feeling you'll be seeing Ryder again sooner than later."

NINE

Coffee cup in hand, Jane strode through the lobby of McKay Industries on her way to the elevator. Dwarfed only by GM's nearby seventy-three-floor Renaissance Center, McKay claimed every floor of the building for its own employees. The glass skyscraper was home to all twenty subsidiaries of parent McKay Industries, six restaurants, corporate apartments, stores, and even a movie theater. It was more than a building. It was a community where executives could live in luxury apartments overlooking the Detroit River and go downstairs to do their grocery shopping or see their physician. Hell, McKay even had its own zip code and its own post office. People from all over the world fought to work there.

Jane didn't take her good fortune for granted. She loved Maddox and being a mother, but she also loved her career. She'd known early on that she had a head for business. At seven, while other girls in her neighborhood had served premade lemonade for a quarter a cup at their stands, she'd made hers from scratch and charged two dollars, pouring the lemonade over ice and serving it in secondhand mason jars she'd bought for a steal. Rather than spend the money on frivolous toys and candy, she'd put it all away in a bank account. In high school, she'd worked part-time for a corporate attorney, which gave her the opportunity to learn some of the legalities of business.

She hadn't ever wanted for money. Her mother had provided her aunt and uncle, who were semiretired by the time they'd become her legal guardians, with a yearly stipend that was well above what they needed to be comfortable. But earning her own money, knowing that she could survive without the help of anyone else, had always been important to her. Now that she was older, she sometimes wondered if that drive stemmed from her mother's abandonment. Her aunt and uncle loved her, but that hadn't kept her from worrying they'd eventually abandon her too.

That drive had gotten her a full scholarship to college and a perfect 4.0 grade point average. And when she'd started as an intern at McKay, she'd worked eighty-hour weeks to prove to both herself and everyone else that she belonged there. It wasn't until she'd gotten pregnant with Maddox that she'd panicked. He'd been a complete surprise.

The best surprise.

She got onto the elevator and pressed the button for the eleventh floor. Mondays were always the busiest day of the week, a fact she was grateful for today. She needed something to keep her mind off Ryder.

Meeting with Evan would definitely help her with that. In between obsessing over what had happened with Ryder and catching up on laundry, she'd thought about Evan's bizarre behavior at the wedding. She'd even tried calling him yesterday, but she'd gotten his voice mail and hadn't heard back from him. Obviously, whatever he'd wanted to talk to her about wasn't important enough to interrupt his day off.

When she got to her office, she unlocked the door and stepped inside, turning on the lights. With a few simple items, she'd made this space her home away from home. A teal pillow on her chair for back support. A few plants here and there. Walls decorated with framed photos of Maddox and Dreama and inspirational quotes by Maya Angelou and Mahatma Gandhi. It wasn't a coveted corner office, but she'd never complain because it was *hers*.

Sitting behind her desk, she flipped on her computer to check her schedule for the day and her work email. Scrolling through it, she confirmed her schedule was packed with meeting after meeting, and that didn't even include the one with Evan in a few minutes.

She clicked open her email and scanned the list, spotting one from Evan sent the night of the wedding, time stamped 8:00 p.m., which was shortly after she saw him. *That's weird.* The email came from the internal network, meaning he must have gone to the office immediately following their brief conversation.

Her stomach plummeted with dread.

He was probably quitting his position at McKay. It didn't surprise her. With his skill, he no doubt had his pick of job opportunities.

Damn. She'd have to call HR to start an immediate

search for a new software engineer. Hopefully he'd give them a couple of weeks before he left.

She opened the email. There was only one line of text.

Thought you should see this.

There was an attachment, but she hovered the cursor over the link. She assumed it was his resignation letter, but he didn't sign his name to the email. What if it was a computer virus?

Biting her lip, she let her curiosity prevail and clicked on the attachment.

Computer code temporarily flashed across her screen before it was replaced by a giant yellow smiley face.

What the hell?

Shit, that couldn't have come from Evan. She'd probably just let a virus infiltrate their network. She quickly deleted both the email and the downloaded file and then ran the virus protection program. Evan would have to check the network to make sure the virus hadn't infected it.

There was a double knock on her door.

Oh good, that was probably him now.

"Come in," she said.

Rather than Evan, her coworker Derek Gardner walked in. He was a newer hire, and he'd been working on developing the restaurant automation line for McKay. In his late thirties, he'd come to the company after freelancing for the last five years in the mechanical engineering field. As vice president of innovation, she spent a lot of hours with Derek in close quarters, and they had become friendly in the last year.

She had a feeling he had a bit of a crush on her. He'd never come right out and said anything, but he tended to find reasons to touch her all the time. Nothing obscene. Just a squeeze of the shoulder or a pat on her hand. Then again, he was friendly with everyone. He was the kind of person who took the time to get to know his coworkers and made sure to never forget a birthday. Not to mention, he always had a smile on his face.

Which was why she was shocked from the lack of it now.

There was something wrong. With Derek's entrance, the energy of the room immediately shifted from peaceful to tense. Something told her he wasn't here to talk about Evan's resignation or a computer virus.

"What's going on?" she asked, sitting up straight in her chair as if she could shield herself from the blow of whatever he was about to tell her.

He exhaled and ran his hand down his face. "Evan Donaldson is dead."

All the air left her lungs. Dead? But...

"Oh my God. I just saw him Saturday night at Finn McKay's wedding." Such a silly thing to say. Why did the fact that she'd just seen him make it that much more unbelievable? "I was supposed to meet with him this morning. What happened?"

His lips curled into a grimace. "He ate his gun. They're saying it was a suicide."

Thought you should see this.

A happy face.

Had the email actually come from him? Was it some kind of message? A weird suicide note?

She couldn't wrap her mind around the fact that he was gone, much less that he'd taken his life intentionally. "Suicide?"

"I know." He came around the desk and rubbed her shoulder. "It doesn't seem real. We went to lunch last week and he was so happy. He'd just found out that his wife was having a baby."

"I didn't know that."

Guilt weighed upon her shoulders. What could have made Evan take his life? She couldn't help feeling that if she had taken the time to talk to him at the wedding, maybe he'd be alive today. But why would he go to her? It wasn't as if they were close.

Lost in thought, she stared at the photo of one-month-old Maddox on her wall.

"You mentioned you saw him at the wedding?" Derek asked gently, sitting on the edge of her desk. "He hadn't mentioned he was invited."

She looked up at him. "I'm not sure that he was. It was weird. He wanted to talk to me and I blew him off. Granted, it was seconds before my mother was about to walk down the aisle, but still . . . I guess I'll never know what he needed to tell me."

"Don't feel badly. You couldn't have known," he said. "He called me Saturday night and left a message to call him back. I didn't. So if you're feeling responsibility, you can share some of it with me. But we weren't the ones who put a gun into his hand and pulled the trigger. That was all him."

It didn't matter if the Pope himself told her not to feel guilty. She hadn't caused Evan's death, but if there was even a slight chance she could have changed his mind, she'd carry that responsibility for the rest of her life.

Strange that Evan had contacted both her and Derek on Saturday night. Whatever he'd wanted to discuss, it had to have been related to work.

Frustrated that she'd never know, she sighed and dropped her head in her hands. "I just wish I'd taken the time to talk to him."

"Did he speak to anyone else at the wedding? Maybe they have some idea what was going on in his mind," Derek suggested.

It was possible, but she doubted it. Something told her he'd specifically come to the wedding for her. But for now, she was going to keep that detail to herself. At least until she could substantiate it. "I honestly don't know."

Derek massaged the back of her neck. "Are you going to be okay?"

Guilt and sorrow be damned, she was a professional. At least for appearance's sake, here at work, she had to keep it together. There was still work to be done and Keane would be counting on her to set an example for the employees in her division. She'd need to go and personally speak with every one of the forty people who worked on their floor.

She took a deep cleansing breath and nodded. "I should call Evan's wife and offer my condolences. See if there's anything McKay can do to help. Be a shoulder for her to cry on." She shrugged. That sounded so trite. She couldn't imagine the pain his wife was feeling. "Maybe she knows what he needed to tell us."

"I'm sure she'd appreciate the call." Derek offered her a

sad smile and slid off her desk. "And if *you* need a shoulder to cry on, I happen to have one readily available to you, day or night."

She stood up from her desk and gave him a hug, her arms wrapping around his warm, burly body.

He was so sweet. If circumstances were different, she may have entertained the thought of dating him. But he was her coworker...

And even if he wasn't, her heart still wanted Ryder.

The phone rang. She pulled back from Derek and picked up the receiver, noting the call was from Keane's secretary's extension. "Jane Cooper."

"Mr. McKay would like to speak to you in his office."

Derek gave her a brisk nod and left her office, gesturing that they'd talk later.

She imagined Keane wanted to discuss the news about Evan. "I'll be right there," she said before hanging up the phone.

A few minutes later, she stepped off the elevator on the building's top floor, a floor strictly reserved for Keane and his three assistants. It always felt as if she were walking into the West Wing of the White House. Everything screamed money, from the gold-painted walls to the cherrywood floors, which was funny once she got to know Keane because the man couldn't care less about his wealth. But it helped him maintain the image of power and worked well to intimidate visitors.

Assistant Number Three greeted her at the desk in the lobby and buzzed her inside without saying a word. Jane went through the door and walked past the boardrooms, kitchen, and library, finally coming to the outside of Keane's office where Assistant Number Two automatically lifted her phone to let Keane know she'd arrived. Jane continued through the double doors into Keane's office. Assistant Number One, a recent Miss America, uncrossed her long legs and stood from her chair across from Keane at his desk. A fire crackled in the fireplace and soft classical music played throughout the room.

Other than his assistants and Finn, Keane rarely brought employees into his inner sanctum. Instead, he'd meet them in one of the boardrooms. But he'd always made an exception for Jane.

When Assistant Number One closed the door behind her as she left, he rose from behind his desk and crossed to her. He took both her hands in his. "Jane. I assume you've heard the news."

Now that she was behind closed doors, her eyes burned with tears. "Derek told me. I just can't believe it. He didn't give any indication that there was anything wrong."

"I know you worked closely with him," Keane said softly. He put his arm around her and led her to the couch by the fireplace. "You're going to need to speak with his assistant, Barbara, and temporarily take over his duties until we can find his replacement. She'll be able to give you his passwords so you can access his files."

It seemed so cold and callous to talk about Evan's work like that, and yet she understood that it was necessary. She couldn't allow her feelings to get in the way of business. She'd show Keane that she could maintain her professionalism in times of tragedy.

She wiped her eyes and settled on the couch next to Keane. "I can do that."

"I should warn you. The police may come by to interview you."

She frowned. "Police? Why would the police be involved?"

Did they know Evan had tried to speak with her only hours before he'd killed himself and that he'd sent her some kind of computer virus?

Keane waved his hand as if swatting a fly. "Standard protocol in a death investigation. They probably won't even require your statement, but I wanted you to be prepared. There are times like these in business when our emotions will try to rule our behavior, but we can't allow that to happen, Jane."

"Of course not, sir."

He continued without acknowledging her agreement. "The company must come first. It's important to stay strong and professional in front of the world. Never give anyone the opportunity to exploit your weakness. Everyone has one. We wouldn't be human if we didn't. But wait until you're home before you crack. Have a glass of wine, hold your baby close, and cry for the senseless loss. Then come back tomorrow with it all behind you."

"Is that what you've always done?"

"It's behind me a moment after I learn the news. I'm not a sentimental man. My first concern is always McKay Industries."

His eyes radiated only kindness but for some reason his words gave her chills. This was the man Ryder had spoken of. Had she been blinded to Keane all along? Or was she imagining things because of Ryder?

She had to understand. Because to her, his lack of feelings made him a sociopath. "But when you're home with your family..."

"McKay Industries is my home. My family. As for my wife, the last thing I would do is show weakness in front of her."

"That seems like a lonely way to live. There's never been anyone you could relax around? Anyone who could share your burdens?"

He sighed and stared at the roaring fire. "There was one...Maria, Ryder's mother. She was a maid in the house. I had just divorced my first wife, Finn's mother, and Maria...she was young. Innocent. Working to help support her parents back in Mexico. She was a special woman."

"What happened to her?" she asked quietly.

"Her mother was ill. I flew her back to her poor rural village in Mexico to visit her. She never returned." His gaze remained on the fire as he paused, seemingly lost in the memory. "Six months after she left, her sister came to my door with a baby—Ryder—and told me Maria had died in childbirth."

Poor Ryder. She ached for him.

"Had you known—"

"No," he said, looking at her, finally out of the spell he'd been under. "I had no idea she was pregnant. If I had known, I never would have allowed her to go. I've had to live with the knowledge that had she stayed, she would've gotten the care she needed rather than having my child delivered on the dirty sheets of her parents' couch by a doctor who never even went to medical school," he said with a curl of disdain on his lips. "Maria... was my last weakness. I never wanted to live through that kind of pain again."

She'd never been in love, but she could understand how someone who'd loved and lost would create a barrier around his heart to protect himself. A man who'd loved like that couldn't be a sociopath.

She took his hand and squeezed. "Keane... I'm so sorry for your loss."

A small smile touched his lips. "It was many years ago. But that brings me to why I called you in here. I'd like to speak to you about Ryder."

Her throat thickened with apprehension. He hadn't called her in to talk about Evan? "Um, okay."

The muscles lining Keane's jaw tightened as he pressed his lips together. "He and I have been... estranged for several years. I've tried everything I can think of to try and repair the rift between us, but he's an obstinate boy. He's determined to forge his own path in life. I get that. Hell, I respect it. But he's refusing to even consider the possibility that he can be a part of our family as well and that one does not negate the other. That's where you come in."

"Me?" she asked, her voice coming out far too squeaky for her liking.

"This has nothing to do with your job here at McKay. I want you to know that. Your job here at the company is secure for as long as you want it."

Until this moment, she'd never doubted that. "That's... good?"

"I sensed a connection between you and Ryder at the wedding."

She brushed her hands down the length of her skirt, nervous by the turn in conversation. What did he know? "You did?"

A small smile played upon his lips and his eyes twinkled. "He was enamored with you. You're a beautiful woman. Who wouldn't be? I believe you'd be good for my son. I'd like for you to become friends with him. Get to know him. Maybe...date him. And while you spend time with him, you can put in a good word about me here and there. Convince him to give me a second chance."

Underneath her blouse, sweat trickled down her chest as the room seemed to heat an extra ten degrees.

She opened her mouth to speak, but the shock from his suggestion left her flabbergasted. While she and Keane were now family, she was also his employee. Asking for her help in swaying Ryder's opinion of him wasn't only inappropriate, but it was also unethical. "I'm not sure I'm comfortable doing that."

She'd defended Keane to Ryder. The Keane she thought she knew wouldn't have made such a suggestion. But now she saw her mentor through new eyes.

"I could pay you," Keane said. "Maybe help with a down payment on a nice house for you and Maddox."

"No!"

Keane cocked his head as if trying to read into her reaction, but his expression gave away nothing.

Did he really believe Jane would take money to manipulate Ryder for him?

Or was he playing with her? Did he know that her connection to Ryder went much deeper than an introduction by Finn before the wedding?

She twisted her fingers together to hide their trembling. As Keane's step-granddaughter, she would have no problem telling him his request made her uncomfortable, but as his employee, she worried a refusal would result in the loss of her job. There had to be a way to get out of this without insulting him or risking her employment.

"That wouldn't be...I couldn't take your money," she said. "Besides, he's my stepuncle now. What would people think?"

He waved a hand. "I doubt it would be a problem. Very few people are aware of your true relationship to Ciara."

She flinched at his painful and insensitive reminder. Keane had never shown such callousness toward her before.

She had no plans on ever taking Keane up on his request, but other than her disgust and disappointment that he had asked her in the first place, she had run out of excuses. "Can I think about it?"

There was a long silence in which she wondered if she'd shown her hand. Keane had a way of reading people that was downright eerie at times. In negotiations, he could see straight through the bullshit and get to the truth before the opposition could think up a better lie. He stood, signaling the end of the offensive conversation.

"Of course, dear. No pressure. It's not as if I'd fire you if you didn't do this for me or remind you of how much I've done for you these past couple of years." His tone was matter-of-fact, without a trace of hostility.

Her stomach sank and a lump formed in her throat.

No pressure?

He was her boss and hadn't accepted the excuses she'd given him. And despite his so-called reassurance not to fire her if she refused, she couldn't help but take the words as a veiled threat.

After leaving his office, Jane made her way back down to her floor and tried to process everything she'd learned from Keane this morning. Between his story about Ryder's mother and his suggestion that she get close to Ryder in order to fix the relationship between father and son, she couldn't miss that Keane had been attempting to manipulate her for his own gain.

While she empathized with Keane's desperation to make amends with his son, she wouldn't allow him to use her. The sad thing was she had already spoken highly of Keane to Ryder and would've continued to do so had Keane not asked her to do it. The conversation had left her with doubts about her mentor.

And doubts about herself.

Had he manipulated her in the past and she'd been blind to it?

She'd been so sure that Keane hadn't stolen Ryder's designs, but what if she was wrong? As vice president of innovation, she was responsible for the department, and any fallout from a theft would fall directly on her shoulders. Then again, why would Keane steal designs from his son if he wanted to reconcile with him?

She took off her glasses and rubbed her temples. She had to get it together before she hit her floor or everyone would know she was off her game today. She pinched her cheeks, bringing some much-needed color to them, and threw back her shoulders. By the time she walked off that elevator, there wasn't a sign she was anything but the consummate professional everyone expected.

The innovation department's floor was mainly set up in a square configuration, with cubicles in the middle and offices on the outside. Generally, assistants and interns sat in the cubicle closest to the employee they worked under.

Jane found Evan's assistant at her desk, typing away with one hand while sniffing into a tissue with the other. Her eyes were teary and her nose was red from crying.

"Barbara," she said softly. "I'm so sorry."

Barbara Spencer had worked for McKay for more than twenty years in one capacity or another. She knew every member of the board, every manager, and at least half of the employees, which ranged somewhere in the thousands.

And the scary thing was she remembered all their names.

Barbara stood and pulled herself together as if she had a spine of steel. "Thank you, Jane. I just can't believe he's gone." She tossed her tissue in the trash. "I've arranged to have flowers sent to his wife and offered to help with the funeral. She expects it will probably be on Saturday since it's Thanksgiving this week and there's an investigation . . ." The poor woman crumpled right in front of Jane's eyes. "I'm sorry. I thought I'd cried my fill already."

Jane gave her a much-needed hug. "Why don't you take the next couple of days off and come back next Monday when we reopen after the holiday?"

"No. No." Barbara plucked a tissue from the box on her desk. "I'll be fine. It will help for me to stay busy. Besides, I've never taken an unplanned day off of work in my life. No point starting now."

"Mr. McKay asked me to take over Evan's accounts until we hire a replacement," Jane told her.

The coding work was too technical for her to complete, but with a basic background in computers, she'd at least have the ability to see where he was in the process.

Barbara composed herself and stopped crying. "Evan was pretty protective of his software designs. He and I had a system of where to hide some of the more"—she paused and put a finger to her lips as if trying to come up with the right word—"valuable files." Nodding, she picked up a framed photo and tapped the back of it. "I'll download everything onto an SD card for you and get it to you by the end of the day."

Jane gave Barbara one last hug and made her way back to her office. She had ten minutes before the rest of the hellish day began. Ten minutes to herself. Ten minutes to remember a time when she didn't have to be strong. Ten minutes to remember what it was like to lose control in Ryder's arms.

She didn't know why she lost all rationality whenever she was around him. That wasn't her. No, she was solid. Dependable. Boring. Dreama was the impulsive one. She had the filthy, unbridled sex with strangers. Not Jane. Jane was the one who carefully planned for every possibility before acting. It had once taken her a month to choose a pair of sneakers. And they only went on her *feet*. Yet she hadn't hesitated to allow Ryder inside her in the most intimate of ways.

Settling into her chair, she picked up a photo of Maddox. He deserved a father. Someone who would always be there to catch him when he fell. But was that Ryder?

She had to give him some credit. He hadn't demanded a paternity test. He'd actually seemed...excited about the possibility of being a father. But then he'd brought up that crap about keeping Maddox a secret because he needed time. Time for what? A part of her wondered whether she should just go ahead and tell Keane he was Maddox's grandfather. Why did it matter to her if Ryder didn't want anyone to know? Maddox wasn't a pawn to be used in some grudge Ryder had against Keane. If he wasn't going to have a father, the least she could give him was a family. A grandfather in Keane. An uncle in Finn. A...well, her mother was both his grandmother and aunt. And wouldn't that mean that Keane was also his step-great-grandfather and Finn his step-grandfather?

She shook her head at the thought of Maddox's twisted family tree.

It didn't matter.

All that mattered was that he'd be loved.

Who was Ryder to deny Maddox that?

And yet...she couldn't do it.

Not after this morning's conversation with Keane. His attempt to direct her into a relationship with Ryder for his own purposes had shaken her confidence in him. She removed her glasses, placing them on the desk in front of her, and hung her head in her hands.

If she could maintain her composure at work on a day like this, surely she could keep her hands to herself. Just because she and Ryder had—what had Keane called it?—a "connection," didn't mean she and Ryder couldn't keep their relationship platonic. For Maddox's sake.

And for hers.

Sleeping with Ryder once had been reckless.

But Saturday night had been a mistake.

A hot, sweaty, orgasmic mistake.

One she wouldn't be repeating.

She glanced at the clock and gathered the items she needed for her first meeting. Sitting on the edge of her desk, her cell phone chimed with an incoming call. She stilled and her heart pounded as she stared at it.

Getting a call on her cell during the workday wasn't unusual. Dreama often called that line rather than using her business number, as did Maddox's day care and pediatrician. In fact, there were dozens of people who could be on the other end of that call.

But somehow, the churning in her gut told her it was Ryder.

TEN

Pacing in his office at Novateur, Ryder held the phone to his ear and listened to it ring as Jane's words repeated over and over in his head.

"I don't want him to know you—to trust that you'll be there for him—only to have you change your mind and leave."

The last thing he wanted to do was hurt Jane or Maddox. But the curiosity had him by the heartstrings, playing him like a damn marionette. Did his son look like him? Would Ryder feel an instant fatherly bond?

The need to meet his son was second only to his need to see Jane again.

Never once had he considered throwing away bachelorhood and settling down with one woman. Not until Jane. She was under his skin, a constant presence that had followed him around since the night he'd met her. Hell, he'd given up sex because of her.

That had to mean something.

Ignoring it would be a big kick to fate's balls.

And he didn't want to piss off fate.

On the second ring, Ryder sat down at his desk and nabbed a cherry Blow Pop out of the middle drawer. It had been years since he'd quit smoking, but the urge to have something between his lips never went away. If he had his way, he'd be sucking on Jane's slippery clit or those perfect tits of hers, but beggars couldn't be choosers.

There had to be a way for Ryder to claim his son *and* keep him safe. Would Maddox be safer having a father there to protect him or would he even need protection if Ryder stayed away from him?

By the third ring, he expected Jane's voice mail, so when he heard Jane's sultry voice saying "hello," it took him a moment to realize it was actually her and not a recording.

"Hello?" she said again.

God, just the sound of her voice made him hot.

He tugged at the collar of his shirt as he sat back in his chair. "It's Ryder."

After a long pause, she spoke. "Ryder. I didn't expect to hear from you."

"I want to see you," he said.

See you. Taste you. Do things to your body you couldn't imagine in your wickedest fantasies...

"I'm not sure that's a good idea."

"Just dinner." He planted his feet on his desk and reclined in his chair. "The two of us sharing a meal in public where we'll remain fully clothed. I promise." When she didn't speak, he added, "We need to talk about where to go from here."

"Does that mean you're willing to acknowledge that Maddox is your son?" she asked, her voice softening.

He answered the only way he could. "Jane, this isn't a conversation we should have on the phone."

"So is Maddox the only reason you want to see me?"

A vision of her riding him, all sweaty and disheveled, with her head thrown back in ecstasy had him adjusting himself. "If I'm honest and tell you it's because I haven't been able to stop thinking about the way your pussy clenched around my cock as you came, would that work for or against me?"

She blew out an audible breath. "Jesus. I can't do this right now."

"How 'bout we do it at six?" When she didn't answer, he laughed, realizing she'd misinterpreted his invitation. "Dinner, Jane. Get your head out of the gutter."

"I can meet you at Andiamo at seven. I want to run home after work and spend some time with Maddox."

"You can bring him," he found himself offering. "If you want to."

She paused. "I think it's better if we wait until we talk. My roommate will watch him."

He was surprised by the disappointment that swept through him.

"Jane? I'll see you at seven." Without giving her a chance to change her mind, he disconnected the call.

He still didn't know how they'd work everything out between them, but he did know he wasn't quite ready to say goodbye to Jane yet or give up the chance to meet his son.

A chuckle came from his doorway. "You look like the cat who just ate the canary," Tristan said. "What's got you grinning so early in the morning?"

Shit, he'd forgotten Tristan was working at Novateur today. He was in town for the Thanksgiving holiday. Since Tristan had taken the professor job in the Upper Peninsula of Michigan, Ryder usually worked alone in the warehouse.

If Tristan hadn't been here to point it out, Ryder wouldn't have known he'd been grinning.

Finished with his Blow Pop, he tossed the stick into the garbage. "Jane agreed to have dinner with me."

As Ryder's closest friend, Tristan knew all about Ryder's yearlong search for Jane and the evidence that had implicated her in the theft of Novateur's designs. Yesterday, Ryder had informed Tristan that he had found Jane and believed she was innocent of the crime, and that she'd had his son.

Tristan strode into the office, stopping in front of Ryder's desk. "You're sure that's a good idea?"

Ryder shook his head as Tristan sat in the chair across from him. "Maybe not, but walking away from her is not an option. Since the moment I saw her at the conference, I've been hooked. There's just something about her that calls to me."

"I get that. I do. It was the same for me when I met Isabella." His friend's brows pinched together. "Don't take offense. I'm worried that you're thinking with your dick rather than your head."

Hard not to take offense.

"Why?" Ryder sat forward, bracing his arms on the desk. "Because I'm not capable of having a serious relationship with a woman?"

"Fuck no," Tristan said, frowning. "I just meant that I knew when you finally fell, you'd fall hard. And that's what worries me. You're not objective when it comes to Jane and as your friend, it's my job to make sure you're not making a mistake with her. A few days ago, you thought she was the enemy working for your father. Now you not only believe that she had nothing to do with the theft, based on her word alone, but you're also accepting her assertion that Maddox is yours."

Hands clenched, Ryder shot out of his chair. "Maddox is mine!"

Tristan was wrong. If anything, Ryder had prematurely judged Jane based on nothing more than his prejudice to-ward Keane.

If Tristan was surprised by Ryder's outburst, he didn't show it. "How do you know?" he asked calmly.

That was like asking Ryder how he knew the sky was blue. It just . . . was. He couldn't explain it, but he knew in his gut that Jane hadn't lied to him about Maddox.

And he didn't need a damned paternity test to confirm it.

"Look," he said, returning to his chair, "I appreciate you looking out for me, I really do, but despite your doubts, I *am* thinking with my head."

"If you say so, then I believe you," Tristan said, picking up a pen from the desk and flipping it in back and forth in his hand.

An awkward cough came from outside his office.

Isaac.

Like a child caught with his hand in the cookie jar, Ryder flushed with guilt. Had he heard Ryder shouting at Tristan?

If he had, Isaac made no mention of it as he entered the room and took the chair next to Tristan. "Good to see you both."

As the silent partner in Novateur, Isaac stayed out of the day-to-day running of the business. The older man had served as a mentor to both Tristan and Ryder during college and had become a friend to them after they'd graduated. When Novateur had required financial assistance, he'd graciously saved their asses from having to close the business or take a risky loan from the bank.

"I didn't know you were coming," Ryder said.

Isaac's gray eyebrows rose. "I wasn't aware I needed an invitation."

"I told him to come," Tristan said, angling his body so that he could talk to both Ryder and Isaac. "You should know that I got another call from the army. They really want to talk to us about the automatous software we've developed."

Ever since Novateur had filed its patent application, several branches of militaries, both in the U.S. and abroad, had been bombarding Novateur with calls about purchasing the patent and offering tens of millions of dollars for it.

And they weren't alone. Since the software could be used in a variety of ways—anything from self-driven cars to robot soldiers—some of the world's biggest corporations had also expressed their interest. Arms producer Sinclair Corp had been one of the most insistent of the bunch, but after blowing off one of its employees at the Mackinac conference, Ryder had refused to speak with anyone who represented Sinclair's interests.

His code for making technology autonomous was not and would never be for sale.

Ryder crossed his arms. "I hope you repeated what I've told them a dozen times."

Tristan gave a curt nod. "I reiterated that we are not interested, but they're determined."

Ryder had been working on the code since high school when his robotics teacher had first discussed the idea of autonomous weaponry. At the time, Ryder and his friends had played around with the idea of building a "killer robot" that would shoot paint rather than bullets. They'd failed miserably at their attempt, but for some reason, the idea remained Ryder's own personal challenge.

And two years ago, he'd conquered it.

Previously, Novateur had been designing automatic kitchens, which required human input. But an autonomous kitchen wouldn't require humans at all.

Grabbing his laptop, Ryder stood. "Come on. I know you're both eager to see our first autonomous kitchen in action."

Tristan and Isaac followed Ryder out of the office and into the warehouse. Novateur currently housed several samples of automatic kitchens for restaurants and bakeries to see in action, each one with different options that ranged in price from a few thousand to hundreds of thousands of dollars.

Ryder led them to the back corner of the warehouse, his

heart racing in anticipation. This was the first time anyone other than him would see his creation.

From the outside, the kitchen wasn't any different from the typical kitchen you'd find in any restaurant. The magic was hidden behind the stainless steel.

Isaac jutted his chin toward a large mixer. "Show me how it works."

With Ryder's press of a single switch on the wall, the entire kitchen went to work. Robotic arms reached from the mixer to the refrigerator and retrieved a carton of eggs. "This particular model is for a bakery. All the software is on my laptop. To make it easy, I've limited the bakery's product to two kinds of cupcakes—vanilla and chocolate—and given the bakery a customer base of one hundred people a day."

After cracking the eggs into the mixer, the robotic arm added the sugar and the mixer came to life with a whir. The ovens lit up as they preheated to baking temperature.

Ryder opened the program on his computer to show his partners and pointed to the columns on the screen. "Right now, the inventory of product is set on zero and based on how I've programmed it, the computer will have the kitchen make fifty of each kind. But suppose the bakery only sells ten of vanilla and thirty of chocolate today. Tomorrow, it will automatically adjust the quantity it makes to reflect that. Over time, it will use the historical data to figure out the necessary inventory and bake the exact quantity the store needs, and it will email suppliers to order the ingredients when numbers get low."

Tristan summed up the difference between their previous

models and this newest one. "The computer learns." He smiled. "Amazing."

That was one word for it.

Dangerous was another.

When Ryder had made his breakthrough with the code, he had gone back and forth on whether to use it in their designs. In the end, he, Tristan, and Isaac had decided so long as the code remained secret, there would be no harm.

But in the wrong hands, the coding could be used for far more nefarious purposes.

Military drones. Guns. Robotic soldiers.

It was coming. The military would eventually develop a code on their own. Ryder couldn't stop it from becoming a reality. But no way in hell would he help them.

Watching as the kitchen went to work filling muffin tins with batter, he grew somber.

Isaac turned to him. "You're absolutely certain that no one will be able to figure out how to replicate our software if they have access to it?"

Ryder paused. "We've done as much as we can to protect it. The code is closed source, so it won't be made public, and we've already filed a patent for it. But even if anyone is able to access it, they won't find it easy to understand. I intentionally wrote it in obfuscated code so that even the most capable of programmers won't be able to crack it."

At least that's what he hoped.

"I would have loved to see Keane's face when he realized the designs he stole left out the part of the code that makes technology autonomous," Tristan said with a smile.

Ryder didn't need to see. He had enough memories of an enraged Keane to imagine it.

"But there's something that doesn't make sense to me," Tristan continued. "What does Keane hope to gain by competing with Novateur, especially if he's unable to manufacture autonomous kitchens?"

That *was* the million-dollar question.

Why start a new division of McKay that was doomed to fail? And why make Jane VP of it?

Ryder inhaled the sweet scent of cake batter. "I don't know yet. But I'm going to find out."

* * *

A few minutes before he was set to meet Jane, Ryder locked the front door of Novateur and walked the couple blocks toward the restaurant. During the summer, the shops stayed open and the sidewalks were filled with people of all ages, but on a fall weekday like tonight, it was much quieter after sunset. He inhaled the scent of Italian food as he made his approach to the trattoria and glanced at the watch on his wrist. Right on time.

He couldn't believe how much he had been looking forward to seeing her again or that only a few days ago, he hadn't known that Maddox existed. Now he couldn't get that pesky F-word out of his head.

Forever.

Hell, he felt like a teenager going on his first date, down to the sweaty palms and damned nervous knots in his stomach. Once inside, he was brought to their reserved table and slid into the black leather booth. When the waiter stopped by the table a few minutes later with a basket of freshly baked bread, Ryder ordered a bottle of red wine.

Twenty minutes later, the wine sat unopened on the table, he'd eaten the entire bread basket, and he was still waiting for Jane.

Maybe she was caught in traffic.

Maybe she'd gotten stuck at work.

Maybe she'd...

He checked his phone again. No missed calls.

His throat grew tight as he realized there was a strong possibility that Jane had stood him up. Disappointment washed over him. She'd given him the impression that she wanted him to be a part of her and Maddox's lives. Had he read the situation wrong?

And then she was there, taking off her coat and collapsing into the booth across the table from him as if she was exhausted. "I'm sorry I'm late."

He blew out a breath and sat back in the booth, releasing the tension in his body.

She'd obviously changed from her work clothes, wearing a pair of jeans and a simple jade sweater. Her hair was up in one of those messy bun things that some women spent forever making look like they hadn't spent any time on, and she wore her glasses perched on her cute little nose. There were remnants of makeup still on her eyes, but her lips were natural and her cheeks were pink from the night air. For some reason, seeing her like this reminded him of how young she really was.

She couldn't be more than twenty-three and she was already a mother. A single mother, raising her son—*their* *son*—practically all on her own.

"I didn't think you were going to show," he admitted as he uncorked the wine and poured them each a glass of the merlot. He looked her over. Her eyes were slightly red and her mouth was pinched with tension. "Are you okay?"

She wrapped her fingers around the stem of her wineglass. "I had a bad day at work. One of our employees—a programmer from my division—killed himself over the weekend. It's taken a toll on everyone, including myself."

"I'm sorry. Were you close?"

"No. It's just—" Jane shook her head. "I'm sure it's nothing. You don't need to hear about my day. That's not what this dinner's about."

She was wrong, but he didn't bother correcting her. He wanted to know everything about her.

"Do you have a photo of Maddox?" he asked, his pulse racing in anticipation of seeing his son for the first time.

She laughed and rummaged through her purse. Once she had her cell phone in hand, she fiddled with the screen. "I have hundreds. Want to see one from today? He was quite proud of himself for spitting his medicine out all over me."

His heart skipped a beat and he shot up tall in his seat. "Is he sick?"

She gave him a slight smile, letting him know she hadn't missed the panic in his voice. "No. He has reflux—don't worry, it's not uncommon for babies—and the doctor put him on this awful-tasting stuff that I give to him in a syringe. Every once in a while, he spits it out. Today, he suddenly learned how to spit it out *at me*, so that we're both covered in smelly medicine. He was pretty proud of himself." She held her phone out to him, her hand trembling. "Would you like to see?"

At that moment, he realized how difficult this was for her, how much she feared his rejection, and it was like a kick to the gut to witness. He was an asshole for making her even doubt for a second how much he wanted them both.

Their fingers brushed as he took the phone from her hand, sending a jolt of lust through him that he felt like a tingle at the head of his cock. *And all from a fucking innocent touch of their fingers.* He'd had women sucking his dick who hadn't gotten him this aroused.

There wasn't a chance in hell he was going to keep their relationship platonic. A fire like theirs didn't burn that strong every day. She was a fucking unicorn in his world, one he intended to ride often and frequently.

But for now, he'd pretend tonight's dinner was only about Maddox.

His eyes landed on the screen and his chest filled with pride.

He hadn't been around a lot of babies and the ones he usually saw all looked the same to him, like bald wrinkled aliens dressed up in Easter pastels with no discerning features or distinct personalities.

But none of them had been his son.

Perfect was the first thing that came to mind.

Maddox was neither wrinkled nor bald. Like Jane, his son

had a crown of curly brown hair, only much shorter. He had golden skin as if he'd spent a lot of time outside, but was more likely a hint of his Mexican heritage. Thank God she hadn't dressed him in pastels. In the photo, he sat in some kind of blue seat that propped him up, wearing a Detroit Red Wings T-shirt, red sweatpants, and a mischievous smile.

But it was his gray irises that had Ryder gasping out loud as any lingering doubt about being Maddox's biological father disappeared. A lump lodged in his throat. "He's got the McKay eyes."

Jane dropped her chin and shrugged. "Yeah, I felt pretty stupid when I realized you, Keane, and Finn all have the same eyes as my son and I never put it together."

"Why would you? You and I met miles away from here. And obviously, my father and brother never mentioned me to you."

"No, they've both spoken about you, but they must not have used your name." She tilted her head and frowned. "Huh. Keane doesn't have any family photos in his office."

While that fact seemed to confuse Jane, he wasn't surprised. Keane had never been a sentimental man. "Of course not. That would mean he actually cared."

"I'm sure that's not why," Jane said quietly.

He wasn't going to start another argument about Keane. They'd just have to agree to disagree. At least for now. Otherwise, Jane would never believe it when Ryder started cozying up to his father. "Let's not waste time talking about Keane. Tell me more about Maddox."

She lit up, her smile widening and her eyes twinkling. "He's brilliant. And I'm not just saying that because I'm his mother."

For the next hour, in between dinner and glasses of wine, Ryder scrolled through hundreds of photos of Maddox and listened to Jane brag about their son. He'd missed so much. The first time he'd rolled over from back to front (he wasn't sure why that was significant, but apparently, it was a big deal). His first smile (Jane swore it wasn't gas). His first Halloween (he greeted trick-or-treaters as a bumblebee). And dozens of other memories that were lost to Ryder forever. Damned if he would miss another.

After she polished off a slice of tiramisu, he returned the phone to her. "Did you have a good pregnancy?"

"Mostly. I was pretty emotional. I mean, I think that's normal. I'd burst into tears at the drop of a hat. Anything from one of those commercials about neglected dogs to breaking the tip of my pencil. My coworkers all kept boxes of tissue on their desk for me. Oh, and I got really huge. I wasn't one of those cute girls with the perfectly round basketballs in the middle. Nope. I can't tell you how many times women came up to me and asked when my twins were due."

"I'm sure you looked beautiful." Just the idea of her swollen with their child had him discreetly adjusting himself beneath the table. "It sounds like you must have been relieved to give birth."

She sank her teeth into her lower lip. "That was...scary. I was actually driving to work when my water broke and

the contractions started. Within an hour, I was ten centime-
ters dilated and ready to push. There was no time to process
anything. It was like one minute I was all alone and then I
blinked and I was a mother. You know?"

"I think I understand what that's like." Two days of
knowing and he could barely wrap his mind around the idea
of being someone's father.

Her eyes widened. "I guess you do. You didn't even get
the nine months to process it."

"I know what would help." He reached across the table
and took her hand. "It's time to meet my son."

ELEVEN

Jane was certain she had never been this nervous in her life. Twice she'd almost pulled over the car on the way to her apartment because her hands were shaking so uncontrollably. She didn't understand it. So Ryder was going to meet Maddox? Why would that make her feel as if she was about to lose everything she'd eaten at dinner?

She took a deep breath as she parked her car in front of her building. Ryder had shown real interest in Maddox tonight. How many men would have patiently listened to her prattle on about her baby all through dinner? There had been pride in his expression as he went through all the hundreds of photos on her phone, especially when he realized they shared the same color eyes. But would that be enough for him to commit himself to becoming a real father to Maddox?

Guess she'd soon find out.

She met Ryder at the front of her building and led him inside to her second-floor apartment. It wasn't much, but it was home. Someday she'd buy a house with a large fenced-in yard where Maddox could chase after a ball and play on a swing set. She could afford that now, but for some reason, she was reluctant to do it. Maybe it was because part of her hoped when she finally did buy a home, it would be with her husband, and if she bought it herself, it would be like admitting that was never going to happen.

For now, she was happy living in her two-bedroom apartment with Dreama. *Oh shit!* As she unlocked the door, she realized that she'd forgotten to call and inform her roommate that Ryder was coming over to meet Maddox. "I'm not alone," she called out in warning.

Dreama strolled out of the kitchen, holding a bottle of baby formula and thankfully wearing appropriate clothes to meet a stranger, one of her own creations—a white T-shirt with black leather and lace adornment over a pair of jeans that were painted with HELL'S LITTLE ANGEL down one leg. "Hey, Ryder. How was dinner?"

Or not a stranger.

Jane's gaze bounced between Dreama and Ryder, a bowling ball of apprehension forming in her stomach. "Do you two know each other?"

"Before you jump to any conclusions," Dreama said, holding up her hand with the bottle, "no, Ryder and I have never slept together."

Dreama knew Jane well. That's exactly where her mind had been going.

Ryder's hand curled around her arm. "Tristan—the friend I told you about—is engaged to Dreama's cousin, Isabella."

Jane tried to wrap her head around it. She shot Dreama an accusatory glare. "You figured it out when I said Ryder's name the other night. Why didn't you tell me?"

"I thought it would be best if it happened organically," Dreama said with a shrug. "That way if he didn't call or you didn't want to see him again, I wouldn't be in the middle."

"Except now that we know the truth, you're in the middle of it anyway," Jane pointed out.

Dreama put a hand over her heart. "Hey, I'm Switzerland. That being said, you're my best friend and I'm always going to be there for you, but it's not up to me to fill you in on the ins and outs of Ryder McKay. That's for you to discover all on your own." She turned her attention toward Ryder and shook a finger at him. "But if you fuck with her, I'll make sure your life is a living hell from that point on. There won't be a woman in Michigan who won't believe you've got three different STDs and a pencil-sized dick that couldn't find a G-spot even with a flashlight and a GPS."

Jane's jaw dropped. Holy shit, her roommate was fierce.

Ryder nodded once, seeming to take Dreama's words very seriously. As he should because Dreama would follow through on her threat if prompted. "Duly noted."

Dreama gave them both a broad smile and passed the baby bottle to Jane. "Good then. I've done my part, so I'm going to take a shower before bed."

As Dreama disappeared into her room, Jane took Ryder by the hand and tugged him toward her bedroom. "Come with me."

A swarm of butterflies flapped their nasty little wings in her stomach. Yeah, so sue her. She didn't understand people's fascination with butterflies. They were worms that turned into flying bugs. Just because their wings were colorful didn't make them any less creepy. And right now, it felt as if there were a whole bunch of the nasty critters recreating an episode of *Dancing with the Stars* inside of her.

By the time she realized she was having a conversation inside her head rationalizing her fear of butterflies to herself, they'd reached her bedroom. Letting go of Ryder's hand, she flicked on the lights and strode over to the crib, where she looked down at her baby boy who was currently sucking on his hand. "Hi, baby. Mommy's home." She scooped him up and kissed his chubby cheek before cradling him in her arms and presenting him to Ryder. "Maddox, this is your daddy. Ryder, this is your son."

Ryder stood as still as a statue and made no attempt to reach for his son, his face unreadable. Before she could question him, he took a stuttered breath and his expression transformed into what she could only describe as one of awe. She knew that because she'd felt the same way the first time she'd laid eyes on Maddox.

He didn't take his gaze off his son. "Can I...?"

She moved closer to Ryder. "Do you want to hold him?"

Still staring at Maddox, he nodded and held out his hands in front of him.

She carefully transferred a cooing Maddox into Ryder's arms.

He held the baby stiffly at first, far away from his body. Then slowly he dropped his shoulders and brought Maddox to his chest. "Hey, little man. It's nice to meet you."

The ice around her heart melted as she watched Ryder get acquainted with his son. He stroked his cheeks and his belly, pulled off his socks to count his toes, and let Maddox use his finger as a pacifier.

Of course, once Maddox realized he couldn't get milk from that finger, his face turned deep red and he began to cry.

Poor Ryder looked horrified. "He doesn't like me."

She smiled as she took Maddox from him. "He doesn't know you. It's just his age. Don't take it personally." Patting Maddox's back, she carried him over to the changing table and set him down. "He's hungry and wet. You'd cry too."

"Isn't he kind of small for being three months? I've held grocery bags heavier than him."

Laughing, she grabbed a fresh diaper. "He's fine. Seventy-fifth percentile in both height and weight."

Now that Maddox had stopped crying, Ryder seemed more comfortable, rubbing Maddox's hand. "And that's good?"

"Yes. That's good."

"He's incredible. Look how hard he can squeeze my finger."

"Just be thankful you don't have long hair." She tossed the dirty diaper in the trash before lifting Maddox off the table and returning him to Ryder's arms.

Ryder popped the bottle into Maddox's hungry mouth and sat in the rocking chair, his finger back in Maddox's grasp.

They looked perfect together. There was nothing sexier than a man holding a baby.

Unless maybe that man was shirtless...

Maddox's eyes drifted shut and his mouth slackened. Ryder continued to rock him as he removed the bottle. "He smells so good. Like...baby powder and hope."

Her heart fluttered. "I wasn't aware hope has a smell."

"Well it does, and it smells like Maddox."

There was a brief knock before Dreama walked into the room. "I'm going to bed. Why don't I have him sleep in the bassinet in my room so you two can chat?"

Right. Jane and Ryder still needed to talk about how they wanted to proceed with regard to Maddox. Although at that moment, the last thing she wanted to do with Ryder was chat. She was acutely aware that Ryder was in her *bedroom*.

"That would be great. Thanks. I'll get him in a little while," Jane said.

Dreama took Maddox from Ryder and gave her a smile. "No rush." On a wink, she left the room, closing the door behind her.

Now that she and Ryder were alone, she didn't know what to say. Where to begin. She stood by the changing table and fidgeted with the hem of her blouse.

She couldn't believe she was here with him. After the wedding, she thought he'd run as far away as he could from her and Maddox. But he hadn't. He'd run straight to them with both arms open.

Ryder got up from the rocking chair and moved closer to her, heat banked in his eyes. She recognized that look. The one that made her feel as if she were the sole focus of his world. "He's beautiful, Jane."

She discreetly wiped her sweaty palms on her pants. "He is."

"So is his mother." He curled his hand around her neck and brushed his thumb across the front of her throat. "There's something about you, Jane. Something...different."

"Different good or different bad?" she asked, her voice coming out as a husky whisper.

"Good." He nodded and swallowed. "Definitely good. There's something you should know about me." His brows pinched. "Something you've gotten a glimpse of that I'd like to explore with you."

"You're talking about BDSM, aren't you?" At his quizzical look, she shrugged. "I kind of figured it out. Dreama and I have had long talks about BDSM, so I'm not shocked. I know she goes to play parties and that she considers herself a sexual submissive."

"Then hopefully it won't shock you that some of those play parties were at my house. In my basement playroom."

Shocked? No. But a white-hot slice of jealousy lanced her chest.

"You're a Dom?" she asked.

"No." The hand around her neck slid upward so that it cupped the back of her head. "I usually refer to myself as a top, but I'm not into any kind of formal power exchange. I like bondage, mainly restraining women with ropes and—"

"Sashes."

He smiled at her reminder of their night at the hotel. "And sashes. And anything else that's handy."

She unintentionally squeezed her thighs together to relieve the growing pressure between her legs. "Why do you enjoy that? I mean, I get why the person restrained would enjoy it—"

"My goal is to bring as much pleasure as I can to a woman." As if he were sharing a secret, he lowered his head so that their faces were inches apart. "It's almost as if I see it as a personal challenge. Bondage, blindfolding, gagging, they all reduce the senses, which can heighten the remaining senses. Not being able to touch me, or to speak, or to see, will allow you to focus on the sensation of whatever it is I'm doing to you. The same thing with impact play. I'm not a sadist. I don't get off on inflicting pain on someone else. I get off on the pleasure that pain causes."

Pain was pain. Wasn't it?

"I'm not sure I understand the difference," she said.

"Did you enjoy it when I spanked you?"

She tried to look away, but his hold on the back of her neck remained firm. "Um...yeah."

"If you hadn't, I wouldn't have enjoyed it either."

She recalled the feel of him underneath her as he'd spanked her. "But you got hard—"

"I was already hard for you, Jane." His voice came out rough, gritty, almost like a growl. "But yeah, my dick really got off on your moans and cries and the fact that you were soaking my thighs with your excitement."

Speaking of soaked thighs...

Her inner walls clenched at the knowledge that her arousal turned him on. "Does that make me a masochist because I like to be spanked?"

"I didn't really smack you that hard. Just enough to pinken up your skin but not hard enough to leave bruises."

Did she want him to leave bruises? She liked the idea of him leaving evidence on her body of their time together. Maybe bruises in the form of his fingertips on her hips from gripping her too hard as he lost himself in her body. Or those bruises resulting from biting and sucking her skin. But from a spanking?

Maybe?

Dreama was a self-proclaimed "pain slut" who loved the rush of endorphins she experienced from pain. For her, the higher the pain, the harder she climaxed. Luckily, she'd never come across anyone who'd taken advantage of her. But it wasn't uncommon for her to come home from a party with welts and bruises. Jane didn't understand the need to take it as far as Dreama liked to go. But she couldn't deny that Ryder's bare hand smacking her ass excited her. "So you don't want to...hurt me?" she asked.

"Hurting you is the last thing I want to do," Ryder said, caressing her lower lip with his thumb. "But seeing you restrained to one of my spanking benches where I can have your ass and pussy at the right angle and level I want..." His eyelids grew hooded. "Yeah. I'd like that a lot."

Goose bumps dotted her arms as she visualized herself bound and helpless. "Despite my actions the night we met and at the wedding, I'm not the type who would have sex with someone I'm not dating." At least she didn't think so. In practice, she'd only ever had sex with Ryder, making her exactly that type.

"I'm flattered to be the exception, but I would hate for you to go against your values." His lips hovered over hers. "I guess that means we're dating."

Liquid heat pooled in her belly. She could barely catch her breath as she anticipated his next move. "Yeah?"

"Consider tonight our third date."

"You know what that means, don't you?"

His mouth brushed lazily over hers. "Why don't you tell me so there's no confusion?"

She playfully bit down on his lower lip. "You're about to get lucky."

He grabbed her wrists with his hands and pushed her back into the wall, and then with an almost brutal intensity, seized her mouth as if it belonged to him. His lips were powerful. Strong. And yet, somehow, oh so soft. His kiss slowed, mellowed. He teased her with the tip of his tongue, offering her a small taste before darting it away.

She moaned and rose up onto her tiptoes to rub her aching core against his hardness, but he stopped, stepping back and leaving her desperate.

She wanted more. *Needed* more. He tasted like the wine from dinner, tart and spicy mixed with what she'd always recognize now as Ryder's unique flavor. She'd thought by now they'd be naked on the bed, halfway to climax, but Ryder seemed to be on his own timetable.

His lips trailed a sensuous path down her neck, sucking, and licking, and biting. She squirmed in his hold, struggling to touch him, but he refused to let go, making it clear to her who held the control.

And it wasn't her.

His breathing accelerated as she fought to get free, making it clear that he was definitely getting off on restraining her.

As if she was afraid, her heart thumped almost violently against her chest and her throat grew thick. But at the same time, her clit throbbed and her folds dampened.

"Take off your clothes, sweet Jane."

If her struggling turned him on, what would he do if she refused? She couldn't wait to find out. "Make me." Ready to run, she twisted out of his arms and dodged away, only to be caught and tugged into his chest.

"You want to play?" He bit the sensitive skin just above her collarbone. "I'm game. Just remember, you asked for it." He swung her around and shoved her facedown onto the bed. Placing his knee on her lower back, he held her down as he pulled up her shirt and unclasped her bra.

Shivers of arousal racked her body as his heat seeped into her and his fingers brushed her skin. She didn't make it easy for him, wanting to see how far he'd take it.

She lay prone, as still as a rock, not giving him an inch but not resisting either. Ryder grabbed the base of her ponytail and wrenched her head back, before tearing the shirt off over her shoulders and leaving it bunched over her upper arms, using it as a makeshift restraint.

He slid down her body, caging her in between his legs. In one swift motion, he jerked her pants and underwear down her legs. For a moment, neither of them moved. Except for their heavy breathing, the room was silent.

She heard the *slap* before she felt the sting on her left butt cheek.

"Son of a—"

The slap on the other cheek mirrored the first.

This wasn't like the spanking he'd given her before. This actually hurt. Not enough to make her cry, but enough that she wouldn't enjoy it.

"You play, you pay," he said as if it was a threat. Which of course, it wasn't. Because she'd asked for this, hadn't she? "You want me to stop, you say the word 'red,' you got me?"

"Yes," she gritted out as he smacked her backside again.

"Repeat it back to me. What word do you say to get me to stop, Jane?"

"Red. Like my poor ass is right now."

He laughed. "Not quite there yet. Do you know why I'm spanking you?"

"Because you're a sadist?"

"Hardly." Instead of slapping her, his touch softened, his fingers rubbing her cheeks lightly. "There are two reasons. First, I'm punishing you because you refused to undress when I told you to. And in the bedroom, sweet Jane, I'm the boss."

Shivering at his proclamation, she looked over her shoulder at him. "Okay, Mr. I'm Not a Dominant. What's the second reason?"

A challenge reflected in his eyes. "You wanted me to. Am I right, Jane?"

TWELVE

Ryder had told himself they could stay platonic.

Liar.

As long as they didn't tell anyone and kept their relationship a secret from Keane, Ryder could protect her and Maddox.

Tonight, in this room, it was only them. Top and bottom. Two lovers safely playing. Discovering. His sweet Jane had shown hints of a wild side. By refusing to undress for him, she'd practically begged for a punishment. Now bent over her bed, hands bound with her shirt and her ass a beautiful shade of red, she was ready to admit to it. "Yes," she said, confirming his suspicion. "I wanted to see what you would do."

"And now that you know? Will you disrespect my wishes again in the bedroom?"

She turned her face away from him, but he didn't miss the cheeky smile on her face. "Probably."

He'd show her cheeky.

Chuckling, he squeezed the globes of her ass and pulled them apart, exposing that secret part of her to his view. His cock hardened to the point of pain as he thought about how tight she'd be inside there. "You're going to be a handful, aren't you?"

"If you're lucky." She jerked as he tucked his pinky between her cheeks and crouched behind her to get closer.

He dragged his tongue up her crack, adding some lubrication to ease his next move.

"What are you doing?" She swept out her leg, attempting to move away from him.

He bit the bottom of her butt cheek in warning. "Stop or I'll give you another ten spanks, only this time, I'll give them to your pussy, and I'll make sure that they fucking hurt." He continued his mission and laved her hole before sliding his pinky in to his first knuckle. She moaned and pushed her ass out, which to him, was like an invitation for more. Unfortunately, it was an invitation he'd have to postpone for another time. "I can't wait to claim this ass."

"Claim it?" Her voice wavered.

Hell yes. When it came to Jane, he felt like a fucking caveman, ready to fight anyone who dared put his hands on her. "I want all of you." He wiggled his finger around to give her an idea of how sensitive the area was and how much she had to look forward to in the near future. "What makes you think I'll let you?" she asked sassily.

"Aw, sweet, sweet Jane." He replaced his pinky with his thumb and pushed it all the way in, enjoying the way she gasped at the invasion. "Because underneath the businesswoman persona that you show the world, you're a dirty girl who's been waiting for the right man to bring her out."

Her muscles clenched around his thumb. "And you think that man is you?"

"Why don't you sit on my face and find out?"

"I don't know what that means," she said quietly.

He momentarily froze. Even knowing she was sexually inexperienced, he hadn't anticipated how much she had to learn.

And how much he was going to enjoy teaching her.

"Give me a moment and I'll show you. Don't move until I tell you." He removed his thumb and quickly snatched a baby wipe off the changing table to clean his hands. When he returned to her, he tugged her shirt off her arms, freeing her from her makeshift bonds. Staring at her ass and weirdly proud of the way it glowed from his hands, he retrieved a condom from his wallet and took off his clothes until he was as naked as Jane. Then he went to the side of the bed and lay down in the middle. After scooting down a few inches, he grabbed a pillow and tucked it under his head.

Jane eyed him warily.

"Come up here," he ordered. Frowning with confusion, she crawled up the bed beside his body. "Now put your knees next to my ears."

Her eyes widened and her lips parted. "Oh."

She got it now.

A blush stained her cheeks. He would've laughed at her naïveté, but he didn't want to offend her and it would probably kill the mood. Besides, he was too busy salivating over the pink flesh she exposed as she spread her legs and lifted herself over his chest.

Her dark curls were slick with proof of her arousal.

He couldn't wait another second to taste her.

"Bring your pussy directly over my mouth and hold on to the top of the headboard. If you let go, I'll stop." He flashed her a grin. "And, Jane, something tells me you definitely won't want me to stop."

Hesitating, she bit her lip, and for a second he thought she might not do it. Although he'd tasted her before, this position was much more intimate and obviously made her uncomfortable.

Bet it would only take thirty seconds before he tongue-fucked the uncomfortable straight out of her.

Gaze locked with his, she slid up his chest, leaving a wet trail along the way, until her sex hovered right over his lips. She reached out and gripped the headboard, putting her at the perfect angle for him to eat her.

Good thing because he was starving.

On a growl, he gripped her inner thighs and swiped the flat of his tongue from her opening to her fully exposed clit. All it would take was a few swirls of his tongue on it and she'd come for him. But he wasn't ready for her to blow quite yet. Not until she was writhing and begging above him, desperate for her release.

His cock was throbbing and dripping with precum, but for the first time, he craved his lover's release more than his own. He dove in, thrusting his tongue as deep as it could go and then flicking it until he found a spot that caused

Jane to buck and moan. Using his hands, he forced Jane up and brought her back down, helping her find a rhythm that would drive her out of her mind. She caught on quickly and rode his tongue as if it were his cock, grinding on it and swerving her hips.

"It's not enough," she wailed with her head thrown back in pleasure. "Fuck me, Ryder. I need you to fuck me."

Hell yeah, he was gonna fuck her. "Not until you come in my mouth." He strummed her needy clit under his thumb and within seconds, felt her channel spasm around his tongue. A rush of liquid bathed his mouth. It tasted different than her arousal. Sweeter. More potent. More...Jane.

On a loud sigh, she lifted herself off his mouth and fell onto the mattress beside him. Her hair was plastered to the side of her sweaty face and her cheeks were red from exertion. She looked well fucked.

Well wasn't good enough.

"On your hands and knees. Ass facing me," he ordered gruffly.

She gave him a lazy smile and, as he snagged the condom off the nightstand, followed his directions without complaint.

His cock twitched when he saw her ass was still red. She was definitely going to feel it tomorrow. Satisfaction filled him from knowing that every time she sat down, she'd think of him.

Doggy-style fucking might seem a bit tame for the average person, but it was all new to Jane. Besides, once he got her into his own bed, he'd explore all the creative ways to fuck her. He could just see her hanging from his ceiling, her legs wide open.

He palmed his length and squeezed. If he could fill both holes at the same time with his cock he would.

But here, now, he was going to take her pussy and take it hard.

He rolled the condom down his length, hissing at his cock's sensitivity, and notched his tip to her opening. "On all fours like that, with your red ass and your juices running down your thighs, you look every bit the dirty girl I knew you were."

She peered over her shoulder. "Only for you."

Her words held magic, feeding the possessive bastard inside of him. He was the first man inside her body and if he had his way, he'd be the last.

"Grab on to the blanket, dirty girl," he warned, sliding his cock into her heat, "'cause I'm about to give you the ride of your life."

Needing an anchor himself, he curled his hands over her hips and pushed himself all the way in, feeling her ripple around him.

From base to tip, hot pressure squeezed him. He groaned, his eyes practically rolling back in his head from the sensation. On the verge of release, his balls drew up tight and liquid heat shot through his groin. Damn it, he hadn't even begun to fuck her yet, and he was about to blow.

Better make it count, then.

His fingers dug into her hips hard enough to bruise her as he slammed himself into her. In fact, if he hadn't been holding on to her, he'd probably knock her right off the bed with the force. But she didn't complain or call out her safe word. Instead, she arched her spine and met him thrust for thrust. Like a song, she chanted his name, every now and then throwing in a few prayers to God to break up the monotony.

"Ryder, I need—"

"I've got you, dirty girl." He reached around and flicked her clit.

It was all she needed. She cried out as her legs trembled and her pussy clamped down on him, over and over. He wanted to hold off, to give her one more orgasm, but he'd been riding the edge for an hour and her contractions set him off. The pressure in his groin hit its pinnacle and his climax barreled into him, emptying his mind and his cock as spurt after spurt of come filled the condom.

He didn't know how it was possible, but every time they fucked was better than the last.

Catching his breath, he wrapped his arm around her middle and pulled her to him. They fell backward and collapsed together on the mattress. Sighing with what he hoped was contentment, she rested her head on his chest and brushed her hand over the patch of hair on his lower stomach.

Her skin was pink and sweaty, her hair frizzy and wild, and all her makeup was smeared around her eyes. And she had never looked more beautiful.

Her hair tickled him as she lifted her head. "I need to tell you something."

"What's that?" he asked, sweeping back the strands that

fell over her eyes and tucking them behind her ear. Of course, her silky hair fell forward almost immediately.

"Earlier today, your father asked me to ... get to know you."

He froze as his stomach rolled and bitterness replaced the sweetness in his mouth. "What?"

Jane pressed her lips together. "He told me that he witnessed the sparks between us and thought I could"—she shook her head—"date you and use the opportunity to convince you that he's changed."

Leave it to Keane to ruin a perfect moment.

Ryder sat up, needing a bit of space. "Is that why you agreed to have dinner with me tonight?"

"No," she said gently. She held the blanket to her chest, covering herself as she sat up too. "Even if I didn't know how you feel about him, I'm not the type of person who would do that. If anything, it made me less inclined to date you."

He wanted to believe her. If she really had slept with him as a favor to his father, she wouldn't have brought this subject up to him, right?

Or had Tristan been right?

Did Ryder suffer from a blind spot when it came to Jane? *No.*

He shook off his doubts, knowing it had nothing to do with Jane and everything to do with his father. Keane was the one he didn't trust.

Running his fingers through his hair, he got off the bed. "Keane wears a very good mask, but make no mistake...

he's a monster, Jane. The things he's done…things he's gotten away with…It kills me to even have you working for him, to tell you the truth. For Keane, people are just chess pieces to move around on a board. He plays with lives without any regard to feelings."

"Okay, I admit he can be manipulative, but a monster?" Jane said, frowning. "That's pretty extreme. Are you sure you're not exaggerating?"

He wished. But after years of witnessing his father's misdeeds, he knew exactly what that man was capable of. "So you've never witnessed anything suspicious going on at McKay?" he probed.

Her eyes widened momentarily before returning to normal. Turning her back to him, she walked to her dresser. "No. Why would you ask that?" She pulled out an oversized Michigan State T-shirt and slid it over her naked body.

He didn't believe her.

But he wouldn't push her on it…for now.

That didn't mean he'd allow her to continue putting herself in harm's way.

He scooped his clothes off the floor and began dressing. "Because I don't have any proof to offer you of my father's misdeeds, but that doesn't mean they didn't occur."

Misdeeds that continued to haunt his nightmares.

Once he finished putting on his clothes, he crossed over to her and took her hands in his. "You and Maddox are mine now and I take care of what's mine. Be a stay-at-home mom to Maddox or find another job that isn't for my father. Anything you want. Just quit your job at McKay."

She wrenched her hands out of his. "Quit? Even if I wanted to—which I don't—I can't just quit. I'm a division head at a multi-million-dollar corporation. I barely know you and you barely know me." Her fists went to her hips. "Just because you're Maddox's biological father doesn't mean you have the right to tell me what to do and how to live my life. I won't throw away my career because *you* have some daddy issues."

He took a step toward her. "Jane—"

She lifted a hand, signaling him to stay away from her. "Get out."

Her rejection was like a lance to his chest.

"I'm not giving up on us, Jane." But he'd give her some time to cool off and reconsider. As he walked out of the room, he gave her one last glance over shoulder. "Happy Thanksgiving."

THIRTEEN

As the elevator closed, Jane pressed the button for the tenth floor of McKay Industries and blinked back the blurriness in her eyes.

It had been only hours since Ryder had walked out of her apartment and she was still furious with him.

She couldn't believe he'd had the gall to ask her to quit her job. Whatever his issue was with Keane, he had no business bringing her and Maddox into it.

Jane took a step back as a few people walked onto the elevator. Normally she'd plaster a smile on her face and make small talk with the other employees, but today she wasn't in the mood. Instead, she kept her gaze on her shoes, avoiding any eye contact.

All night she'd lain awake trying to make sense of Ryder's request. She knew that he harbored anger at his father, but was that any reason to expect her to quit her job?

She didn't understand Ryder.

Yes, Keane had been out of line in asking her to date Ryder to put in a good word for him, but that didn't make him a monster.

Ryder didn't know how fortunate he was to have a father and brother who not only loved him, but also wanted him to be a part of their lives. She would have given anything to have that.

But she didn't have to think about Ryder now. At work, she could focus on the tasks for the day and put all her personal crap on the back burner. Between her own accounts and the ones she'd taken on for Evan, she had plenty to keep her busy. And she still needed to tell Keane about Evan's email.

She headed down the hallway to her office, noting the unusual hush on the floor. A foreboding crept down her neck. Passing by Barbara's empty desk, she immediately knew something was wrong. The woman had never missed a day of work and by this time of day, even if she wasn't behind her desk, she always had a steaming mug of tea waiting for her on it.

Jane didn't bother going to her office. Instead, she turned around and got back on the elevator, hitting the button for the top floor. She pulled at the collar of her blouse, the fabric suddenly too tight around her neck. Sweat popped up on her forehead as she told herself she was probably overreacting. Barbara deserved a day off. Perhaps she had finally decided to use it. Or maybe she had taken her tea with her when she'd been called to someone's office. Maybe Jane would get off this elevator and go to Keane's office where she would find Barbara, tea in hand. Maybe she had been reassigned and the icy hot prickles snaking around Jane's chest were a result of no sleep.

Maybe...

As the elevator dinged, the doors slid open and Jane heard the weeping confirmation. The first thing she saw was Keane's third assistant dabbing at her eyes with a tissue while speaking to a uniformed policeman.

As if it would keep the bad news at bay, Jane held her breath as she approached Keane's office. She didn't bother stopping to talk to anyone or wait for permission from his first assistant to go through Keane's closed door. With shaky hands, she turned the knob and strode inside. Keane spoke to a police officer in a hushed tone. His eyes were narrowed, his hands clenched, and his posture ramrod stiff as he spoke in a hushed tone. To her, he looked as if he was reprimanding the officer. But why?

Almost immediately, Keane's gaze fell upon Jane and his whole demeanor changed. His shoulders slumped, his eyes softened, and his hands opened.

A shiver passed through her.

Keane nodded once, acknowledging her presence. "Jane."

For some reason, she stayed by the door. "Tell me," she demanded, surprised by the steel in her voice.

"This is Jane Cooper," Keane said to the officer as he motioned for her to join their little tête-à-tête by the desk. "She also works in the innovation division."

She strode to them and read DETECTIVE MORAN off the name tag he wore over his right breast. "Who is it this time?"

Keane took her hand and patted it. Maybe he'd meant for it to come off as comforting, but instead she felt patronized. "Barbara. She died last night."

She removed her hand from his grasp and crossed her arms. "With all due respect, there are two policemen here. I think there's more to the story."

"Ma'am, we're here because a neighbor used her key and found your coworker and her husband deceased in their bed after she heard an alarm going off in their home," Detective Moran said. "The neighbor called the ambulance and by the time paramedics got to the home, the woman who reported it had passed out. Testing showed it was due to carbon monoxide poisoning."

She blinked back the tears. At least Barbara died in her sleep. "Oh my God."

"It was likely an accident," the detective said, glancing at Keane before returning his attention to her, "but we have to investigate, especially in light of your other coworker's recent suicide."

What was that look for?

"Do you think it was related?" she asked, a heaviness filling her chest.

"I'm sorry. I can't comment on an ongoing investigation. When was the last time you spoke with Barbara?"

He was asking the right questions. Maybe she'd misinterpreted his interactions with Keane.

"Yesterday right before I left," she answered. "Around five. She said she was staying late because she was copying files for me."

"Well, that's all I need at this time." Detective Moran shook Keane's hand. "Mr. McKay, thank you for speaking with us." He turned to her and handed her a card. "Ms.

Cooper, if you have any information that might aid us in this investigation, please call me."

After the detective left, Jane turned to her boss. He owed her some answers. "Keane."

He opened his arms wide, inviting her in for a hug. "Come here, Jane."

Wary, she went into his embrace, but instead of staying there and allowing him to comfort her, she gave him a brief squeeze and took a step back. "I just don't understand. First Evan and now Barbara."

If he noticed her acting unusual, he didn't say anything. "It's a damn shame. I've known Barbara for many years. She was a part of the McKay family."

"Keane, be honest. Do you think it's possible that Evan and Barbara were murdered?"

He harrumphed and waved a hand, dismissing the idea. "Don't be ridiculous. They're completely unrelated tragedies."

"But even the officer—"

"Drop it, Jane," he said. His jaw was noticeably rigid. "Let the police do their jobs and stay out of their way."

How could he be so certain? Evan and Barbara were both in the innovations department. For heaven's sake, Barbara worked directly for Evan. What if Barbara had figured out Evan's death wasn't a suicide?

"But if—"

His face turned red. "Let it go, Jane!"

She flinched at his tone. Never once had he lost his temper with her. Her heart was beating like a drum against her chest as every word Ryder had ever uttered about Keane suddenly rang true.

He was hiding something from her just as she was hiding something from him. But not telling him that he was Maddox's grandfather wasn't the same as lying about two employees' deaths.

Before, she'd been certain about the type of man Keane McKay was.

Now she realized she barely knew him at all.

She covered her heart with her hand and sniffed, playing the part Keane expected her to play. The naïve protégé who followed his every instruction to the letter and never challenged him. "I'm sorry. I guess I'm just emotional."

"Of course you are," Keane said, buying her act. "That's understandable. But I have every confidence you'll put it out of your mind and be a role model for the others. Later this morning, I'll be issuing a statement to all the employees and speaking to all of management personally, but in the meantime, I don't want to hear any rumors or innuendo about these terrible tragedies being related."

Two of his employees had died and he was worried about interoffice chatter?

Any lingering idea of informing him about Evan's email died.

Maybe Ryder had been right.

Was she truly in danger by working for Keane?

She adjusted her glasses. "I can't stop people from wondering."

"No, but you can make sure people are performing their

jobs to the best of their ability, which means they'll be too busy to gossip."

"I'll do my best."

He put a hand on her shoulder. "I know you will. Have you given any thought to what we discussed?"

This was the moment.

She should tell him why his request had been inappropriate and that she wouldn't do it. At least if he fired her, she'd be safe.

But instead, she found herself saying, "Yes, I've decided I'd like to help you. In fact, Ryder and I had dinner last night."

If Keane was involved in anything criminal, she needed to find out. And she wouldn't be able to do that if she no longer worked at McKay Industries.

If Ryder had been telling her the truth about Keane, then she couldn't let him find out that Ryder was Maddox's father.

Or know that she had feelings for Ryder.

Not until she figured out what Keane was hiding.

Until then, she'd play along.

"Good. Good," Keane said, bobbing his head. "I'm sure he has some strong opinions of me, but I hope you know me well enough to realize Ryder's thoughts are filtered through his own biases. I admit to making mistakes with him, but it's time to leave it all in the past before it's too late."

"Too late?"

What did he mean? Was that a threat?

He gave her a sad smile. "I'm not a young man, Jane. I'd like to make peace with my son before I die. You can't know how much it means to me to have you on my side."

Guilt swarmed her and her stomach twisted. As a rule, she hated lying. But what choice did she have? If Keane did have something to do with Barbara's and Evan's deaths, then lying was a necessary evil.

Jane didn't believe for a second that their deaths weren't related. Maybe she could believe it if Evan hadn't come to the wedding to talk to her or hadn't sent the email. Maybe if Barbara hadn't been Evan's assistant.

After leaving Keane's office, she headed to her own. A few people tried to stop and chat with her along the way, but she apologized for not having time to talk and kept going. She was determined to see if Barbara had left her the SD card with the files on them as she'd promised.

Once inside her office, she scanned the room, but nothing appeared out of place and there was no sign of the SD card. Standing nervously at her desk, she listened to her messages and checked her emails, surprised that there wasn't one from Barbara.

Did that mean she hadn't finished copying the files for Jane?

Jane spent the rest of the morning consoling employees. Unlike her, no one seemed to link the two deaths together, and several times, she found herself wondering if she was just being paranoid. But then she'd remember the way Keane had acted earlier, how he'd seemed to be admonishing the cop when she'd walked into his office, and how he'd grown angry when she questioned him about the possibility of the two deaths being connected, and she knew deep in her gut that he knew more than he was telling her.

Evan and Barbara had been her employees. That made Jane responsible for them. She owed it to them to find out the truth.

She had to search Evan's office and Barbara's desk. For what she wasn't certain, but they must have left some clue behind. Something that would indicate a reason for their senseless deaths.

By six, most of the employees had left for the day, giving Jane the perfect opportunity to do some sleuthing. She started in Barbara's cubicle. It felt odd to be sitting in the same chair where Barbara had sat only the day before, alive and well. The elderly woman had kept her space immaculate. Other than a couple family photos and knickknacks, the desk was clean of clutter.

Jane turned on Barbara's computer. Its low hum filled the quiet as it booted up.

Her pulse sped up and her knee nervously bounced as she waited. A pins-and-needles sensation crept up her neck. She had the feeling of being watched. She peered around the cubicle, but no one was there.

The computer beeped, drawing her attention. Once it displayed the home screen, she clicked on File Explorer and searched the recent documents. There was no record of Barbara copying any files.

She smacked her forehead with her hand. *Of course.* Barbara would have used Evan's computer.

Inside his office, everything had been packed into boxes except for his computer and a single picture frame.

She pressed the power button on the CPU, but nothing happened. Frowning, she checked the wires to make sure the computer was plugged into the electrical outlet. That didn't appear to be the problem. Again, she tried to turn on the computer, but it was dead.

Damn it. She'd have to call IT and see if they could fix the problem or at least extract the files for her.

Striding out of Evan's office, she slammed into a hard body. "Oomph." She looked up at Derek. Her heartbeat accelerated. She hadn't known anyone else was here.

"I'm so sorry," she said. "I should've been watching where I was going."

He rubbed her shoulder. "Don't worry about it. After hearing the news about Barbara, we're all a bit lost in our own heads today."

"What are you doing here so late?" she asked, searching his face for a sign of... she didn't know what.

"I had to make a few calls since I'll be gone for the rest of the week," he explained.

McKay would be closed tomorrow through next Monday for the Thanksgiving holiday.

Someday, Jane would have a house big enough to host her own Thanksgiving. Everyone would be welcome. Family, friends, coworkers. The more the merrier. There was nothing worse than being alone on the holidays.

"Right." She blew out a breath. "I'd forgotten about that."

After wishing him a happy holiday, she casually strolled down the hall and onto the elevator, trying not to peer over her shoulder to see if Derek was following her.

Before this week, she would've never believed anyone she knew could be a murderer.

Ryder had her doubting everyone and everything.

Including herself.

FOURTEEN

Is that apple pie I smell? Forget dinner. When's dessert?"
Ryder asked Tristan as he stepped into the Lawson home.

Cars were lined up on the street outside the house, and judging by the dozens of different voices, Isabella's entire family had come for Thanksgiving dinner. Isabella came from a large Italian family with several sisters, a brother, and lots of cousins. Three little boys ran down the wooden staircase, their feet making much more noise than Ryder would've thought possible.

He saw Maddox in every one of them.

It had been three nights since he'd held his son or heard from Jane. He couldn't count how many times he'd picked up his phone to call her, before hanging up because he'd left the next move to her.

But damn it, he didn't think she'd take this long.

It was a gamble he'd hated to wager. But if she wasn't ready to hear his story, he couldn't make her listen. Wagging her finger, Mrs. Lawson came up behind Tristan. "I'm going to pretend I didn't hear that. You eat dinner, you watch some football, and you'll make the space for dessert."

"Thank you for including me, Mrs. Lawson," he said, handing her a bouquet of orange lilies and a bottle of wine.

"You always have a place at our table, Ryder." She reached up and patted him lightly on the cheek. "Come in and let me take your coat. We'll be having dinner shortly, but if you're hungry, I have some appetizers set up in the living room."

Even though she was about a foot shorter than him, she had a way of making him feel as though he were a five-year-old. Vulnerable but safe. Loved unconditionally. His throat thickened with emotion as he tried to recall the last time he'd felt that way around his father.

Had he ever? Ryder often wondered what his life would have been like had he grown up with his mother. Would she have made their cold, impersonal mansion seem more like a home? Welcomed family and friends to their house for the holidays? Would he have spent the day after Thanksgiving decorating the Christmas tree with her?

The image of the woman with the long black hair rose to the forefront of his mind. He didn't think of her often, but on days like these, he couldn't help but wonder if she had been real or just an imaginary by-product of a recurrent nightmare from his childhood.

After Mrs. Lawson took Ryder's jacket and reintroduced him to a half-dozen relatives, Tristan smacked him on the back and led him to the family room, where a group of mostly men had congregated in front of the television to watch football. As soon as he approached, Isaac stood from the couch.

The Lawsons had also "adopted" Isaac and his wife, Cassandra, into their family. Ryder held out his hand. "Isaac, Happy Thanksgiving."

Of course, Isaac would have none of that. He pulled Ryder into a bear hug and thumped him between the shoulder blades. "Ryder. Good to see you."

"Lions winning?" he asked, not really caring but making an attempt at small talk.

Isaac snorted as if he couldn't believe Ryder was asking. "What do you think?"

If he was a betting man, he'd put money on them leading the game early on but later losing to the opposing team.

Kind of like he was doing with Jane.

He snagged a beer from the table and snapped off the cap. "Where's Cassandra?"

Isaac's wife was a regal and charming woman who adored her husband. And from what Ryder had witnessed, the feeling was mutual.

Isaac surprised Ryder and grabbed himself a beer to drink. He wouldn't have pegged the older man as a Canadian beer drinker. "Cassandra's in the other room with the women." He arched his brow and smiled. "You know how she gets when she's around children. I don't think she'll ever give that poor baby back to his mother."

Something stirred between his ribs. "Baby?"

"Jane's here with Maddox." Isaac spoke casually, but the twist of amusement to his lips gave him away. "You know Jane, right?"

"We've met," he said, playing along to see where Isaac

was going with this charade. He obviously knew something. But what? Had he overheard Ryder's conversation with Tristan at Novateur? "She mentioned my father called you personally to request her as an intern."

"He did."

"And you didn't think to tell me?"

Isaac had the audacity to appear perplexed, but Ryder knew the man. Very little caught him off guard. "Why would I do that?"

Ryder glared at Isaac. "Because it's my father."

Isaac's face soured. "I know how you feel about him, but that has nothing to do with my duty to my students as dean of the business school. Despite any opinion I may have about him, I felt it was in Jane's best interests to allow her to decide whether or not to accept the internship."

Ryder wanted to argue, but it wouldn't be worth the energy he exerted because of course Isaac was right. Didn't mean he had to like it. "You should have told me."

"Did you even know Jane back then?"

"No," Ryder admitted.

Isaac's gaze twinkled and the corners of his mouth lifted. "Her son is a handsome guy. His eyes are quite unique. I've rarely seen that gray before."

Isaac knew.

Ryder glanced at the other men in the room, relieved to see that they were all focused on watching the game. Still, he dropped the volume of his voice. "Did you overhear my conversation with Tristan at Novateur?"

"You mean, when you shouted that Maddox was yours?"

Isaac asked, keeping his voice quiet as well. He smiled at Ryder. "But even if I hadn't overheard, one look at that boy and I would've known he was a McKay."

It had been just as obvious to Ryder.

Which led him to wonder...

Had Keane figured it out too?

And if so, what game was he playing?

* * *

Jane hadn't gotten a chance to hold Maddox since walking into the Lawsons' house. For more than an hour, he'd been passed from woman to woman, leaving Jane with her hands free for a glass of white wine and her attention free to engage in conversation. And other than his happy baby babble, she hadn't heard a peep from him.

Was this what it would be like to have a supportive family?

The Lawsons' house was by no means a mansion and yet practically every inch of the main floor was filled with family, friends, neighbors, and strangers like herself. It was crazy loud inside with all the laughing and talking of adults and the whining and screaming of overtired children. She was grateful to Dreama for bringing her here tonight, but at the same time, it hit her how much she was missing.

Jane's mouth watered at the scents coming from the kitchen. Turkey, cinnamon, apple...and oregano. The Lawsons were Italian and, according to Isabella, served various Italian dishes along with the traditional Thanksgiving foods. And since they owned a bakery, their dining room was already overflowing with at least a dozen desserts ready to be served after dinner was eaten. Needless to say, Jane wouldn't go home hungry that night.

She scooped a handful of cashews from the bowl on the coffee table as Isabella sat down beside her and kicked off her heels on a groan.

"Rough day?" Jane asked.

Isabella smiled. "New shoes. I should know better by now not to break in a pair of heels when I'm going to be on my feet most of the day, but I couldn't resist them." She leaned over and whispered, "And neither could Tristan."

Dreama had introduced Jane to Isabella and Tristan when they'd first arrived at the Lawson house. Jane had taken an instant liking to them, especially Isabella, who welcomed Jane with a large hug.

Isabella massaged the bottom of her foot. "It's crazy how Ryder spent the last year obsessing over you and you were practically right under his nose the entire time. Jane's such a common name, I never thought to put you together with the girl Ryder was looking for. Besides, Dreama always refers to you as 'Chickie' whenever she talks about you."

Jane wanted to ask Isabella if she knew where Ryder was spending the holiday.

Was he alone?

She'd picked up the phone a half dozen times in the last couple of days, but she couldn't find the courage to call him. What would she say? "When I answered her ad for a roommate, she told me I didn't look like a Jane. She's called me

Chickie ever since." After a lifetime of feeling as ordinary as her name, she had loved having a nickname with some personality.

"I think Jane's a beautiful name," Isabella said. "*Jane Eyre* is one of my favorite books."

Hers too. Not because the heroine shared her name, but because in the end, the orphaned Jane found the family she'd always wanted. "Ryder doesn't have a crazy wife locked up in his attic, does he?" Jane asked on a giggle.

"No, but if I did lock one up," came a deep rumble of a voice into her ear, "I'd keep her in my basement playroom where I store my restraints."

Holy shit.

He was here.

She hopped up from the couch and spun around. "Ryder." Her heart banged like a stick on a drum. She had so much to say to him, but now that he was in front of her, she didn't know where to start. "Happy Thanksgiving."

"Happy Thanksgiving, Jane."

His gray eyes were dark as a storm cloud as his gaze locked on to hers and refused to let go. All the people and all the noise in the house disappeared from her consciousness until it was only her and Ryder and that sizzling connection between them.

"Can we talk?" he asked.

"Use my old bedroom," Isabella said, jarring Jane from the trance she'd fallen into. "It's up the stairs, second door on the left. If any of the kids are in there, feel free to kick them out. They know they're not allowed."

Ryder circled around the couch and, taking her by the hand, led her up the staircase to Isabella's room.

Her pulse quickened as she tried to find the words she wanted to say. She had plenty of experience negotiating in the boardroom but had zero experience navigating the intricacies of her personal life. He flicked on the lights and led her inside before closing the door behind them. Her eyes barely had time to adjust before he caged her in against the pink wall and his hard chest.

"Time's up. I'm done with giving you space."

Moisture pooled in her panties and her nipples went crazy hard, poking out of her blouse like an invitation to Ryder's mouth. It had been only two days since he'd touched her, but it felt as though it had been years. The heat of his body radiated from him, making her sweat in anticipation.

Or maybe that was from the erection pressing into her hip.

"While I appreciate you giving it to me, I've always thought that space was overrated."

He clenched his jaw, the muscles around his mouth tightening. A low growl emanated from deep in his chest. "I'm not going to fuck you."

Oh God.

Her cheeks heated.

She'd misunderstood.

Mortified, she would have figured his rejection would have killed her arousal, but nope. *Still horny as hell for him.*

"Okay. Is that what you wanted to say to me?" she asked, her voice cracking.

His eyes widened. "Shit, I didn't mean to say that out loud. It was more of a warning to myself." He framed her face between his palms. "Make no mistake. I want to fuck you so hard and so filthy I can barely see straight. But we've spent too much time fucking and not enough talking. So for now, I'm gonna keep my hands and mouth off you. At least until we get things worked out."

Jane bit the inside of her cheek to keep from crying out as her sex quivered and clenched in what felt like a mini-orgasm.

He'd almost made her come.

From his words alone.

Trembling, she reached out and set her hands on his chest. "Things?" she asked. His navy sweater was soft under her fingertips, but beneath that, his hard muscles flexed.

"I'm sorry I asked you to quit your job. It isn't my place to tell you what to do." He covered her hands with his own. "It's been a long time since I cared for anyone, and I'm out of practice."

He cared about her?

Wasn't it too soon? They were virtually strangers.

Yet she had to admit . . . she cared about him as well.

Her body grew warm and floaty as if she'd drank a double shot of vodka. "I should've given you the opportunity to explain." She tilted her head to look into his eyes. "I'm not used to anyone having a say over my life. For as long as I can remember, I've always had to take care of myself. The aunt and uncle who raised me loved me, but they weren't exactly affectionate people. They taught me to be self-sufficient."

He cradled her face in his hands. "I'm not asking you to change. Just know that if you ever fall, I'll be your safety net. From now on, we're in this together."

"If that's true, then I need you to be honest with me. You called Keane a monster..." She clenched his sweater in her hands. "Tell me why you hate him so much."

He traced her cheekbone with his thumb. "You're sure you want to know?"

"No," she whispered. "But I'm sure I need to." After losing two of her employees and witnessing Keane's bizarre behavior, she had no choice. She had to learn the truth about the man she'd considered her mentor.

But more than that, she needed to understand the man in front of her.

FIFTEEN

Ryder wrapped his arm around her waist and pulled her sideways onto his lap. Once they settled at the headboard of Isabella's squeaky old twin bed, Ryder rested his chin on top of her head.

He didn't like to think about his childhood. For so long, he'd locked away those memories and thrown away the key.

Walking through life being angry at his father was easy.

But talking about his past...that was fucking hard.

He swallowed hard, easing the tension that had built in his throat, and took a deep breath. Jane didn't rush him. Instead, they sat in silence, simply holding on to one another. He buried his nose in her hair and inhaled her fresh scent. She fit so perfectly against him.

He could get used to this.

After a few minutes, he found himself ready to tell her about his darkest days...and his biggest regrets. "One of my earliest memories is sitting on my father's lap," he said, staring at the pink wall in front of him, "eating a cookie as he talked to three men about setting a fire to someone's house to teach them a lesson. I couldn't have been more than four and I was already terrified of him. Afraid of what he'd do to me if I ever disobeyed him."

"What were you afraid he'd do?" she asked, laying a gentle hand on his shoulder.

His recurrent nightmare of a woman covered in blood flashed through his mind.

"When you hear your father complimenting one of his enforcers for shattering the bones of someone's legs with a baseball bat, you tend to have an active imagination when it comes to the idea of punishment."

She grew rigid in his arms. "Did he ever—"

"No, Keane never laid a hand on me." He hadn't needed to. Not when fear had worked so well. "My father never hid his crimes from Finn or me. He was grooming us to take over McKay Industries, just as his father had groomed him. But Finn and I made a pact. We would never become our father. Never join the family business. Never provide Keane with any heirs for him to mold."

Her eyes softened with understanding. "That's why you don't want Keane to know about Maddox."

"He's not done with me, Jane. I haven't figured out why he set up a business to compete with mine or how you fit into it, but I swear, I will never allow Keane to get his hooks into our son."

She gave him a small smile as she soothingly ran her fingers through his hair. "I know you won't."

A wave of relief crashed into him. "You believe me?"

"I do." She frowned. "Did you think I wouldn't?"

Only a few days ago, she'd been firm in the belief that Keane hung the moon. What had changed since he'd last seen her?

"Other than talking about it with Finn, I kept it all to myself for a long time," he said. "When I finally did tell someone, it didn't go well."

"What happened?"

"The day before I started college, I went to the cops. Unbeknownst to Keane, I had won a full ride to Edison University and was leaving for good. I spoke to a detective for three hours and gave him everything I knew about Keane's illegal dealings."

Jane's brows dipped in confusion. "Then why didn't they arrest him?"

"Three hours and the cop never wrote down a damned word. At the end, he warned that if I ever made another false report, he'd have my ass thrown in jail."

Ryder recalled it as if it were yesterday. The feeling of betrayal and helplessness that came from discovering the people who were supposed to protect you were instead the ones who would harm you. "Until then, I hadn't realized just how powerful of a man Keane was. I never made that mistake again." He stared into Jane's eyes and made a vow. "And I never will."

Her lips parted and her pink tongue darted out to moisten them. She was so beautiful, her cheeks flush with color and her wild hair framing her face. His cock began to harden. He knew she felt it when her breathing hitched.

Suddenly, they were kissing, hard and fast as if they were starving for one another. His hands plunged into her hair. She shifted on his lap, facing him, and ground her core against the bulge in his pants. They moaned in unison.

"We shouldn't. I swore I wasn't going to fuck you tonight," he reminded her.

He could've cried when she ceased her grinding and lifted herself off him. But she shocked the hell out of him when she ran her hand down his length.

"Then let me take care of you tonight," she said, her voice as sweet as honey. Her fingers went to his fly and nimbly unbuttoned his jeans.

He stilled her hand. "Get off the bed."

She rolled off him and planted her feet on the ground beside him.

"Can you snap?" At her nod, he continued. "If you need me to stop, snap your fingers." Because her mouth would be too full of cock to speak. "Any other time, you use a safe word. A word you don't normally use in conversation and something you'll easily remember. A standard one is 'red,' which is why I chose it for you to use before, but you can pick anything you want."

Her cheeks blushed a dark pink. "Red. I'll remember that."

He swung his legs over the edge of the bed, facing her. "Take off your shirt and bra."

Creases formed on her forehead. "I thought I was—"

"Jane. Don't ask questions. Just do it." Preferably, before his cock punched its way out of his jeans.

His heart pounded as he watched her follow his orders. Her hands were shaking a bit as one by one, she undid the buttons of her blouse. Her breathing was rapid and her pupils blown up like round, black balloons eating up the brown irises of her eyes. All signs she was as excited as he was for this.

Keeping her gaze on him, she peeled her blouse off her shoulders and let it fall to the floor, then reached around to undo the clasp of her lacy white bra. His breath came out as an audible hiss when she bared her pert tits to him.

"Now remove your pants and your panties." His voice came out as if he'd swallowed sand.

Snagging her lower lip between her teeth, she hooked her thumbs into the waistband of her underwear and slowly— much too fucking slowly—dragged them down her thighs and stepped out of them. With her hands hanging at her sides, she stood before him, her back straight and her chest out. He allowed himself a moment to take in the lovely view of her.

From the wild strands of her hair teasing the tops of her breasts to the light stretch marks on her belly, she was so fucking perfect. He groaned at the sight of the glistening curls of her mound.

"You like me telling you what to do in the bedroom, don't you?" He didn't wait for her to answer. He stood up from the bed and unzipped his jeans. "Prove it to me. Get on your knees."

She sank to the floor and looked up at him through heavy-lidded eyes.

Standing right in front of her, he pushed his jeans and briefs down to just below his knees. His cock sprang free, the wet tip of him smacking him in the navel. A little smirk played at Jane's lips.

He'd wipe that smirk off soon enough.

His cock twitched and a bit of precum dripped from his tip. He swiped his finger through it and wiped it across Jane's lips. Her eyes went glassy as she licked it away.

He laid his hands on her cheekbones and pulled her head forward. "Open up. You don't have to do anything but relax your mouth and let me in."

He couldn't wait any longer. He surged forward, giving his sweet Jane the first couple inches of his cock. Her tongue caressed the underside of his crown, bathing it in her warmth. He fought against the urge to shove the entire length down her throat.

Sweat beaded on his forehead. He took a deep breath as he slipped his cock farther into the hot cavern of her mouth. She peered up at him wantonly. Slowly, he pumped himself in and out of her, getting her used to the sensation of having her mouth invaded. When she didn't panic, he pushed her head farther onto his cock, careful not to reach the back of her throat.

He knew that this was the first time she'd ever given head and that if he ever wanted it from her again, he better not scare her off. They'd have plenty of time for her to become an expert and learn how to swallow down his entire length into her throat without gagging.

But a simple blow job wasn't enough for him. Not with

Jane. With her, there was an underlying need that had never been there with any other woman.

The need to dominate.

Control.

Consume.

There was a connection between them he couldn't deny, and he was drawn to her like no other.

He moved his hands from her cheeks to the back of her head and propelled her forward on him in tempo with his thrusts. Her lips stretched and tightened around him, and he watched in fascination as his cock slid in and out of her. The inside of her mouth was soft and wet and so fucking hot he couldn't hold on much longer.

But he would.

For Jane.

Because he wasn't the only one who was going to come.

"Play with your pussy," he commanded. "Use one hand to rub that slippery clit of yours and shove the fingers of the other inside of you pretending it's my cock."

She didn't hesitate. Immediately, he heard the sound of her fingers pumping away inside of her wetness. Her eyes fluttered closed and she moaned around his cock, the vibration racing along the length of him to his balls.

"Are you going to come, my sweet Jane?" he asked. "I bet you are. You love having your face fucked by my cock, don't you? You're so good at this, baby. You're making me feel so good. I want to do the same for you. I don't want you to hold back. I want to feel you scream around my cock."

Her lids briefly opened and their eyes met before she

closed them again on a whimper. A fine sheen of perspiration broke out along her collarbone. Her body trembled and her skin flushed. Suddenly, she screamed, the sound of it muffled, and her body jerked as her release crashed over her.

The tremor of her scream on his cock and the vision of her coming was all he needed to push him over the edge. His balls drew up tight to his body. He lightened his hold on her head. "Jane, I'm going to come. If you don't want to swallow it down, snap your fingers."

Her eyes shot open and she gave the subtlest shake of her head.

No snap.

White-hot tingles raced down his spine and wrapped around his testicles before traveling up his length. His toes curled into the carpet and he held his breath. His cock pulsed and then his climax hit him. His come spurted into her mouth—once, twice, so many fucking times—coating her tongue and pooling in her mouth. As his cock slipped out from between her lips, Jane closed her mouth and swallowed his come down her throat.

Sexy as fuck.

He tugged her to her feet and pulled her toward him as they fell back onto the mattress. He kissed her, not minding the taste of him inside her mouth. If anything, it made him hot. Even though he'd just come, his cock was stirring, ready for more. He loved her weight on top of him and the way she was tall enough so that their bodies lined up just right. If he hadn't stupidly vowed not to fuck her and had been wearing a condom, he could easily slide inside her tight heat.

But he could make her come one more time before they went back downstairs. This time with his mouth.

He rolled her over, trapping her beneath him.

His cell rang in his jeans pocket, which, after everything, were still halfway down his legs. He didn't want to take it. Probably just Tristan telling him to get his ass downstairs for dinner. But he grabbed it anyway and checked the display, not recognizing the number.

He moved off Jane and sat up to answer. "Ryder speaking."

All the tension that Jane had sucked out of his body returned as he listened to news on the other end of the call. He answered a couple questions before hanging up and then immediately began getting dressed.

Jane got off the bed. "Who was that?"

"That was the alarm company," he told her. "Someone broke into Novateur."

SIXTEEN

Jane hadn't expected to get to see Novateur tonight. She'd been looking forward to turkey with all the trimmings and taking pictures on her phone of Maddox's first Thanksgiving. But once Ryder received the call that his business had been broken into, all of it fell by the wayside. Although he'd insisted she stay, she'd made arrangements for Dreama to bring Maddox home with her. It wasn't as if there weren't a dozen people at the Lawsons volunteering to hold him for her.

She followed Ryder's car as they drove the ten minutes from the Lawsons to Novateur. Unlike McKay Industries, which was located downtown on the Detroit River, Novateur was housed in a modest one-story brick building in the suburbs, not far from where she'd met Ryder for dinner the other night, or her apartment. She wondered if Ryder lived nearby too.

A police car was parked on the street in front of the building, its blue lights flashing. She hoped that the alarm had been set off by accident, but with the things that had been happening this past week, she wouldn't discount anything. Especially since someone—possibly on Keane's orders—had already stolen Ryder's designs. Would a break-in at Novateur be that hard to believe?

Still, it was likely her mind was running away with her.

As she approached the building, Ryder, along with passengers Tristan and Isaac, was already speaking with two officers who were standing in front of Novateur's broken glass front door.

Ryder went inside and turned on the lights. She waited until all the men had entered before she stepped into the warehouse.

It was much bigger inside than she'd anticipated. There were three rows of kitchens, stretching back as far as her eyes could see. It was nothing like McKay, where all their designs from the innovation department were virtual and made off-site by the manufacturing divisions. She rarely got to see them in action. And their restaurant kitchen demos were still being tweaked because of the software failure. Although now with Evan gone, it was doubtful they'd ever get it working. After hearing the truth about Keane from Ryder earlier, she had to wonder if the software problems stemmed from the fact that her company hadn't written the software—but had stolen it from Ryder.

The taller of the two cops waved his arm. "The alarm probably scared them off, but you might want to look around to make sure they didn't take anything."

Ryder took her hand and led her toward the right side of

the warehouse. They followed along the wall, passing a half-dozen kitchens, before he brought her to an open door.

His lips pursed and his eyes narrowed. "I know for a fact I closed this door before I left work yesterday."

He went inside and turned on the lights.

It was an office.

It wasn't large or lush. More...functional. A large steel desk covered with forms and papers and the typical office supplies. She walked around the perimeter, taking it all in. There were a couple framed photographs on the wall. Both of the Detroit Tigers. One from the 1984 World Series and the other of the victorious final championship game for the eleventh American League pennant.

Guess he was a Tigers fan. Just a reminder of how little they knew one another.

He went through his drawers like a madman, opening them, staring at them for several moments, and then slamming them closed again. He slid open the thinnest drawer, where she would normally keep her pens and pencils, and frowned. He lifted up a Rolex watch. "My watch is still here. If they were after valuables, don't you think they would've taken this?"

The expression on his face was one she'd never seen before. His pupils were tiny pinpricks and his nostrils flared.

On one hand, his anger scared her. But not enough to run the other way.

Hoping to calm him down, she went to his side and put her hand on his shoulder. "Ryder—"

"This wasn't a random break-in," he said firmly. "Whoever it was knew what he was looking for and it wasn't a Rolex."

Tristan and Isaac strode into the office.

"Like what?" she asked.

He turned his head and stared at the Tigers World Series photo. "The only thing of real value in this place."

What?

"Where's your laptop?" Tristan asked.

Ryder stormed over to the frame on the wall and removed it. There, behind it, was a hidden safe built into the wall. He plugged in a series of numbers and, on a beep, opened the safe. He pulled out a laptop and brought it to his desk.

"Thank God whoever it was didn't find it," he murmured. He looked up at Tristan and Isaac. "But my records were rifled through."

She was confused. What exactly did Ryder keep on that computer and why was it so valuable it needed to be locked in a safe?

"So were ours," said Isaac. "Not that we keep much here."

Ryder flipped up the top of the computer and turned it on.

"What are you doing?" she asked.

"Checking the footage for the past hour. Novateur has video cameras set up throughout the warehouse." He clicked on a tab and brought up a video. He slid the time backward until a shadow appeared by the front door. She watched as the guy busted the glass with some kind of tool and was able to turn the locks of the door.

Although the video was dark, a small stream of light from the streetlamp gave them a glimpse of the intruder.

"Shit, he was wearing a mask," Ryder said. "And the video is too grainy to see anything other than one person with broad shoulders and a manly gait."

"Great," Tristan said sarcastically. "At least we've narrowed down fifty percent of the population."

She squeezed Ryder's shoulder. "You should give it over to the police. Maybe they can enhance it."

"Even if they had the capability to do that," Ryder said, "the cops aren't going to take time to investigate a break-in when nothing was taken."

She wondered if there wasn't another reason he didn't want to involve the cops. After what he'd told her tonight about his past experience with a detective, she understood how he might not trust the police.

"What's so valuable on your laptop that someone might have broken in for it?" she asked.

The room went silent.

Ryder shut down his computer and pushed back from his desk. After returning the computer to his safe, he directed his attention to Isaac and Tristan. "Guys, why don't you let the cops know nothing was taken, then go back to dinner and enjoy Thanksgiving with your families? I need to talk to Jane."

After they left, she hoisted herself onto the edge of Ryder's desk and waited for him to tell her what the heck was going on.

He paced the width of the room. "The designs McKay is developing for the restaurant automation line. How's that going? Having trouble with the technology?"

She jerked back, wondering how he knew that. He'd already made it clear he believed his father was behind the theft of his designs off his computer at the conference. "Do you think Keane had something to do with this break-in?"

Deep creases formed above his brows. "The short answer is...I don't know. From the military to your grandfather, there's been a lot of interest in the technology I've developed. That's why I've taken extra precautions to keep it safe."

"What technology?" she asked, confused. Yes, restaurant kitchen automation was on the cutting edge, but it didn't seem valuable enough to warrant that amount of interest.

"Other than for general hardware schematics and basic automation, the designs stolen from my laptop on Mackinac were worthless"—he rubbed the back of his neck—"because I'd omitted a part of the coding in the software. The part that enables a computer to *learn*."

Her jaw dropped. "A computer learn? That's not possible."

"It's not only possible, but I also developed it."

"Okay, but why would the military want it?"

He stopped his pacing and turned to her. "How familiar are you with autonomous weapon systems?"

Weapons? What did weapons have to do with restaurant automation?

She tipped her head to the side. "Not much." *More like nothing at all.*

"Automated weapons are already a reality," he explained. "They'll only do what they're programmed and/or directed to do. An example is a C-RAM system."

Having no idea what he meant by a C-RAM system, she shrugged and shook her head.

He took a step toward her. "The counter-missile systems that shoot down rockets. Those systems have radars and sensors that can detect a missile threat, warn us about the threat, and utilize built-in weapons to shoot it down before it can reach land. These still utilize human supervision and give the government owner the opportunity to shut it down, if needed. But an *autonomous* weapon system doesn't rely on *any* human intervention. For all intents and purposes, it's artificial intelligence, able to process and act all on its own."

She sat quietly for a moment, allowing herself to process the information. Was he really saying he'd written software that could be used to make a weapon autonomous?

How was that possible?

"Your software can do that?" she asked, doubt evident in her tone. "The software you wrote for Novateur."

A small grin pulled up the corners of his lips. "Yes. The software I created can be used in a variety of ways. Anything from kitchens to robots to weapons."

"Keane has never mentioned anything about autonomous technology," she told him. Even if he had, she never would have put it together with something like weapons. "As far as the innovation department is concerned, we're purely working on restaurant automation." She moved off the desk. "But you were right. As you suggested, the software isn't working." She paused, something nagging at her. "The programmer I mentioned who'd committed suicide...he was the person working on fixing it."

Ryder's jaw grew rigid. "How did he kill himself?"

"Gunshot to the head. He didn't leave a note and his wife was pregnant." She took a breath. "Ryder, there's something else. Evan's assistant, Barbara...She and her husband were found dead in their home. Accidental carbon monoxide leak. I'm worried their deaths are related in some way. Especially since..."

"Since?"

"Evan tried to talk to me at the wedding. It was right before the ceremony, so I told him we'd meet Monday morning. That was the last time I spoke with him. And yesterday, I saw Keane speaking with one of the police officers as if...I don't know..." She shook her head. "I just got the feeling that Keane was keeping something from me about Evan's and Barbara's deaths."

She regretted not taking a minute to hear Evan out. If she had, would he still be alive today? A lump of sorrow caught in her throat.

She wasn't sure if he noticed her melancholy, but Ryder wrapped his arms around her waist. "You have no idea what he wanted to talk to you about?"

"No." She thought back to that night. "But he seemed nervous. He was sweating. When I got to work on Monday, there was an email from him in my inbox. But it didn't really say anything and the file he sent was corrupt."

He rubbed circles on her lower back. "Probably a computer virus. You should have the IT department check your computer."

"Right. I was going to do that but with everything that's

happened and then the holiday, I never got the chance." Besides, she'd deleted it from her computer and the antivirus program had come up clean. When she returned to work next week, she'd call IT to take a look at her and Evan's computers.

"I want to help you find out if Keane was behind the theft of your designs."

"Oh hell n—"

Before he could finish, she put a finger to his lips. "Hear me out first, okay?"

At his nod, she continued and wrapped her arms around him, setting her hands on his lower back. "Keane trusts me. If he believes you and I are dating, and I convince him that you're starting to come around to the idea of letting him back into your life, he'll have no reason to doubt it. And then I can get him to lower his guard, confide in me as to whether he stole your designs and had anything to do with this break-in."

Ryder didn't hesitate with his answer. "No. I accept your decision to keep your job at McKay, but that doesn't mean I like it. The more you interact with him, the more you're putting yourself in his crosshairs." The muscles in his back tensed under her hands. "You said it yourself—two people have died in your department. If Keane gets suspicious that you're setting him up, who knows what he'll do."

Jane weighed the risk. Honestly, what would Keane do? Fire her? Despite what she now knew about him, she couldn't imagine him physically harming her.

"I understand your concern, but at this point, I don't

think I'm in any danger. The second that changes, I promise you I'll quit." She reached up and sifted her fingers through his hair. His eyes closed and his jaw slackened as he curled into her touch.

"Jane," he whispered, burying his face into her neck and holding her tightly to him. "Please, don't do it. If anything happened to you..."

She held on just as tightly. "He won't suspect a thing. Trust me, nothing will go wrong."

SEVENTEEN

Ryder was slowly creeping his way into every part of Jane's life—and her heart. In the month since Thanksgiving, not a day had gone by that they hadn't seen each other, even if it was just for an hour after she got home from work.

Jane had started to look forward to it.

Started to *count on it*.

She'd been used to doing everything alone, along with Dreama's help. Now, bit by bit, he'd been taking on some of Maddox's strict nightly routine. Her heart ached whenever Ryder held Maddox in his strong arms. It was everything she'd dreamed of for her son and—if she was being honest— for herself.

After they put Maddox to bed, she and Ryder would spend time talking . . . and kissing. Lots and lots of kissing. But nothing more. Not because they didn't want to. Lord, there were times he left her so aroused, the second she slid under the bedsheets and touched herself, she went off like a grenade.

But because they were taking the time to get to know one another before they made love again.

Now nine at night, Jane passed by Keane's empty assistants' desks and worried she'd miss Ryder's visit. She'd been working twelve to fourteen hours a day the last week finishing up a multi-million-dollar acquisitions deal for McKay. While she found it exciting and rewarding work, she would rather be home.

It didn't help that the innovation department was currently understaffed. Finding someone to fill Evan's position was no easy feat, and since it was the holiday season, no one would be hired until after the New Year. Their IT department hadn't been able to fix Evan's computer or access his files, and although Evan was supposed to have saved his projects on the McKay network, IT reported he'd never done it. That meant extra hours of work for Jane since she was the one who had to renegotiate vendor and customer contracts.

The SD card that Barbara had promised never materialized.

And as far as she knew, no evidence of foul play in Evan's and Barbara's deaths had materialized either.

She told herself that Evan's strange behavior at the wedding and his weird email had caused her to overreact. But if that was true, why hadn't she mentioned it to anyone at McKay? Even when IT had checked her computer for viruses, she hadn't told them *who* had sent the suspicious email. Luckily, they hadn't found anything on her machine.

"I have the Donnelly paperwork for you, sir," Jane said as she entered Keane's office.

But for a small desk lamp and the lights from the parking lot filtering through the window, the room was shrouded in darkness. Snow fell lightly outside and everything was eerily quiet.

"Wonderful. When is the closing scheduled for?" he asked softly.

He looked up from his computer, his face weary. His skin had taken on an almost grayish tone in the past month and he'd been coughing more and more. He worked long hours, longer than even her, and she wondered if it was beginning to take its toll on him.

"Tomorrow at three. But I've organized it so that you don't have to attend." She handed him the thick stack of paper. "Just sign and return the documents to me by noon and I'll make sure to take care of it."

He gestured for her to sit in the chair in front of his desk. "Jane, you've gone above and beyond for me on this deal. I just wanted you to know it hasn't escaped my attention."

That wasn't the only thing she'd "gone above and beyond" for him. Over the past month, she'd been feeding information to Keane about Ryder. None of it real and all of it to convince Keane that Jane could be trusted.

She took a seat, wishing she could take off her heels. Her feet were killing her. "Thank you, Keane. I hope you know that you can count on me."

"I do. You wouldn't be VP of innovation if I didn't."

Even though she'd defended her promotion to Ryder, she'd always had doubts as to whether she'd earned it. "I guess a bit of me worried I had gotten the job because of Ciara."

His brows dipped. "Your connection to Ciara may have gotten you the internship, but it's your hard drive and intellect that got you the promotion."

Was it? Or had Keane promoted her for another reason? Until Ryder, she'd believed everything that came from Keane's mouth. Now she knew that she'd been naïve.

She rolled her lower lip between her teeth. "What made you decide to contact me at school and offer the internship?"

He leaned back in his chair and folded his arms across his chest. He waited a beat before answering, "Your mother asked me to."

His words floored her. That was the last thing she ever expected to hear. "I don't understand. She asked you to give me an internship?"

"She mentioned she had a daughter who was graduating top of her class from my alma mater and that I'd be a fool to pass you up." He appeared genuinely confused. "I thought you knew that."

Was this another one of Keane's manipulations? "I don't get it. She's never shown a speck of interest in my life or reached out to see me or Maddox. She's ignored me practically my entire life. I didn't think she cared."

Keane got up from his desk and walked around it, stopping by her chair. He put his hand on her shoulder. "Sometimes a parent doesn't know how to show their child that they care or they do it in the wrong way. We make mistakes we can't take back. I can't pretend to understand why Ciara keeps herself at a distance from you and Maddox, but I do know she's very proud of you and everything you've accomplished."

Nodding, she blinked back the tears that threatened to fall. Why did Ciara do it? Why not tell her? And why act so cold toward her when they *were* together? None of it made any sense.

Keane coughed into his hands, loud coughs that racked his entire body.

"Are you okay?" she asked. She knew he suffered from a chronic cough, but this was much worse.

He waved her off and grabbed a bottled water off his desk. As he returned to his chair, he drank down half the liquid before the coughing slowed. "Sorry about that." He opened a desk drawer and pulled out a cough drop, then popped it in his mouth. "So how are things going with Ryder? Are you making any progress?" His voice was hoarse and whispered, as if he couldn't get enough oxygen.

"A little. We had dinner yesterday." She considered Keane, noting his pallor and weary eyes. He was weak right now. Tired. His defenses might be lowered. "He's still hurt that we're competing against Novateur. And he mentioned something about stolen designs."

He pursed his lips, but other than that, he gave nothing away. "Stolen designs?"

She mirrored his expression. "Mmm-hmm. Apparently someone copied some of his design files and he was concerned you might be involved. Of course, I told him you weren't and that as head of innovation, I would know if something I was working on had been appropriated through illegal means."

"Did he believe it?"

How should she answer?

"I'm not sure," she said hesitantly. "But I think it would help maybe if I could tell him why you started a competing business."

He folded his hands on the desk. "As I told Finn, I began the restaurant automation company at McKay for Ryder. I thought that it and you would entice him to give up Novateur and come to work here."

"Me?" She couldn't keep the surprise from her voice. What did she have to do with it?

He smiled at her. "You're just the kind of woman I've always wanted for my son. You're smart, beautiful, and loyal. From the moment I met you, I knew you would be perfect for Ryder. That's why you have to get him to forgive me. After I'm gone, the two of you, along with Finn, can run all of McKay Industries together."

Was that all one elaborate lie to throw her scent off the trail? Or was he telling the truth?

She just didn't know.

But he obviously wanted her to believe it was true.

She responded as if she was flattered. "Keane. I'm...I don't know what to say."

He opened his mouth to talk but he broke out into another coughing fit. His shoulders shook and his face turned red as he unwrapped another cough drop with shaking hands.

Regardless of her feelings toward him, she was concerned. She stood from her chair and went over to him. "Are you all right?"

He nodded as his coughing slowed. "Just a lingering cold. Don't worry about me. It's late." He looked up at her and smiled again, albeit this time weakly. "Go home to your son and get some rest."

She almost felt sorry for him. He was obviously sick, and as far as she knew, he had no one to take care of him. At the same time, she had to remember, he reaped what he sowed.

"Oh, one last thing," he said hoarsely. "I meant to tell you that someone from HR will be by tomorrow morning to remove the items left in Evan's and Barbara's offices. I told them to report to you first."

"Okay." She nodded and gave an awkward wave as an invisible band wrapped around her chest and squeezed. "Well, good night."

Back in her office a few minutes later, she put on her coat with the intention of leaving. She rubbed her chest, still feeling that tightness that had formed upon hearing that Barbara's and Evan's offices would be emptied.

It was late. She was exhausted. She still had a dozen things to accomplish at home. And she didn't want to miss seeing Ryder.

But she couldn't get herself to go home.

Not until she checked Barbara's and Evan's offices one last time.

She had to be overlooking something. Barbara had promised she was working on copying the files for Jane and she wasn't the type of employee who would've shirked her responsibilities. Jane thought back to the last day she'd seen her. Barbara had told her she was staying late to finish copying the files. So if Barbara had copied the files onto some sort of SD drive, where would she have left it?

Passing the elevators, she headed toward Evan's office. It wasn't the first time she'd been alone here at night, but for some reason, she felt...uncomfortable.

Like she was being watched.

Goose bumps broke out on her arms, and she shivered underneath her winter coat.

Starting in Barbara's cubicle, she searched every drawer and every nook and cranny of her desk for an SD drive, but came up empty. It was bizarre. All of the office supplies were still there. But there wasn't a single SD drive. Even in Jane's own desk, she must have a dozen of them lying around. They were pretty standard around McKay.

So where were Barbara's?

She sat in Barbara's old chair and swiveled around in a circle. A shadow climbed the wall by Evan's office. She stopped and stared. Her pulse kicked up. Was someone there with her?

"Hello?" she called out.

No one responded.

She shook her head. Her imagination was running away with her. It was time to go home.

As she stood, the photo on Barbara's desk caught her eye. Jane recalled Barbara tapping the picture frame of her and her husband during the discussion of how she and Evan would hide messages for one another. She hadn't thought much of it at the time, but now she wondered.

Had she been giving Jane a hint as to where to find the SD card?

Was it inside the frame?

Her hands trembled as she excitedly pulled the frame apart...

And found nothing but the photo.

Damn.

But she wasn't done yet. She crossed the hallway from the cubicle to Evan's office and flicked on the light. Just like the month before, everything was boxed up except for the framed photo sitting on the desk. Why hadn't Barbara packed it with the rest of his stuff?

Jane picked up the frame and removed the back from it.

The SD card fell out onto the desk.

Anticipation thrummed through her. Since Evan's computer was dead, she went back to Barbara's cubicle. She powered up the computer and when the welcome screen appeared, she inserted the card.

There was a loud whirring noise and then the computer screen went black. The computer's power shut down, but the light on the monitor confirmed the screen was still working. She tried to turn on the computer again, but nothing happened.

It was as dead as Evan and Barbara.

Whatever was on this SD card had not only crashed the computer, but it had also destroyed it. But why? Did it have some kind of virus on it? Or was it something more?

She had to give it to Ryder. Maybe he would know how to fix it.

Dropping it into a pocket in her purse, she headed to the elevator.

A few minutes later, she was in her car and on her way home. She cranked up the heat and set her windshield wipers to medium speed to brush away the accumulating snow.

As a native Floridian, she'd yet to become comfortable with winter driving. Her fingers tightened around the steering wheel as she got on the four-lane main road. The roads were slick, but traffic was light, so she stayed in the right lane and drove under the speed limit.

When she checked her rearview mirror, a single headlight behind her snagged her attention. She couldn't tell if it was a motorcycle or a car, but whatever it was, it was coming up on her much too quickly.

Out of instinct, she sped up. Her mouth went dry and her heart felt as if it had jumped into her throat. The headlight got brighter and brighter as it approached.

She braced herself for impact.

It never came.

At the last second, the car—which she could now see it was—swerved into the middle lane. She took a breath as it passed.

And screamed when it cut back in front of her.

She slammed her foot on the brakes.

Her vehicle fishtailed as she desperately tried to regain control. She took her foot off the brake. Another vehicle appeared in the left lane. Her breath stalled. She was going to hit it.

She fought the urge to close her eyes and instead attempted to stabilize her car. A second later, she slid off the road into a ditch and her head bounced off the leather-wrapped steering wheel.

Lifting her head, she saw that a car had pulled onto the side of the road about twenty-five feet ahead of her. It shut off its lights and began backing up.

Her heart was beating so fast, it was hard to catch her breath.

Why had the driver turned off the headlights?

There was only one reason she could think of.

Because he didn't want anyone to see him.

Was it the same driver who'd run her off the road?

Hands shaking, she rummaged through her purse for her phone and found it dead.

She hit the gas, but she couldn't get the traction to escape the ditch.

She was trapped.

EIGHTEEN

Checking the clock again, Ryder decided he couldn't wait any longer.

It was time to call the police.

Jane had told him she'd be working late tonight, but it was nearly eleven. His calls had gone straight to voice mail and no one answered at her office. He'd been pacing the floor of the family room for nearly an hour to stop himself from thinking the worst. What if something had happened to her? What if Keane had—

He heard the sound of the apartment door opening and turned that way. Jane's coat hood was pulled over her head and snow blanketed her.

"Jane," he said, his voice coming out on a huge sigh.

Her gaze jerked toward him and surprise widened her eyes. "You're still here. I'm sorry you had to wait for me."

Sorry? He'd been worried sick, and she was sorry he'd had to wait?

His gut burned as he fought the urge to bend her over his

knee for a spanking. "Of course I'm still here. I wasn't about to leave until I knew you were safe. Where have you..."

She removed her coat.

Was that dried blood on her forehead?

He rushed over to her. "Jesus. What happened?"

She looked at him blankly. "I had a minor accident."

"Minor? You're bleeding."

Her hand flew to her forehead. "It was nothing. I hit my head on the steering wheel when I slid into a ditch."

Nothing?

What was the matter with her? How could she act so calm?

Was she in shock?

He bent over, putting a hand behind her knees and another at the small of her back, and lifted her into his arms.

"Ryder! What are you doing? Put me down!"

At least *that* got a reaction out of her.

"Why didn't you call me?" he asked as he sat on the couch and placed her on his lap.

"I was going to but my cell was dead. I..." She shook her head and her eyes filled with tears.

He swept the curls off her face. "Jane."

She trembled against his chest. "I think someone intentionally ran me off the road."

Intentionally? What the fuck?

Acid churned in his stomach. "Start at the beginning, sweetheart."

She gripped his biceps. "I found an SD card hidden behind a picture frame in Evan's office. I think it might have something to do with why Barbara and Evan died. Ryder...I think they were murdered."

As warm as it was in the apartment, cold seeped into his skin. "Did you tell anyone you found it?"

"No. Even though I was alone, I felt as if I was being watched. I put the card in my purse and left to come home." Tears slid down her cheeks. "The roads were slippery. A car behind me was speeding and I thought I was going to get hit. But at the last second, he went into another lane. I had about two seconds of relief before he cut back in front of me, causing me to lose control of my car. That's how I ended up in the ditch. I was only there a minute before a salt truck driver stopped and helped push me out of it."

Thank goodness she hadn't had to wait long. The idea of her sitting in her vehicle, helpless at the side of the road, made him sick. They'd have to talk later about keeping her phone charged, but now wasn't the time.

"And the car that ran you off the road?" he asked, sensing there was more to the story.

Her bottom lip quivered. "Whoever it was pulled over to the side of the road and started backing up toward my car. But the weird part was whoever it was turned off his headlights, as if he didn't want to be seen."

It could have been some harmless prank.

A teenager or some random asshole.

But his gut said otherwise.

He could have lost her tonight.

He kissed her forehead. "I think it's possible someone at

McKay saw you with the SD card and intentionally ran you off the road to get it."

"How? My car and Keane's were the only ones in the employee parking lot. There was no one else at McKay but us."

"None that you knew of, but you said you felt as if you were being watched." He brushed his hand down her arm. He couldn't stop touching her. "What made you decide to look for the SD card again?"

"Keane told me someone from HR was coming by to clean out Evan's and Barbara's offices. I thought it would be my last chance to search for it. But he was still in his office when I found it."

Keane. It all came back to him.

"That doesn't mean he didn't have some security camera set up," he pointed out. "He could've seen you find it and either went after you himself or sent someone else to do it."

That would explain her feeling of being watched.

Jane chewed on her lip. "Why did he run me off the road? Why not go after me when I was still in the building?"

"I don't know," he said. "Maybe because his henchman hadn't arrived in time?"

Or more likely Keane hadn't wanted anyone to tie her death to McKay.

"From now on, I'll drive you to and from work. It's dark when you leave in the morning, and it's dark when you return at night. It's not safe." He didn't give her the opportunity to protest. "We need to see what's on the SD drive. You said it's in your purse?"

"Yes, but it's not going to be any help. I already tried to

open the files at McKay and it ended up crashing Barbara's computer." She frowned. "I'm wondering if it might have done the same to Evan's because his was also dead."

"I think you and Maddox should move in with me."

"No. I'm not going to be run out of my apartment," she said vehemently. "We don't even have any proof that the SD card had anything to do with tonight's accident. Besides, I can't just leave Dreama here."

He nodded once. "Then it's settled. Until I know you're safe, I'm moving in."

Ryder didn't need any proof. He wasn't going to take any risks when it came to Jane's and Maddox's lives.

"Are you sure? My apartment isn't very big. You won't have any privacy."

She needed to know how much she meant to him and that there was nothing he wouldn't do for her. Losing her would be like losing the air he breathed. He wouldn't survive without her.

Didn't she understand that?

He wrapped his hand around the back of her neck and stared into her eyes to make his message clear. "I don't need my damned privacy. I don't care if I never have a moment of privacy ever again. I just need you and Maddox safe."

She blinked rapidly, her eyes glassy. What was going on in that gorgeous mind of hers? After a deep breath, she put on the fakest smile he'd ever seen and slid off his lap.

"Thank you for staying here tonight. Did Maddox have his medicine? Did you give him a—"

"Jane. Stop." He jumped to his feet and tugged her to him

before she could put any more space between them. That's
not what either of them needed tonight. "I did everything.
Bath. Reflux meds. Warm bottle of formula. Fresh diaper.
Rocked him for five minutes, then put him to bed on his
tummy at ten p.m. Let someone take care of *you* for a change."

The tension in her shoulders eased as he held her. His
sweet Jane was so used to being in control, she didn't know
how to let go.

She needed his help.

She needed *him*.

In the past, women had wanted him. Wanted what he
could do for them. But they hadn't truly needed him. Then
again, before Jane, he hadn't had the capacity to do anything
but take.

He tipped back her head to look in her eyes. "Why don't
we take a shower and wash that blood off you?"

"A shower?" she repeated on a squeak.

He loved that he could so easily shock her. Her innocence
turned him the hell on. "You know that thing you do when
you want to get clean? How 'bout I show you how fun it is
to use it instead for getting dirty?"

She snagged her lower lip in her teeth and nodded.

He snatched her hand and pulled her to the bathroom,
where he shut the door behind them. The room wasn't very
big, but she'd made it her own. While the walls and cabi-
nets were all white, she'd added a colorful purple flowered
shower curtain with matching bathroom set. It was cute and
girly and smelled like his sweet Jane.

She reached into the shower and turned on the water. He

couldn't help but be pleased that he was the lucky bastard who got to initiate Jane into the joys of sex. She was so vibrant and full of sensuality, from the wildness of her hair to the way she moved her hips back and forth when she walked.

She completely undid him.

And she had no idea.

He removed a condom from his wallet and swiftly shed his clothes. She, too, undressed, showing no sign of the shyness she'd exhibited a month ago when she'd stripped for him on Thanksgiving.

Condom in hand, he stepped into the tub and, once she joined him, pulled the curtain closed. He set the condom on an empty soap dish and moved closer to her. Steam enveloped them as he lowered his mouth to hers.

Their kiss started with a slow exploration of tongues and soft caresses of lips. He tried to keep it controlled, but just like always with Jane, he struggled to rein himself in. He was hungry for her. Fucking starving. He spun her around and pushed her back up against the wall. She was just as hungry for him, kissing him with the same intensity.

They moaned into each other's mouths, their tongues thrusting and sparring with one another. Her soft tits brushed against his chest, her raspberry nipples poking him. Teasing him.

His throbbing cock was hard as steel. But it would have to wait. Because this wasn't about him. It was about giving her what *she* needed.

And what she needed was to be dominated.

He dipped his head to her breast, taking her nipple between his lips. He bit down on it, first gently, then a bit harder, before soothing it with the flat of his tongue. Her hand curled around the back of his head as he moved to torture her other nipple with the same treatment.

He crouched to the level of her navel and looked up at her. "I need you to stay quiet for me. Can you do that, baby?"

The last thing they needed to do was wake up Maddox or give a sleeping Dreama an earful.

Jane's moans were for his ears only.

On her nod, he dropped to his knees and leaned toward her pussy. Her fragrant arousal was a heady aphrodisiac. He needed to taste it. Craved it like a drug.

To give him better access, he lifted her leg and hooked it around his neck. She put a hand on the wall beside her and rested her head against the back wall to balance herself.

He swiped a finger up her slit, finding her already drenched. "Such a pretty pussy," he crooned. Spreading her folds apart, he bent forward and licked a path from her entrance to her clit. Her spice hit his tongue, awakening all his senses. He used the tip of his tongue to tease her clit out from beneath its hood and felt it swell in response.

Jane let out a muffled moan. He couldn't see her, but it sounded as if she'd put her hand over her mouth.

She was such a good girl, following his instructions.

He worked her clit relentlessly, sliding his tongue back and forth and up and down until he found the rhythm that made her cry out the hardest. She rocked her hips, fucking herself against his tongue. Her uninhibited response was so fucking sexy, he could easily do this for hours and never get tired of it. Pleasuring her made him feel powerful and filled him with pride, as did the way she sweetly submitted to him.

Her bud swelled beneath his tongue to nearly twice the size it had been and her thigh trembled on his collarbone. She glided her fingers through his hair, her nails digging into his scalp.

He sensed she was close.

And he knew just what would push her over the edge.

He reached between her legs to the crack of her ass and carefully inserted the tip of his pinky inside her. Her body jerked and her clitoris pulsed. On a muffled scream, she came. He moved his tongue to her opening, bathing it in her sweet release.

He removed her leg from his neck, then stood up and seized her lips, giving her a taste of his favorite dessert. Without taking his mouth off hers, he blindly grabbed for the condom, and once he found it, ripped the package open and rolled the latex down his painfully sensitive cock.

He wasn't going to last long. "Turn around, bend over, and brace your hands on the wall in front of you."

She got into position, pushing her ass out to him and tantalizing him without even knowing it. He just couldn't help himself.

He smacked his hand against one globe, the sound of it reverberating in the space. She peered up at him over her shoulder and stuck her ass out farther. That was all the invitation he needed. Not that he needed one. She had a safe word and if she asked him to stop, he would.

He didn't go rough with her. For about a minute or two,

he playfully swatted the flesh of her behind in a steady rhythm. She moaned over and over until finally, he couldn't take it anymore. Bending his knees, he aligned his cock to her opening and surged forward, sliding his entire length inside of her in a single thrust.

Holy shit, she felt amazing at this angle. Her walls clung to him tightly, so tightly, he swore he could feel her heat and every ridge of the flesh inside of her, even through the condom.

He drove himself in and out of her, the force of it pushing her onto her tippy toes. Setting a fervent pace, he held her hips and pushed her back onto his cock as he thrust into her.

"Oh God," Jane cried. "Ryder, I'm coming again."

Thank fuck.

Tension wound tight in his lower abdomen, stretching, and then finally breaking. "I'm with you, baby. I'm there too." Liquid heat darted up his cock and shot out from the tip into the condom, over and over.

Breathing hard, he rested his head on Jane's back, suddenly noticing and not caring that the water of the shower had turned cold.

This. This was what he'd been missing out on all these years.

Before Jane, he hadn't truly understood Domination and submission. It had all been kinky games to him. But he got it now. The connection between Dom and sub. The rush that came from bringing pleasure to a partner.

He got it.

And he'd do everything in his power to keep it.

NINETEEN

If this was what it would be like to live with Jane, where did he sign up?

Waking up with a soft, warm Jane in his arms had felt...right. Who cared that it had been six in the morning and they'd only gotten three hours of sleep? Or that the minute he'd slid his fingers inside a wet and willing Jane, Maddox had cock-blocked him by waking up ready for breakfast?

It had taken a lot of convincing, but he'd gotten Jane to take the day off of work. She'd been in a car accident, her life could be in danger, and she was worried about overseeing some closing that afternoon. Keane could take care of it his own damned self.

But someone had to look out for Jane.

And that someone was Ryder.

Since they had the whole day together, Jane had suggested they walk to the neighborhood's community center where Maddox could have his first photo with Santa Claus.

Frankly, Ryder thought it was kind of silly since Maddox didn't have a clue about Christmas yet, but he'd smartly kept that to himself. Jane seemed pretty excited about it.

From the couch where Ryder was feeding Maddox his bottle, he watched Jane shove about a dozen diapers into a bag. "Do you really have to pack that much stuff with you every time you leave?"

Dropping a cold pack into a side compartment of the diaper bag, Jane laughed. "If I have Maddox with me I do. You'll learn soon enough. Always plan for the unplannable."

Words to live by, and not only when it came to having children.

His son's mouth glommed on to the bottle's nipple as if he hadn't eaten in days. Holding Ryder's finger in his little fist, Maddox gazed up at him.

The love Ryder felt for his son was overwhelming. He'd never experienced anything like it. His chest tightened. His throat thickened. And *damn it*, his eyes even burned. How could he have gone so long without knowing he could love someone so much?

How could his own father have held him as a baby and not felt the same love surging through him? Was Keane simply incapable of love? Or was it that Ryder wasn't worth loving?

Before knowing that Keane might have something to do with the deaths of two people who worked for him, Ryder had already been worried about what Keane would do if he discovered Maddox was his grandson. But knowing now that someone had might be after Jane, Ryder was consumed with fear and rage to the point he could hardly contain it inside. If Jane knew the kinds of thoughts he was entertaining, she'd probably have him committed.

There was nothing he wouldn't do to keep Jane and Maddox safe.

Nothing.

And that included going after Keane before he had the chance to hurt them.

What if Keane had ordered those deaths over whatever was on the SD card? If he discovered that Jane now had the card, would he go after her next? Is that why she'd been run off the road?

Keane seemed to have a soft spot for her. After all, he'd hired her as an intern and had given her a job that gave Jane the means to financially support her son. From what Jane had told him, she and Keane had been close. If that was true, would Keane really harm her? Or would his ruthlessness and greed win out?

Whether Keane had anything to do with it or not, Ryder would never allow him to be a part of Maddox's life. He'd proven time and time again that he didn't know the first thing about raising a child.

He hated all the unanswered questions. Not only those related to whoever was after the autonomous software, but also what the hell was on that SD card.

There was only one way to find out.

Fix that card.

Not so easy. Not even for a computer geek like himself with a gift for programming.

Noticing the bottle of milk was now empty, Ryder plucked it out of Maddox's mouth and like a pro (if he did say so himself), gently patted his back to burp him. Within ten seconds, his son let out a loud belch followed by a giggle.

"Good one," Ryder told him, getting up from the couch. He dressed Maddox in his winter coat and hat, and then brought Maddox to his car seat, where he belted him in to get ready for their walk. Jane covered Maddox with a blanket.

A haggard-looking Dreama stumbled into the room coughing. Although she was wearing sweatpants and a hooded sweatshirt, her teeth chattered. "Oh. I thought you'd be at work," she said to Jane. She gave Ryder a quick wave of her hand in acknowledgment and then turned back to Jane. "Do you have any cold medicine? I ran out," she croaked.

"Yeah. It's in my bathroom, underneath the sink," Jane said, her brows knitted in concern. "You look terrible."

Dreama blew her nose into a tissue. "I feel terrible. I think I have the flu. I'm calling into work and going back to bed." She spun around, wobbling a bit before she put a hand out to the wall to steady herself.

Jane jumped into action and threw an arm around Dreama's waist to help her to the bathroom. Was it wrong of him to worry Dreama would get Maddox sick?

Ryder crouched down by Maddox. "Maybe you and your mom should stay with me at my house until Dreama's better."

A short time later, a door closed and Jane returned to the family room.

"Should we be worried?" he asked her.

With her purse and the diaper bag slung over one arm, Jane frowned as she lifted Maddox's carrier and they headed to the front door. "No, she'll be fine."

"I meant Maddox." Did she really need all that stuff just to go down the block? Figuring it was the least he could do, he took the diaper bag from her. "She looked pretty sick. What if she does have the flu and Maddox gets it?" He dragged the stroller outside and hefted it down the stairs to the first floor.

Jane popped the car seat into the stroller and smiled as wide as the Grand Canyon. "He'll be fine. I doubt she has the flu and even if she does, this isn't the first time one of us has gotten sick since Maddox was born. We just have to keep the two of them separated for the next couple of days."

"How long have you known Dreama?" he asked.

"A couple years."

"You're pretty close."

Jane pushed the stroller along the sidewalk. "When I found out I was pregnant...I was scared. I couldn't find you and it's not as if I had family support. But Dreama was there for me every step of the way. I don't know what I'd do without her."

He walked side by side with her. "I'm glad you have her, but you don't have to do it on your own anymore. I want us to be a family."

She sucked in a breath. "Ryder—"

"I'm not saying we should get married tomorrow or anything," he said. Although he wouldn't complain if they did. "But I want to be there. For you. For Maddox."

"I'd like that too. But we don't have to rush it. Maddox and I aren't going anywhere." She turned her head to look at him. "Besides, we hardly know each other."

He smiled at her, not hiding his smugness. "I think I know you pretty well."

At her blush, he laughed.

Sure, he knew her sexually, but that wasn't what he'd meant.

Giving a little chuckle, she shook her head. "You don't know me as well as you think you do." Her brows rose in amusement. "What's my favorite color? Food? How do I take my coffee?"

"Those things are superficial." He wrapped his hand around the handle of the stroller next to hers. "I know you're a great mother and a loyal friend. You try to see the good in everyone. You're driven. Smart. Kind. Beautiful. Sexy. Submissive." He paused, lowering his voice. "Forgiving. And more than anything, you want a family to love."

She stopped walking. Let out a huge breath. And reached up to cup his cheek. "Ryder."

He nodded. "So yeah, I know you."

She leaned up and kissed him lightly on the lips.

And that kiss meant more to him than all the ones that came before.

They headed down the street toward the community center, which was located only a couple of blocks away. The residential area where Jane lived was built up around a bunch of shops and restaurants, giving it a small-town feel despite its city location. He lived in a similar community, but he had a house with a yard...

And a playroom that was *definitely* not meant for Maddox. "Have you thought of a way to read what's on the SD card without infecting the computer?" she asked.

"There's a couple of programs I'm familiar with that will help remove a virus from a memory card and recover lost data. But there's something I've been trying to figure out. From what you've explained, Barbara used the SD card to download Evan's files, right? But his computer was dead when you tried to read the card, which means the virus didn't activate until that file was downloaded."

She frowned. "You lost me."

"I think Evan designed the virus himself."

She pulled a set of plastic keys out of the diaper bag and shook them in front of a fussy Maddox. "Wait. You think Evan added the virus to his *own* computer?"

He nodded. "Barbara downloading the file onto the SD card activated the program that crashed his computer."

"Then I transferred the virus to her computer when I tried to read the SD card. So now that we know how it got on there, do you know how to fix it?"

"I can try all the usual antivirus programs, but if I were Evan, I would've written my own. If that's the case, the question is going to be where did he hide it?"

Arriving at the community center, Jane retrieved Maddox from his car seat and parked the stroller with a dozen others outside the front door.

Wearing a puffy brown coat and a hat that reminded Ryder of a giant blueberry, Maddox was oblivious to his new surroundings.

Jane's eyes narrowed on the adjacent parking lot. "I think that's Ian's car over there."

He turned his head and spotted a black Rolls-Royce. Not exactly the type of car one saw in this part of town. Ian Sinclair got out of the back of the car (of course he had a driver) and walked toward them.

What the hell was *he* doing here?

"Jane," Sinclair said as he approached. "I thought that was you."

Clear shock evident on her face, she went over to greet him. He kissed Jane on the cheek and awkwardly patted Maddox on top of his blueberry-hat-covered head. "I was just on the way to meet Ciara for lunch at a bistro near here when I saw you through the window and had my driver stop so I could say hello."

"I thought she and Finn were still on their honeymoon," Ryder said.

Sinclair smiled. "They came back early. Been in town for almost a week." His curious gaze bounced between Ryder and Jane. "I wasn't aware that the two of you were friends."

"Do you have a problem with that?" Ryder asked, taking a step closer to Sinclair.

"I'm just surprised. You only met—what—a month ago? And here you are together, the three of you, like a little family." He paused and rubbed his chin, looking at the three of them. "Then again, you are family, aren't you?"

Ryder's blood went cold.

Had Sinclair figured it out?

"Family?" Jane asked, a slight blush on her cheeks that Ryder hoped Sinclair would attribute to the cold air.

"Ryder's your stepuncle now that Finn and Ciara are married." Sinclair raised a brow, seemingly confused. "Why? What did you think I meant?"

If Sinclair was playing a game with them, this was the time to throw all the cards on the table. "Are you trying to insinuate something?" Ryder asked. "If so, I'd rather you not waste our time and just say it."

Jane's jaw dropped. "Ryder—"

"It's fine, Jane," Sinclair said, waving his hand as if brushing away a pesky fly. "If you two are seeing each other, I'd like to know what exactly is your intention toward my granddaughter?"

Ryder huffed in annoyance. "What makes you think you have any right to ask that? For twenty-three years, you've ignored her, denied her the birthright she deserved, not caring about her feelings, and all of a sudden you're interested in who she spends time with?"

"I have always cared about Jane," Sinclair said. "If I'd had my way, I would've raised her as my own. But Ciara, she was...headstrong. Wild. Alcohol, drugs, promiscuity. She managed to stay sober once she learned she was pregnant, but I feared it wouldn't last. I offered to hire full-time help to raise Jane so she could grow up in our home, but Ciara wouldn't hear it."

"Right," Ryder said. "You cared about Jane so much you've had nothing to do with her in all these years."

"Ciara threatened to"—Ian winced—"hurt Jane if I didn't

send her away. Giving her to my deceased wife's sister was a compromise of sorts. Jane remained in our life, but Ciara didn't have to see her if she didn't want to. I've kept an eye out for her, even though she lived far away. Now that she's finally home where she belongs, my love for her has only strengthened."

Jane's expression softened. Sinclair had all the right words, but Ryder didn't believe his sincerity for a minute. Men like Sinclair, like Keane, didn't love anyone but themselves.

"That's a nice story," Ryder said, not bothering to keep his doubt from his tone.

"It's the truth. I don't want to see Jane get hurt." Sinclair angled his body toward Jane. "You need to understand there will be people out there who will try and use you for your connections. People who have an ulterior motive for becoming your"—he glanced at Ryder before looking back at Jane—"friend."

Amusement played at Jane's lips. "I'll keep that in mind, Ian."

Ryder fought the urge to roll his eyes. Couldn't she see through Sinclair's act? He didn't care about Jane any more than Ciara did.

Sinclair beamed at Maddox. "Can I hold him? He's getting so big."

Jane nodded and transferred the baby into Sinclair's arms. Two seconds later, Maddox burst into tears and wailed loud enough to be heard across town.

Apparently, Ryder wasn't the only one who disliked Sinclair.

"He's just tired," Jane said apologetically, taking Maddox back. The baby instantly stopped crying.

"Why don't you join your mother and me for lunch?" Ian asked Jane.

Ryder noticed Sinclair had not extended the invitation to him.

Jane's eyes momentarily lit up. Then she glanced at Ryder. "That's probably not a great idea," Jane said. "I wanted to get Maddox's photo with Santa and then Maddox really needs to go down for his nap. Routine and all. But thank you for asking."

Sinclair flashed her a smile that reeked of insincerity. At least it did to Ryder. "You are always welcome, Jane. You're part of the family. Never forget that." He gave her a hug and thankfully retreated back to his car.

Did she regret turning down the lunch invitation? She shouldn't.

"Your grandfather gives me the creeps," he said, breaking the silence. And what the hell was he really doing in her neighborhood?

"Ryder," she said in a chastising tone. "That's mean."

"Just saying how I feel. Even Maddox can't stand him." He crouched lower to talk to his son face-to-face. "Can you, buddy?" Maddox energetically punched his fists in the air and gave a slobbery grin. "He doesn't seem tired now, does he?" Ryder pointed out to Jane. "He just didn't want the scary old man to hold him."

"Ian isn't that bad."

Yeah, well, pneumonia started out like an ordinary

cold before it attacked the lungs and made it difficult to breathe.

The next half hour was spent in what Ryder could only describe as Christmas Hell. Whining children and impatient parents filled almost every inch of the community center as they waited in line for Santa. By the time they reached the front, Maddox was sound asleep.

But as Ryder looked at the photo of Maddox sprawled across Santa's lap, he had to admit it had been worth it.

Not speaking, Ryder and Jane began their trek back to the apartment. Jane seemed lost in thought.

A few minutes later, they climbed the stairs of her building. A knot of unease formed in his neck when he saw Jane's front door wide open.

He was certain Jane had locked it before they'd left.

It was probably nothing—maybe Dreama had opened it for some reason and had forgotten to close it—but he wasn't going to take any chances with Jane's and Maddox's lives.

"Stay out here," he ordered Jane. "I'll go check things out."

At Jane's nod, he went inside, his body on full alert, not knowing what he'd find.

It didn't take long to find out.

A bloodied Dreama was lying on her stomach in the hallway by the door, as if she'd been struck down trying to flee. Blood flowed freely down her legs…her arms…her head. A red-stained baseball bat was by her side.

Was she alive?

His own breath stalled in his chest and his hands shook

like a junkie needing a fix. He dropped to his knees, Dreama's blood soaking into the fabric of his jeans.

"Jane! We need an ambulance. Call 911!" he yelled.

Dreama was so still.

Too still.

Dread wedged like a rock in his throat.

Who the hell had done this to her?

He bent low to talk in her ear as he put two fingers over the pulse point of her neck. "Dreama? It's Ryder. Don't worry, Jane's calling 911. We're going to get you to a hospital. You'll be fine."

He wasn't sure who he was trying to convince—Dreama or himself.

Especially because he couldn't find a pulse.

TWENTY

Jane had never thought that sitting could be so exhausting. For eight hours, she'd just been sitting in the hospital waiting room's hard orange chair. Couldn't they at least make the chairs a bit more comfortable? There was a new product for McKay's innovation division. She'd get right on it...as soon as she got the news Dreama was going to live.

As soon as Ryder had screamed for her to call 911, she'd known something terrible had happened to Dreama. Her mind had conjured up a dozen reasons Dreama might need an ambulance. Not one of them came close to reality. Holding Maddox close to her chest, Jane had cautiously stepped inside her apartment. What she'd seen would haunt her until her dying day.

Dreama broken and shattered like a china doll.

Her legs twisted and bent in the wrong direction.

Blood splattered all around her. On her. On the walls. On Ryder.

It was like a scene out of a horror movie.

Jane couldn't help but wonder, if she hadn't gone to the park with Ryder...

Could she have protected Dreama?

Or would that have been *Jane* lying lifeless on the bloody carpet?

What if Maddox had been there?

She shuddered to think about it.

The minutes that followed were a blur. As the paramedics worked on Dreama, the police checked the apartment to make sure the attacker was no longer there. Then the cops had asked Jane and Ryder a whole bunch of questions, one right after the other. She couldn't even remember answering them. But one thing remained vivid. When the paramedics had taken Dreama away on a stretcher, Jane got a close look at her ravaged face.

She wasn't embarrassed to admit she'd vomited right then and there.

Before Jane had recovered, Dreama was already in the ambulance and speeding to the nearest hospital.

The police had allowed Jane to change her clothes and pack a bag for her and Maddox. The apartment was officially a crime scene and off-limits for the time being.

Not that she wanted to stay there.

Somehow, Ryder had stayed calm throughout the ordeal, calling Tristan so that he could tell Isabella and notify Dreama's parents. It hadn't taken long before they'd shown up at the hospital, along with Dreama's aunts and uncles and cousins. There were so many of them. Dreama had so many people who loved her. They practically filled up all the seats of the waiting room. All except Isabella.

She refused to sit.

Instead, she paced back and forth across the waiting room. Every once in a while, Tristan would stop her and hug her, whisper something in her ear. She'd nod, and while she'd resume her pacing, it was slower, her body more relaxed. Jane wondered what he said to calm her.

Jane hated that she was jealous. Not only because Isabella had someone who so obviously loved her or because she had an entire family there for support, but because she could *feel*. Isabella had cried and raged and at one point had even smiled. In fact, everyone in the room had been teary-eyed.

Not Jane.

To her, everyone else was running at super-speed while she was stuck in slow motion. She didn't have the energy to do anything. Not even cry.

She was completely numb.

Thank God for Ryder. He hadn't left her side for a second, sharing the responsibility of tending to Maddox, without caring who noticed. It just wasn't important at the moment.

Nothing was important but Dreama.

It was just after eight p.m. when Dreama's surgeon came into the room, wearing fresh scrubs and a blank expression. Everyone went silent as Dreama's parents stood for the news.

A buzzing permeated her body, yanking her out of the uncomfortable numbness. Her pulse began to race as the fear she'd first experienced upon seeing Dreama after the attack returned with a vengeance. Jane's heart physically hurt, like it was being squeezed in a vise, and she couldn't catch her breath. Dark spots began clouding her vision and the room spun.

Was Dreama alive?

Ryder shifted Maddox on his lap and grabbed her hand. The simple touch grounded her, reminded her she wasn't alone. The pain in her chest diminished and she found herself able to breathe again. As if he was her anchor in a storm, she gripped his hand tighter.

"How is she?" Dreama's father asked the doctor, his tone weary and nervous. He held his wife close to his side.

"She's out of surgery and doing well," said the doctor loudly, knowing everyone was listening. He then lowered his voice, but Jane was close enough to still hear him as he continued. "We were able to stop the internal bleeding, but I'm sorry to report that despite our best efforts, we had to perform a complete hysterectomy. There was just too much damage from the beating. We also removed her spleen and repaired a nick to her right kidney. She has numerous broken bones that will need setting once she's strong enough to go back into surgery. For now, we've just stabilized them with casts." He paused and put a hand on Dreama's mother's shoulder. "Also, I thought you'd want to know that we found no evidence of sexual assault."

"When can we bring her home?" Dreama's father asked.

"Expect her to be in the hospital for at least six to eight weeks and physical rehabilitation after that." The doctor raised his voice again. "We'll be moving her into a room soon, but she's probably going to be unconscious for several more hours. I suggest you all go home and get some rest.

Visiting hours begin at nine a.m. for immediate family members only."

She wasn't surprised when Dreama's mother shunned the surgeon's advice and announced her decision to stay. If it were her child, she'd do the same.

God forbid.

Jane took a deep breath and bowed her head, relieved Dreama had made it through surgery and was alive. Her eyes burned as if tears were about to form, but they refused to come.

No longer holding Ryder's hand, Jane stared at the spot where the surgeon had announced the news. She knew it was time to go but she couldn't get herself to move. The chatter around her grew quieter and quieter until Ryder stood in front of her with Maddox in his car seat.

"Come on. It's time to go home," he said gently, as if she were a child who needed coaxing.

Home?

She didn't have a home anymore. She couldn't live in that apartment. Not without Dreama.

Lacing his fingers with Jane's, Ryder pulled her to her feet and with an arm around her shoulders, led her out of the cold, sterile hospital and into the night. She didn't know what road lay ahead for her, but one thing was clear.

She couldn't navigate it without Ryder.

* * *

Ryder slid into the driver's seat of Jane's car and closed the door, hoping it wouldn't wake Maddox. Of course, judging by what he'd seen today, the kid could just about sleep through anything. Still, he didn't want to take the chance. Not now when Jane so obviously needed him.

She was in shock.

Pale and listless, she hadn't spoken much all day. Hadn't eaten more than half a candy bar. Hadn't smiled or cried or even met anyone's gaze. It was as if she was physically there but the rest of her had checked out.

Everyone else had been too caught up in their own grief to notice.

But not him. Except for Maddox, no one mattered more to him than Jane.

Sitting by her side for eight hours, he realized if he hadn't been there, she would've been on her own. And that was fucking unacceptable to him. Someone as warm and funny and caring as Jane deserved to have a room full of people who were there to take care of *her*.

He drove out of the hospital parking lot onto the dark street and headed toward his house. A single headlight made the same turn. For a moment, Ryder thought it was a motorcycle but as he looked in the rearview mirror, he realized it was a car with only one working headlight.

Like the one that had run Jane off the road.

For the time being, he kept the news to himself. Jane had gone through enough today. She didn't need to worry about anything else. Besides, plenty of cars fit that description. Still, he'd stay extra vigilant and keep an eye on it.

Staring out the passenger side window, Jane finally broke the silence. "Who would hurt someone like Dreama?"

He wasn't sure whether she was talking to herself or to him.

"I keep going over the what-ifs. What if Dreama hadn't been sick and had gone to work as she'd planned? What if we hadn't gone to the community center? What if we hadn't run into Ian? Would we have gone home earlier and stopped it from happening? I can't help but thinking if only I'd done something different, anything different, Dreama wouldn't be in the hospital fighting for her life."

The car wasn't exactly the best place for a conversation like this, but it couldn't wait until home. "Or it could have been you. None of this was your fault. The blame falls on the person or persons who hurt her." He didn't believe in coincidences. The police theorized that Dreama had interrupted a burglary and frankly, Ryder didn't bother correcting them. Informing them that they were wrong would prove futile when his father was concerned.

She turned her head to look at him. "I didn't think…" Her voice cracked. "I should have warned her."

The guilt in her eyes slayed him. "You had no reason to think she was in danger."

"I'm not sure I believe that. Not when two people in my department just died and I'm walking around with an SD card that may be the reason why."

Noting the car with the one headlight was still behind them, Ryder turned his car into his neighborhood. He breathed a sigh of relief when the other vehicle didn't follow, but instead, continued straight down the main road. "I know I wanted to wait until we found the antivirus program, but I think it's time we check what's on that SD card."

She blinked a few times as if coming out of a fog. "Do you have a computer you're willing to lose if the antivirus software doesn't work?"

"I've got two old ones I've kept for backup in case. Why don't you get Maddox settled and I'll grab them from my home office?"

Inside his house, Jane pulled the SD card from her purse and dropped it into his waiting palm. He showed her the extra bedroom where she could set up the Pack 'n Play for Maddox.

If they weren't in such a hurry, he would've given her the grand tour. He would love to see her face as she saw the potential his house held. Would she like the kitchen or was it too small? What did she think of the neighborhood? Could she imagine herself and Maddox living there? And wait until she saw his huge fenced-in backyard.

After retrieving his old computers, he placed them on his dining room table. He decided to hit the virus with the most comprehensive program he had available, but his gut told him he was about to destroy yet another computer. Two people had died because of whatever was on that SD card. Even the most powerful antivirus programs probably wouldn't be enough to fix the card so that they could access the files.

Jane's soft footsteps pattered on the hardwood floor as she entered the dining room. "He's sound asleep for the moment." She put a baby monitor on the table. "His schedule is off for the day, but I think we should have a couple of hours before he wakes up for his last night feeding." She gestured to the computer as she sat in a chair beside him. "Any luck?"

"Just starting, but I wouldn't get your hopes up." She watched in curious anticipation as he inserted the card. He ran the antivirus software on the SD card. A few minutes later, a message popped up that the software did not detect any viruses or malware. "Fucking genius," he mumbled.

He tried opening the file. Normally, if a card was corrupt, he'd receive an error message.

That wasn't what happened.

Code scrolled up the screen like the credits of a *Star Wars* movie. And then on a loud buzz, the screen went completely black just as Jane had described to him.

"Yeah, that's what happened when I tried opening it. But I didn't see the code before. That's new."

Because the virus was learning.

"I've never seen anything like it in all the years I've been playing around with computers," he said in awe. "This isn't the typical virus or worm you pick up on the Web. I was right. Evan intentionally designed a virus to protect the contents of the file. Every time someone tries to open the file, the virus adds another layer of protection to it. Eventually, it will become impossible to open, even if we find the antivirus program he wrote for it. Tomorrow morning, we need to go search his office. It has to be there somewhere."

Jane went quiet, her brows knitted in a frown and her finger to her lip. "Is it possible to email an antivirus as a file?"

"I suppose it's possible. Why?"

"Remember I mentioned Evan had sent me an email but that the file was corrupted?"

He thought back to that conversation. He'd been so focused on the SD card, he hadn't paid much attention to anything else. "Tell me about the email."

"The message of his email said, 'Thought you should see this.' When I clicked on the attachment, a bunch of code flashed on the screen and then a giant yellow smiley face filled the screen."

"A yellow..." Ryder scratched his head for a moment as he processed Jane's information. "Did your computer still work right after?"

"Yeah," Jane said, fidgeting with the ends of her hair. "I thought I'd gotten lucky."

"Maybe you did," he murmured. A rush of excitement stirred in his belly. "When you clicked on the attachment, it's possible you downloaded the program that will allow you to read the files on the SD card. Your work computer is immune from the virus."

Guilt flickered in her eyes. "But I erased the email and whatever downloaded onto my computer."

Ryder bit down on his lip to keep himself from swearing out loud.

Jane might have ruined their only chance at finding out what the hell was on that card.

"We need to access your computer at work and see if the antivirus program is still on it." He stood and offered his hand. "But not tonight. You should rest. Come to bed. I promise I won't lay a hand on you. It's enough that you and Maddox are here safe with me. Just let me hold you."

She intertwined her fingers with his but didn't get up from the table. "What if I told you that isn't going to be enough for *me*? Would you do something for me?"

Didn't she realize by now there was nothing he wouldn't do for her? "Anything. Everything."

Staring into his eyes, she stood. "Take me downstairs."

TWENTY-ONE

Downstairs," Ryder said, parroting her words. He swallowed thickly. "You mean you want to see my playroom."

If Jane wasn't so serious, she would've laughed at Ryder's shocked expression. And honestly, she'd surprised herself. But after witnessing Tristan with Isabella in the hospital waiting room, she wondered if his ability to soothe her was more attributable to him being her Dominant than her fiancé. And it had led Jane into thinking about some of the things Dreama had told her about Domination and submission and why she practiced it.

Dreama had explained that giving up control helped release everything she'd kept bottled up inside of her. She'd also told Jane there was no one right way to practice BDSM as long as the participants followed the safe, sane, and consensual creed (Dreama had also mentioned something about RACK, but Jane couldn't remember what that meant), and that everyone had their own reasons for being in the lifestyle.

Ryder had claimed he wasn't a Dominant and that for

him it was solely about sex and fun. Well, tonight she
wanted to challenge that statement.

"Not just to see it," Jane said, curling her hand around
his neck. "I want to *use* it. I can't stop thinking about
Dreama lying there broken and alone. I don't want to think
about it anymore. Can you help me forget? Just for a little
while?"

He tucked her hair behind her ear and cupped her face in
his hands. "Are you sure?"

"Yes. I've never been surer of anything in my whole life."

He snagged the baby monitor off the table and slipped
his arm around her waist. She should've felt something—
nervous, excited, horny, but instead, she remained numb
and detached from her own body. She wanted to stop thinking and feel. Pleasure. Pain. She wanted it all. And she
wanted Ryder to give it to her.

His house had surprised her. It wasn't the kind of place
she would've thought he would own. This was a family's
home. She'd cut through the neighborhood a few times to
avoid construction on the main road, and there were always kids riding their bikes or playing ball out on the lawn.
There was even a park in the middle of the neighborhood.

But it was the inside of his house that had really thrown
her for a loop. She'd assumed he'd have the typical bachelor
pad. Black leather couch, glass coffee table, large-screen TV.
Instead, it was so...homey. Not a television in sight. Lots
of bright pictures on the wall, a burgundy couch, plants in
well-placed spots.

"Your home is beautiful. Did you decorate it yourself?"

His brows rose. "Is that your not-so-subtle way of asking if I had a woman's help? Maybe an ex-girlfriend?"

"No." *Who am I kidding?* "Okay, yes."

He smiled as if her answer pleased him. "All me. I grew up in a cold, sterile home. So I made it the opposite. I'm glad you like it." He brushed his hand over her hip. "And, Jane? I've never had a real girlfriend. Not until you." She closed her eyes, allowing his admission to wash over her. In her head, she knew before tonight those words would have thrilled her. But the connection between her head and heart was severed.

He led her past the kitchen to a set of stairs that led to the basement.

"I didn't believe you," Jane said as she took in the space Ryder called his playroom.

While upstairs was perfect for a family, downstairs was definitely adults-only. Silly her. For some reason, she'd envisioned white walls, unfinished floors, maybe a couple of floggers and ropes lying around.

She was so naïve. Even though he'd admitted to having parties at his home, how could she have known he'd stocked his basement with enough equipment to keep dozens of people entertained?

He'd painted the walls a dark blue, which should have made the room look smaller, but with the off-white faux stone floor, it seemed larger than the entire first floor upstairs. Hanging on the walls were floggers, whips, paddles, and other "toys" she didn't recognize. But it was the rest of the room that had her jaw dropping. There were benches, tall X-shaped pieces, a weird-looking chair with a hole on the seat, and a steel frame with a swing attached to it. She couldn't even begin to imagine what they were all used for.

It was like a kinky amusement park.

And she was about to go for a ride.

She couldn't wait.

She walked over to where he hung his floggers and ran her hands down the length of the buttery leather handles and then played with the ends, surprised by their softness.

How could something so soft cause pain?

Did she want to find out?

Ryder's eyes burned with heat as he watched her touch the toys on the wall. Was she imagining him using them on her? Which one was his favorite?

"Most people bring their own personal equipment with them to the play parties, but I like to keep a few on hand in case anybody gets an itch to try something new," he offered, his voice deeper than usual.

She turned to him. Her heart was beating so quickly she felt it as a tremor throughout her entire body. "Now that we're down here, what do you want to do to me?"

He grabbed her hips and slammed her up against the wall. A flogger fell to the floor with a thud. His hard body caged her in as if she were an animal in need of taming, when in actuality, he was the wild prey.

Only he could never be caged.

His teeth grazed the side of her neck. "What do I want to do? I want to take care of you. Tonight is about what *you* need. And what I can give you. I'm going to push you farther than you ever thought you could possibly go. Tonight, in this room...I own you."

"Own me? You can't own me," she said, purposefully challenging him when in truth, there was nothing she wanted more.

This was what she needed.

To be fucked.

Dominated.

Consumed.

Until all the day's memories washed away like the shore at high tide.

He bit into the skin of her neck and growled. "You're wrong. I can own you. And you know how I know that, sweet Jane? It's because *you already own me*. You have since the moment I first saw you."

Pressure built in her core and her clitoris throbbed in time with her racing heart.

And she was wet.

So wet, she could actually feel it coating her inner thighs.

The need to come overwhelmed her. Seeking relief, she couldn't stop herself from grinding her pelvis against him.

He laughed as he took a step back, depriving her of the friction she so desperately craved. He gripped her wrists and raised her arms over her head. "Now tell me. Who owns you?"

She swallowed, catching her breath. "You do, Ryder."

"Damn right I do. I'm your body's master. The man who holds your power in his hands. Who tells you when and *if* you are allowed to come. Who chooses whether to give you pleasure or pain." He rested his forehead against hers. "The only thing you have to do is surrender...and feel."

Her head was swimming.

All her emotions were there, right under the surface of her skin, just waiting to be exposed. The fear of submission. The excitement of the unknown. The exhilaration of knowing how much she meant to him. But Ryder's words and the promises they held weren't enough to release her emotions from their prison.

She needed more.

He was right.

She had to surrender to him.

She let her body go slack, no longer struggling against him. "Please."

"Mine." A rumble vibrated from his chest. "All fucking mine."

His lips covered hers, stealing her breath and her sanity. Arms overhead, body trapped, she relinquished her power and truly put herself in his care. There was nothing soft about this kiss. His mouth demanded rather than cajoled. Compelled rather than offered. He alone had control, leaving her with nothing to do but *feel*.

She felt as though she was both spinning and floating at the same time. If his body hadn't been pressed against hers, she was certain she would have crumbled to the floor.

He tore his mouth from hers and whirled her around so that she faced the wall. "Your safe word is *red*. Don't hold back if you need to use it." He reached around her torso and with a hard tug, tore open her blouse. Buttons scattered. "Clothes off."

He didn't give her the chance to undress herself before

the blouse was sliding down her shoulders, baring her naked back to him. The rough stubble on his face abraded the length of her spine as he sank to his knees and quickly removed her pants so that she stood in front of him wearing nothing but her panties.

She looked over her shoulder at him. "I would have worn sexier underwear if I'd known you were going to rip my clothes off of me."

He cupped her ass in his hands and kneaded it like it was clay. "You underestimate the power of plain white cotton. It's sexy as fuck. At least on *your* ass. But they're in my way." In one deft motion, he whipped her panties down her legs.

Cool air drifted over her exposed skin.

A quick nip to her butt cheek and he was up on his feet, his arm banded around her chest. He marched her over to the unusual chair and pushed her onto it. Made of dark wood, the chair was padded with black leather both on the thin panel that supported her back and on the seat. It wasn't uncomfortable per se, but it wasn't exactly a chair she'd offer to a guest. Especially since there was a hole in the seat. Still, she had no idea what he could possibly do to her while she was sitting with her legs together.

Eyes dark as twilight, he circled around the chair as if he was wondering what to do with her. He didn't fool her for a second.

He'd known exactly what he planned to do before he'd forced her into the chair.

She startled at the sudden jostle of the chair. From behind her, Ryder seized one arm of it and lifted it to shoulder level.

Leather wrapped around her biceps, securing her to a horizontal piece of padded wood. After Ryder repeated the action with the other arm, he kneeled on the floor in front of her, where he bound her ankles to the front of the chair's legs.

Looming over her, he licked his lips. Her gaze dropped to the large bulge in the placket of his pants. She'd never get over having the ability to arouse him. It did something to her. Gave her a rush of adrenaline that shot through her heart to settle between her thighs. Although she was naked, she grew hot all over.

A snarl played at the corner of his mouth. He bent at the waist to grip the top of her thighs, putting his face at eye level. Holding her captive by the intensity of his gaze, he snapped her legs apart, spreading them as wide as possible, and then tipped the entire chair back so that she was looking up at the ceiling.

In that position, she could keep nothing hidden. Ryder would become intimately acquainted with her innermost secrets.

She was on full display.

Her heart thumped wildly as a tendril of fear snaked through her abdomen.

Fear.

She was starting to feel again.

Heat suffused her as he kneeled between her thighs and stared. The longer he stayed like that, not speaking, not touching, the more uncomfortable it made her. It was humiliating to be that exposed and helpless. Even more so because her arousal was trickling out of her.

His warm breath whispered along the insides of her thighs, light as a feather. "Do you have any idea how beautiful you are?"

She snorted. "I'm not sure *beautiful* is the right word to describe what you're looking at right now."

"You've never gotten to see your pussy up close and personal. You'll have to trust me on this. You. Are. Beautiful." He kissed one inner thigh and then the other. "Inside and out."

Smiling devilishly, he stood and walked to the corner of the room, where he retrieved a small leather bag off a table. After returning to her side, he bent and took out a bottle of lube and a pink item she didn't recognize. Narrow at the top, it progressively widened along its length. He squirted an obscene amount of lube on it until it glimmered from its slickness.

Suddenly, she realized the purpose of the item and the reason for the hole in the chair. "There's no way that's gonna fit."

"Oh, it will fit," he said, dripping cold lubrication between her ass cheeks. "But if you truly don't want this, you can use your safe word."

The word *red* was on the tip on her tongue, but then she thought about their shower and how hard she'd come when he'd slipped his pinky into her behind.

"I'm not using my safe word. I want this. But I don't want the plug. I want your cock."

Ryder's pupils dilated and his eyes grew hooded. "I want my cock in there too, baby. But I have to stretch you first with the plug so that I don't hurt you."

He teased her with the tip of it, rubbing the lube into the

sensitive skin there and making her muscles involuntarily clench. "Just relax and breathe." On that, he started slowly pushing the rigid piece of plastic inside of her.

Her body flushed as she yearned to touch herself in order to relieve the growing ache in her core. But she couldn't. All she could do was sit there and take whatever he chose to give her. She wanted to say it hurt, but if she did, she'd be lying. There was pressure and a burn and *wait*. She moaned and her eyes rolled back in her head as Ryder slid the plug back and forth, awakening nerves that had never been touched. She found herself trying to push her body toward it, but the restraints held her immobile.

The sensations rolling through her reminded her of when she'd lost her virginity. There had been a fullness then, too, and even a bit of pain as she'd become accustomed to being stretched. But discomfort and pain had turned to pleasure once he'd moved his cock in and out.

She hissed as the burning increased.

Maybe it wasn't *exactly* the same as when she'd lost her virginity.

But even as it burned, her clitoris began to throb relentlessly as if it had its own little heart beating inside of it. All her nerves flickered to life like a match to a candle. The stretch, the burn, it all intertwined until she could barely catch her breath from the overwhelming need to come.

He tapped the end of the plug a couple of times. "How's that feel?"

Thoughts floated in her mind, but she couldn't translate them into words. Instead, all that came out was another moan.

"Fuck." He took a step back and admired his work. "It looks sexy as hell. But I think you're missing something." He went back into the bag and pulled out another pink object, one she recognized.

This time, he didn't bother with the lube.

She didn't need it.

She was already sopping wet and ready to be fucked.

He dragged the dildo over her lips. "I bought this a couple days ago hoping you'd give me the chance to use it on you."

Her core quivered at the thought of him picking out sex toys specifically for her. And then he started inching the dildo into her and she wasn't thinking of anything except how was he going to get it all the way inside her with the plug making her channel tighter than normal.

"Breathe, sweet Jane. I promise I wouldn't give you this if I didn't think you could take it."

She sucked in a breath through her nose and tried to relax, but the growing tension in her belly from the double penetration didn't make it easy. It was similar to the feeling she'd get right before she climaxed yet sharper. More intense. At the same time, it wasn't going to be enough to push her over. Instead, as he slid the entire dildo inside her, she hovered on the precipice of something larger than an orgasm. Her limbs stiffened and shook uncontrollably.

But apparently Ryder wasn't done with her. He strode over to the wall and walked the length of it, trying to decide what instrument to use to torture her next. After making his choice, he returned to her with a black crop in his hands.

He didn't give her the chance to panic before he smacked the top of her mound with it. She clenched around the objects inside of her, sending a wave of heat through her core, and her body jolted as if electrified. The crop rained down. Each cheek. Her thighs. Her labia. Her clit. Her nipples. Over and over until she was a throbbing, writhing mess of pure sensation.

Each slap of the crop was like a balm to her ragged soul. Not because it hurt. It was nothing she couldn't handle. But because she could feel more than the physical. As Ryder turned her skin pink, every blocked emotion bubbled to the surface and boiled over.

Tears rolled down her cheeks and a sob escaped her chest. As the need to come increased, she couldn't hold anything back. Pain. Pleasure. Fear. Rage. Sorrow. Grief. All of it poured out.

Ryder dropped the crop to the floor with a thud and wedged himself between her thighs, covering her bare skin with his still-clothed body. He wiped away the tears from her face and kissed her gently on the mouth, his demeanor changing from dominating to comforting. It was as if she'd been a piece of glass that he'd shattered into pieces, and now with every slide of his lips, the touch of his thumb over the pulse point on her neck, and the caress of his tongue along hers, he was putting her back together again.

His kiss meant everything. He was breathing new life into her and all of her cells buzzed in celebration. She was ready for him. Ready to be claimed in the most primal of ways.

And when he took a step back and removed his clothes, she knew he was ready too.

His gaze stayed on hers as he rolled on a condom and added a generous amount of lube to the length of him. He carefully pulled out the dildo first, making her core clench and release several times. Then the plug was gone and with a quick adjustment, he tilted the chair to put her at the right angle for his cock.

He didn't pause. Didn't give her more than a moment to process the emptiness before he was pushing himself into her. He was much larger than the plug, stretching her almost beyond her capacity, and she didn't think she'd ever been more aroused. Her clit felt as if it had grown to ten times its size and her inner walls seemed to rub against each other as his cock took up space inside her body. There was a burn. Pressure.

"Fuck, you're tight," he said through clenched teeth. Sweat dripped down his neck, and the muscles of it bulged as if strained with tension.

She wanted to lick that sweat clean off. "You don't have to go slow. I'm—"

She didn't get the rest of the words out before he closed his eyes and drove himself fully into her. Leaning forward until they were chest to chest, he grabbed on to the arm boards and began fucking her ass, each thrust bringing his pelvis into direct contact with her engorged bundle of nerves.

An inferno of tension blazed in her lower belly. His mouth took hers in a brutal kiss that branded her as his and made it clear that he was claiming her. Possessing her. Owning her. They were two slick bodies on the cusp of something larger than themselves.

She had Ryder's cock in her ass and yet she'd never felt so safe. So cherished. So...

Loved.

Her tears came harder now and she let out a sob.

Between kisses, he made his demands. "Let it out, sweet Jane, and surrender. Give me your tears. Your worries. Your climax. I want it all. *Right. Fucking. Now.*"

She broke.

There was no other word for it.

Head to toe, she shook as hot pleasure flooded her core and blasted outward to every muscle, every vein, every organ. Especially her heart. She had to bite down on her lip to keep from saying the words that repeated over and over in her head: *I love you. I love you. I love you.*

"I can feel your ass clenching around my dick," Ryder mumbled against her mouth. "It's too good. I can't hold back." On the next thrust, he threw his head back and surrendered to his climax.

Overcome with exhaustion, she closed her eyes.

She couldn't love him.

Not yet.

It was too soon.

Wasn't it?

TWENTY-TWO

Since having Maddox, Jane was used to being awoken by the slightest of noises. Her eyes flew open and she bolted up in bed. Was Maddox crying? It was still night, the moon still looming large and bright in the sky. She was confused by the feel of the sheets on her naked skin until she remembered she was in Ryder's bed.

She had a vague recollection of Ryder tending to her. He'd carried her upstairs and placed her in a warm bath to soak her sore muscles and other areas and later rubbed some cream into her skin as she lay on the bed. And when Maddox had woken up hungry, Ryder had taken care of him and allowed her to sleep.

Which meant it was too early for Maddox to have another bottle. She waited for him to cry out again, but the monitor was silent. Sometimes he would cry and immediately fall back to sleep.

Too bad she wasn't as lucky. Once she was up, it would take her at least fifteen minutes to relax enough to do the same.

She rested her head on the pillow and flipped on her side toward Ryder. The moon gave enough light that she could see the outline of him.

Flat on his back, he slept restlessly, his body twitching and his head turning from side to side.

She placed her hand on his chest and whispered a "shush," just as she did with Maddox sometimes. It seemed to do the trick. On a large sigh, his body stilled.

Thanks to Ryder, yesterday's horrible events were clear in her mind, but she was no longer a prisoner to them. Crying in Ryder's arms had cathartically washed away the guilt she'd been holding inside. Her heart still ached for Dreama, but there was also fierce determination to punish the one or ones responsible.

But in freeing her emotions, Ryder had opened the floodgates. Her late-night revelation had thrown her for a loop. She certainly cared about him, but was it love?

They had so many hurdles to jump over before they could even talk about something permanent. He'd professed that he wanted to be a part of both hers and Maddox's lives and earlier tonight had pronounced his ownership of her.

But what was to prevent him from changing his mind once he really got to know them? What made him different from Ciara or Ian?

Loving him would only make it that much harder when he left.

Whimpering, Ryder rolled to his side and curled into a ball. *"Él es mío, no tuyo! Él es mío, no tuyo!"*

Was he speaking Spanish?

There was so much she didn't know about him.

She sat up and inched closer to his side, brushing his arm reassuringly. "Shhh."

He thrashed around violently. "Nothing happened. It was a dream. You belong to me," he yelled over and over.

She'd heard that you shouldn't wake someone from a nightmare, but she couldn't stand to watch him suffer. Kneeling over him, she gently shook him to coax him awake. "Ryder. It's Jane. You're having a nightmare."

He whimpered like a wounded puppy before growing completely still. "Jane?" he asked in a voice thick with sleep.

She ran her fingers through his hair in an effort to soothe him and found him drenched with sweat. "Sorry to wake you but you were having a nightmare."

There was such a long pause that she almost thought he'd fallen back to sleep. "Yeah. I get them sometimes," he said quietly. "Thanks for waking me. I'm sorry I woke you. I'm fine now. Go back to sleep."

"I'm not tired and don't apologize for waking me. That seemed like much more than a nightmare. You were talking in your sleep. I think you even spoke some Spanish."

He jackknifed up in bed, pulling the blankets off both of them. "I did? What did I say?"

"I don't speak Spanish, so I'm not sure, but you kept repeating, 'It was just a dream. Nothing happened. You belong to me.'" She waited a beat and, when he said nothing, asked, "Does that mean anything to you?"

He reached over to his nightstand and flicked on the lamp. Light flooded the room, momentarily blinding her.

"I haven't had that nightmare in ages, but I used to," he said, his voice sounding as if he'd swallowed sandpaper. "Every night. For years and years." He shook his head and covered his face with his hands. "I think seeing Dreama like that after her attack might have triggered it. The blood..."

Since watching *Wizard of Oz* as a small child, she'd suffered recurrent nightmares about tornadoes, but each one was different. She'd never heard of having the same nightmare over and over. And to have it for years?

She stroked his back. "Sometimes they say talking about your nightmares can make them go away. Would you tell me about it?"

Body trembling, he shuddered and blew out a breath. She wanted to be there for him like he'd been there for her. But at the same time, she didn't want to push him if he wasn't ready.

Still, it twisted her insides to see him like this.

When he finally spoke, his voice was so quiet she almost thought it was someone else speaking. He averted his gaze, keeping it trained on the blanket in front of him. "It started when I was around five, I guess? I don't know. I can't remember a time when I didn't have it, but Finn said that's when I started climbing into bed with him because I was too scared to sleep alone." He paused to take another deep, stuttered breath. "It's always the same. My father is struggling with a woman who is screaming in Spanish. She says my name. There's a loud bang and then she's covered with blood. Keane stands over her with something in his hands. I think it's a gun. And then she's gone and I'm the one lying bloody on the floor."

"Ryder, who is the woman in the nightmare?"

He raised his head and looked at her with red-rimmed eyes haunted with a child's terror. "I think she was my mother."

She instantly threw her arms around him and pulled him close, feeling his heart racing against her chest. No wonder he hated Keane. "Keane told me she'd died during childbirth in Mexico," she told him. "That he'd loved her."

But now that she'd learned about the terrible things Keane had done, did she believe him?

Ryder gritted his teeth. "I doubt he's ever loved anyone in his life. He believes because I'm his son that automatically means I belong to him. Like I have no will of my own and my sole reason for existing is to do whatever he tells me to do. If he had his way, I'd be just like him. A murderer without a conscience."

"He's wrong." She climbed onto his lap and placed her palms on his cheeks. "You could never be anything like him."

She pressed a soft kiss to his lips, her intention only to ease the anguished look in his eyes, but the moment their mouths connected, Ryder seized control and the kiss morphed from one of tender compassion to frenzied passion. He poured his desperation into her and she accepted it. Took everything he had to give and made it hers.

Holding her tight to his chest, he propelled her onto her back and braced himself over her. "How long do we have before Maddox wakes up?"

She quickly did the math in her head. "Maybe two hours?"

"I need you," he said hoarsely.

"You have me. Whatever you need, I'm yours."

It didn't matter that they hadn't been together long. Now that he'd trusted her with his most vulnerable thoughts, his darkest fears, she could admit the truth to herself.

She was totally and irrevocably in love with him.

She'd always be there for him.

Even after he broke her heart and left.

* * *

Jane believed him.

After years of trying to convince himself that his dream was only that—a dream—he'd finally admitted the truth out loud: He'd witnessed his father killing his mother.

But Jane had been wrong. Telling her about his recurrent nightmare hadn't helped. Each word was like a bullet that ricocheted around inside of him, leaving an eviscerated mess behind.

With her generous spirit and tender heart, Jane alone had the power to heal him. In fact, it had already begun. Before her, he'd never wanted a family. Yet she and Maddox filled a void he hadn't known he'd been missing. And now that he had them, he would never let them go.

The way she'd trusted him in the playroom and surrendered to him so completely had done as much for him as it had for her. He'd never expected to find serenity through Domination. But in breaking down Jane's walls earlier tonight, he'd also broken down his own, walls he hadn't even known existed.

He'd lied to her.

Dreama's attack hadn't triggered the nightmare, at least not directly.

It was knowing that it could have been Jane.

He wrapped his hand around his cock and slid it up and down her slit, getting himself nice and wet. Her eyes darkened with desire and she let out a little moan as he rubbed his cockhead in circles over her clit.

There were important words for him to tell her, important words that would change their lives forever, but tonight wasn't the right time for them. Tonight he would have to settle for showing her.

"No restraints," he said. "No toys. Just you and me. Let me make love to you."

He wanted to fuck her bare, feel her tight heat gripping his cock, but as greedy as he'd admitted he was for her, it was something he refused to demand. One day when they both decided they were ready, he'd take her that way, over and over, with the intention of getting her pregnant with his child. He wasn't going to miss out on watching her body change or hearing the baby's heart beating for the first time. Not again.

At her nod of consent, he reached over to the nightstand and grabbed the condom off of it. He ripped open the package and unrolled it down his length, then with his hands behind her thighs, placed her legs around his waist.

He took his sweet time sliding into her, memorizing all the sights and sensations of the moment. She was so hot inside, he could feel it through the rubber. Wet, too, the sound of his dick moving farther into her mingling with their panting breaths. And she was so fucking tight, it was as if he were taking her virginity all over again.

When his cock glided over a certain spot, she moaned and dug her fingernails into the skin of his back.

He smiled at her responsiveness. She held nothing back during sex. Instead, she made it so damned easy to find what pleased her the most. And pleasing her... pleased him. There was power from making someone come, and when it was Jane, it took it to a whole other level. She arched her back and bit her lip, her reactions pure and innocent. Only she wasn't so innocent, was she? And no one else would ever know that because it was all for him. No one else would ever get to take the gift of her virginity because he'd stolen it for himself. *Twice.*

There was so much to teach her, so many things to do *to her*, *with her*, and he couldn't wait to begin.

Starting now.

Vanilla sex didn't mean boring.

He shoved his hands under her ass and tilted her pelvis up, then jerked her legs apart. "Better hold on tight to me because the ride's about to get a bit rocky," he warned.

She smiled up at him. "I can take it."

He couldn't wait to prove her wrong. "We'll see. Keep those legs up or I won't let you come."

The second she opened her mouth to respond, he dragged his cock back over that spot again, over and over, faster and faster, until her eyes rolled back and closed. Her abdomen trembled underneath him as she neared her first climax. Refusing to blow until she'd come at least twice, he fought against the tingle behind his balls signaling his own impending orgasm.

He didn't have to wait long before she was rocked by climax number one.

Her core quivered around his dick, and she burrowed her face into his neck to muffle the sound of her cries. Again and again, her walls clamped down on him, each time making it more and more difficult to hold back.

"One," he counted smugly, causing her to open her eyes.

For the next hour, he made love to her relentlessly. On her back. Her stomach. Her knees (his personal favorite). All the while, he had to think about baseball and politics to keep himself from coming. But he was rewarded greatly for his delayed gratification. Four orgasms and counting, Jane was a writhing, moaning, sticky mess.

"No more, Ryder," she said, whimpering. He currently had her bent over the bed and was slamming into her from behind. "I can't come again."

"One more time." He reached around to pluck her clit. "We'll go over together this time."

Slamming into her, he finally allowed himself to let go. Only a few thrusts later, when she pounded the mattress with her fist and said, "I'm coming," did he close his eyes and bask in the sensation of her swollen pussy gripping around him.

Low in his belly, a storm grew out of control and his balls drew up tight to his body. White-hot ecstasy shot down his spine and up through his cock as spurt after spurt of come filled the condom.

Fuck, he couldn't remember a time he'd climaxed so hard.

Both of them were slick with sweat.

He picked her up and carried her across his room to the bathroom. "Let's take a quick shower before Maddox gets up."

She curled her hand around the back of his head. "I could get used to this."

His chest was bursting with unspoken emotion.

Now was the time. He couldn't hold back any longer.

"Jane. I—"

Her cell phone rang, the noise freezing him in his tracks.

Their eyes met as they both realized there was something wrong. It was five o'clock in the morning.

Dreama.

TWENTY-THREE

The hospital was quiet in the early morning hours. Jane hadn't seen a single doctor as she and Ryder took the elevator up to Dreama's floor or walked down to her room. The silence made the sound of their footsteps on the linoleum sound much louder than normal. It was jarring. She felt as though she and Ryder were starring in some B horror movie and the psycho villain with the chainsaw was about to attack.

Guess that wasn't far off from the truth.

Only the psycho in this particular movie wielded a baseball bat.

After receiving the phone call from the hospital an hour ago that Dreama was awake and requesting to see her, Jane had jumped into the shower—alone—and quickly got dressed while Ryder gave Maddox a bottle. Ryder showered next and drove them in her car to the hospital. In his carrier, Maddox had already fallen back to sleep.

Once in the waiting room, she handed Maddox to Ryder

and went over to speak to Dreama's parents, who were sitting in the same chairs as last night. A few empty coffee cups and candy bar wrappers littered the small table beside Mr. Agosto.

"How is she?" Jane asked Mrs. Agosto, bending down to give her a hug. The Agostos appeared as if they'd managed to age a decade over a few hours. Their eyes were bloodshot and both of them were drawn, their wrinkles more apparent with their paler skin.

Jane didn't want to imagine what they were going through.

"The doctor said she's stable. Whatever the hell that means," Mrs. Agosto muttered, sounding eerily like Dreama. "She woke up for a few minutes and asked for you, but she's been unconscious ever since."

"How did she take everything?"

Jaw tense, Mrs. Agosto glanced at her husband. "I don't know. My pigheaded daughter refused to see us. Refused to see anyone." She stood to her full five-foot frame. "Anyone but you."

"What?" Shock blasted through Jane and her hands began to tremble. Ryder came over and put his arm around her waist, giving her support. "Why would she only want to see me?"

"Other than Isabella, you're her best friend," Mrs. Agosto said. "Sure, my daughter and I talk every day. We're close. But there are things a girl doesn't always want to tell her mother. And Isabella . . . she experienced her own tragedies. Dreama admires your strength . . . and your compassion. She might put on a good show, but inside, she's still a scared little girl who hides under the bed whenever she hears an unfamiliar noise. I'm afraid..." Raising a hand to her mouth, Mrs. Agosto choked on a sob. "I'm afraid she won't deal with this well. There are things she went through as a child...things we never mention...How many challenges should a person be given in one lifetime?"

Mr. Agosto took his wife into his arms, as she could no longer hold back the tears.

Jane saw the question in Ryder's eyes. What had Mrs. Agosto meant when she said Dreama had gone through challenges? Her friend had never mentioned anything negative about her childhood other than having two overprotective parents.

She took Ryder's hand and squeezed. "I'm going to go see her. Maddox should—"

"I've got Maddox." Ryder jutted his chin toward the exit. "Go. Dreama needs you."

On a nod, she let go of his hand and gave the Agostos a weak smile. The walk to Dreama's room was like trudging through three feet of snow. Exhausting and hard. Her legs were so wobbly she could barely remain upright. But her friend needed her and she wouldn't let her down. Especially now.

Jane's pulse roared in her ears as she entered Dreama's room, but a steady beeping automatically replaced it. Lying in the bed, Dreama looked better than she had the last time Jane had seen her.

But not by much.

Her battered face was swollen to twice its normal size and her skin was bruised to a grotesque purple. They'd set casts on both arms and both legs and effectively immobilized her by a pulley that elevated all four limbs above her torso. Several wires hooked her up to a monitor that spit out second-by-second information. As she quietly tugged a chair to Dreama's bedside, Jane couldn't help the tears from spilling. Dreama might be the one lying in that bed, but Jane had never felt so helpless.

She plucked a tissue from the box on the metal tray that served as Dreama's nightstand and collapsed in the chair.

"Hey, Chickie," Dreama croaked. She sounded as if she'd swallowed sandpaper. Her lids were open, but her eyes were so bruised, they were narrow slits.

Jane popped out of her chair. "You're awake."

"How long have I been here?"

Didn't she remember waking up earlier?

"About eighteen hours," Jane told her. "The hospital called me and said you'd asked for me. I just saw your parents. They're really worried about you. I know they'd love to come visit you."

"No," her friend said firmly. "I don't want to see them."

Now wasn't the time to push away the people who cared about her. Dreama was going to need everybody's help to get through the next few months as she healed. "Dreama—"

"How bad is it?"

Jane's heart skipped a beat. No. She didn't want to be the one to tell her. "How bad is what, sweetie?"

"What did that sicko do to me?"

Glancing at the door, she shuffled from foot to foot. "Maybe I should have the doctor—"

"No. I don't want to hear it from someone who just sees me as another number in his win column. I need to hear it from you."

Jane would rather break her own arm than have to tell her the news. She retook her seat and moved her chair so that Dreama only had to turn her head to the side to see her.

God, with Dreama in traction, Jane couldn't even hold her hand. What kind of comfort could she possibly provide?

If it were her lying in that bed, she would want the whole cruel truth up front. Just blatant facts with no false promises of quick healing. The road ahead of Dreama would be a rocky one. Yet Jane had no doubt that Dreama would soon have to endure people who would minimize and dismiss her injuries with platitudes like "it could have been worse."

After a long silence, Jane made up her mind. Right now, Dreama didn't need the compassionate, motherly Jane. She needed the detached and professional one. "The doctor confirmed there was no sign of sexual assault. But you have a lot of broken bones. Arms, legs, nose, cheeks, ribs. You had internal bleeding. They removed your spleen and fixed your kidney…"

Even wearing the persona of workplace Jane, she couldn't get the next words out. She had to look away from Dreama to keep herself from falling apart.

"What are you not telling me?" Dreama asked, knowing Jane all too well. "Come on, Chickie. I'm a big girl. I can take it."

Life wasn't fair. Dreama had never said one way or another whether she wanted children, but now the choice had been taken away from her by a monster with a bat.

Jane took a cleansing breath and gave it to Dreama straight. "In order to stop the internal bleeding, they had to do a complete hysterectomy," she said quickly, like ripping off a Band-Aid. "I'm sorry."

Dreama turned her head away and looked up at the ceiling. "It is what it is."

They sat together in silence as Dreama processed her injuries and the way her life had been changed forever. Jane wished there was more she could do for her. Some way to comfort her. There was no part of Dreama's body that wasn't broken or bruised and because of that, there'd be no hugs in Dreama's immediate future. The only option was to comfort her with words. And Jane couldn't even do that for her.

"What happened, Dreama?" Jane asked softly, not even knowing if Dreama was still awake. "Do you know who did this?"

As if she'd been prepared for the question, Dreama turned her head back to Jane and immediately began speaking. "I was sleeping, and you know how deeply I sleep, especially when I'm sick. But I woke up with my heart pounding and a feeling like something was wrong. I heard a noise from the family room, and I knew, I just knew, it wasn't you. Noises like that are never good. I can't describe it except to say it was like I knew evil had entered our home." Her eyes watered as she paused to take a breath.

"But I still hoped that I was having some sort of cold medicine–induced paranoia," Dreama continued. "I grabbed a baseball bat from my closet. And when my door opened to a man wearing a face mask and gloves, I swung that bat like I was *Ty fucking Cobb*. But he grabbed that bat out of my hands so quickly, I almost could've believed he'd expected it. I managed to run past him, but I wasn't fast enough. He hit me from the back and I fell." Her tears streamed down her face and her scratchy voice was full of pain.

Jane didn't want to hear the rest. But she knew her friend needed to say it. And she owed it to Dreama to listen.

"I thought he'd leave, you know?" Dreama asked, more to herself than to Jane. "Most burglars would've run out of there. But he kept hitting me. Over and over, so hard I thought he'd break my spine. There was a ten-second reprieve when I thought, 'He's gone. It's over.' Then with his foot, he rolled me over and looked down at me."

She started shaking as the monitor's beeping got faster. "I'm a parole officer. Some of my parolees are rapists and murderers. But this guy... I swear his eyes belonged to the devil. He was getting off on it. And then he started swinging again. I wanted to lose consciousness so badly, but I couldn't escape it. I thought, 'I'm gonna die. It can't get any worse.' And then... he got on top of me. He was gonna rape me, Jane. And I would've preferred death to that."

Oh God. Jane swallowed the rising bile burning her throat. The attack was even more brutal than she'd thought. How did someone recover from something like that?

Dreama should have asked for Isabella, not Jane. Isabella would have known the right words. The right way to comfort her. All Jane could do was sit there and try to not throw up. "What stopped him?"

"His phone rang and it seemed to snap him out of whatever frenzy he was in. He answered the phone and told whoever was on the other end that he hadn't found the SD card. And then he left."

Jane choked on the bile that had risen into her throat.

The attacker had been looking for the SD card.

He'd been there because of Jane.

Because she had the SD card. And the attacker knew it.

She had to tell Dreama the truth. That Jane had led the attacker straight to their doorstep.

"I'm so sorry, Dreama," Jane said, tears burning her eyes. "I should have never have left you alone."

"It's not your fault, Chickie. How could you have known someone would break in?"

Her friend's words dug the knife deeper into Jane's heart. "Dreama, there's something you should know."

The speed of the monitor's beeping increased. Within seconds, Dreama's lips seemed to have taken on a slight bluish tint. She winced.

Worried, Jane shot out of her chair. "Are you in pain?"

Fear reflected in Dreama's eyes. "It's...hard...to... breathe."

Loud chimes joined the beeps as Dreama's eyes rolled back in her head and she went absolutely still.

"Dreama!" Jane yelled. "Somebody help!"

A stream of doctors and nurses stormed into the room, pushing Jane out of the way.

What was happening?

A nurse took her by the arm and steered her into the hallway.

"What's going on?" Jane asked, her entire body trembling.

"We need you to go sit in the waiting room," the nurse said softly.

How the hell could the nurse be so calm?

"Not until you tell me what's wrong."

The nurse glanced back at the room. "Your friend isn't getting enough oxygen into her lungs and her heart is under distress." She put a hand on Jane's shoulder and squeezed. "The doctor will be out as soon as we know."

Know?

Jane's stomach cramped as she realized what the nurse had meant.

Her legs folded beneath her and she fell to the cold linoleum floor.

That might have been the last conversation Jane would ever get with her best friend.

Dreama was dying.

And it was all Jane's fault.

* * *

Sitting in the waiting room, Ryder sipped on his coffee, his leg nervously bouncing as he waited for Jane. She hadn't been gone long before Dreama's family began to fill all the seats in the room. It wasn't even seven in the morning and yet a dozen aunts, uncles, and cousins had congregated together to support one another. Isabella and Tristan were the first to arrive, followed by Isabella's parents and siblings. They'd brought freshly baked donuts and muffins to go along with the terrible free hospital coffee, but no one was eating. Instead, they made strained small talk. It was a vast improvement over yesterday's tears, but still, everyone waited with bated breath for Jane to return to the room with news about Dreama.

So when Jane finally did return, only as pale as a ghost with tears streaming down her cheeks, Ryder's heart sank. Something was wrong.

After handing off Maddox to Isabella, he strode to Jane and gathered her in his arms. Her body shook from the force of her tears.

"Everything's okay," he whispered, although he had no idea if that was the truth. "I've got you." When a doctor came into the room to speak with the Agostos, Ryder knew something had gone terribly wrong. Jane sniffed and wiped her tears with the back of her hand. "We need to talk out in the hall."

He took her hand and led her just outside the waiting room. "What happened in there?"

"I'm not sure. One minute she was talking and the next minute alarms were going off and the hospital staff threw me out of the room." She started crying again. "She couldn't breathe. Dreama is going to die, Ryder. And I never got the chance…I was going to tell her the truth."

"What truth, sweetheart?" he said quietly, rubbing her back to try and calm her.

She let out a shuddered breath. "The attack wasn't random. She remembered hearing her attacker on the phone saying he didn't find the SD card. He was there because of me."

He cradled her face in his hands. "You listen to me," he said firmly. "You didn't cause this and it doesn't help to dwell on it. Dreama is a fighter. She's going to make it. I promise you, I'll find who did this. Dreama *will* get justice."

He couldn't sit in the waiting room while the person who put Dreama in the hospital walked around scot-free. Not when Jane could be next.

The safest place for her and Maddox was here in the hospital, surrounded by Dreama's family. No one would dare to harm her in such a public place. As long as she stayed here, he wouldn't have to worry about them.

He needed to see what was so important on the SD card that it was worth killing two people and attacking one more. Even though Jane maintained she'd deleted the possible antivirus program from her computer and it was probably a long shot, he had to try to open it on her work computer. If Evan was as good as a programmer as he appeared to be, it was possible he'd included a second antivirus program to be hidden somewhere else in Jane's computer files. That's what Ryder would have done. "Give me the SD card. I'm going to McKay," he said, drying her eyes with a brush of his fingers. "And I want you to stay here."

Her eyes darted from side to side as she considered the options. She was torn. He knew she wanted to go with him, but at the same time, she didn't want to leave her friend, especially while Dreama's fate was up in the air.

He didn't push her. Instead, he waited quietly until she came to her own decision.

She placed her hands on his chest. "You won't be able to just walk in on a weekend and let yourself inside my office. There's a guard. Locked doors."

"It won't be a problem."

Not when he was a McKay. And he had a way inside.

His brother.

Unless Finn...

He shook his head as if in doing so he could knock the thought right out of his brain.

Finn had nothing to do with the murders or the attack. His brother simply wasn't the type of man who would exchange his morals for money. Ryder still had no idea why he was working at McKay or why he'd married Ciara, but he refused to believe the man who'd bought Ryder a flashlight out of his own allowance so that Ryder wouldn't have to sleep in the dark could be part of a plan that involved the murder of innocents.

When it came down to it, Ryder would have to trust his brother if he was going to get inside Jane's office. And if he was wrong, if his brother was sleeping with the devil, then Ryder needed to know that too.

He loved his brother. But he wouldn't hesitate to give him up to the authorities if he'd done anything to put either Jane or Maddox in harm's way.

"What are you going to do once you find out what's on that card?" Jane asked him.

He wanted to say he'd take the evidence to the cops,

but who's to say they'd believe him? By the end of the day, there was a chance Ryder would have blood on his hands . . . Maybe he wasn't so different than Keane after all.

The thought didn't sit well, but he would do anything to protect Jane and Maddox. "Whatever I have to," he simply said.

He didn't fool her. It was there in her sharp intake of breath. In her rigid spine. In her teary eyes. Her hands fisted his shirt. "I hate that you're going all alone. What if something happens to you?"

The tears in her eyes undid him. He wouldn't bring her along, but there was a way to compromise. "I won't be alone. I'll take Tristan with me."

That way if things went to shit, at least he'd have his best friend watching his back.

Still holding on to his shirt, Jane rested her head on his chest. "Promise you'll come back to me. I can't lose you."

"You won't lose me. I promise." Not if he had any say in it. He kissed her lips, taking her essence into his mouth, his lungs, his heart, and gave her his in return. "Hopefully by tonight, all of this will be over."

The doctor strode past them and quickly disappeared down the hall. Isabella stumbled out next with a fussy Maddox in her arms, immediately followed by Tristan.

His eyes met his friend's. Whatever the doctor had told them in there, it hadn't been good. "How's Dreama?"

Tristan pressed his lips together and shook his head. "The doctor thinks she has a blood clot that traveled to her lung. That's why she couldn't breathe. They took her back into surgery."

As the women spoke about Dreama, Ryder pulled Tristan aside. "Hey, I need your help with something."

"Sure. What do you need?"

Other than the fact that the people who'd died worked for Keane, Ryder had no evidence to suggest he was behind their deaths. But if he was...

"Keep me from committing murder."

TWENTY-FOUR

Catching Tristan up on almost three decades of events surprisingly didn't take as long as Ryder thought it would, considering he had only twenty minutes between the hospital and McKay's offices. Obviously, he didn't have the time to tell him everything, but he managed to hit the highlights and the most recent events. By the time Tristan parked the car, Ryder finally stopped talking and gave his friend the chance to respond.

Tristan stared at him, slack-jawed. "Shit, you've been holding out on me. Here I thought I knew everything about you and you go ahead and pull a couple of dead bodies out of your pocket."

Ryder snorted. "You don't have to sound so impressed."

"I'm not impressed." Tristan undid his seat belt and turned toward him, shaking his fist. "I'm fucking mad as hell. You should have told me everything a long time ago."

"Yeah, well, I'm telling you now," Ryder said, opening his car door, "so quit whining like a two-year-old and let's go see what's on the SD card."

Thankfully, Tristan didn't hold grudges. He shrugged it off and got out of the car, gesturing to the mostly empty lot. "Is Finn here yet?"

Ryder had called Finn as he and Tristan were leaving the hospital. If his brother was surprised that Ryder wanted to meet him at McKay, he hadn't expressed it.

Which in itself raised a few red flags.

It was almost as if he'd been expecting Ryder's call.

Tristan whistled as they stepped inside the marble lobby. "Hard to believe you gave all this up willingly."

"Remember, marble might look shiny and pretty, but it's also cold and hard. I much prefer Novateur's look, with its open ceilings and wood floors, to this. Unlike McKay, we've got nothing to hide."

"Not to mention we couldn't afford an office with marble," Tristan pointed out.

Ryder shrugged. "Yeah, there is that."

True, the building that housed McKay Industries was impressive. But Ryder had grown up in a mansion just like this building, and he was tired of all the secrets hidden behind its walls. McKay Industries was a house made of straw and Ryder was the Big Bad Wolf about to blow it all down.

As Ryder and Tristan approached the guard, an elevator chimed and Finn stepped off.

He strode over to them and shook Tristan's hand, then gave Ryder his brotherly half-hug, half-back pounding. He turned to the guard. "This is my little brother, Ryder. Make sure to tell security he's always welcome in the building. I'm taking them both upstairs to Ms. Cooper's office."

Finn waited until the elevator's doors closed to ask, "Want to tell me what's going on?"

Ryder folded his arms over his chest. "It depends. What can you tell me about McKay's two most recent employee deaths?"

His brother's eyebrows furrowed in what appeared to be true surprise. "This is about Evan and Barbara? What interest could you possibly have in them? How do you even know them? And why the hell are we going to my stepdaughter's office?"

Tristan started laughing. "Sorry. I'd forgotten Ryder and Jane are related now." He turned to Ryder. "Hey, if you married Jane, wouldn't that make Finn your stepfather?"

"What am I missing?" Finn asked Ryder. "You and Jane...? But how? You just met."

"Actually, we met a year ago at a conference up on Mackinac Island." He paused, torn as to whether to tell Finn the truth. "Maddox is my son."

The elevator door opened. Tristan stepped off, but Ryder and Finn remained frozen.

Finn swallowed tightly and ran his hand down his face as the elevator doors closed again, leaving him and Ryder alone to talk in private. "You need to get Jane and Maddox to leave the state," he ordered. "Hell, the country. It's not safe for them here right now."

Ryder grabbed his brother by the collar and got up in his face. "What do you know?"

If Finn had intentionally left Jane and Maddox in the line of fire, knowing their lives were in danger, Ryder would never forgive him.

"Officially, I can't tell you," Finn said. "But I swear, Ciara and I have done everything we can to protect them."

Officially? What the hell did that mean?

"You've got to be kidding me," Ryder said bitterly. "Ciara has never done a thing for Jane other than abandon and neglect her."

His brother didn't fight him. "You don't know the first thing about Ciara," he said quietly.

Ryder pushed his brother back into the elevator wall. "What the hell are you talking about?"

"Fuck it." Finn blew out a breath, his shoulders dropping in surrender. "She's going to kill me for telling you, but it's time for the truth to come out." Anger and sorrow were etched on his face. "Ian...he molested Ciara. From the time she was twelve. At least that's the first time she remembers it happening. She actually doesn't have any memories of him prior to that."

Twelve. Jesus Christ.

"Ciara's mom died that year," Finn added. "She suspects that her mother's death might not have been an accident."

Apparently, Ryder and Ciara had more in common than just Jane.

Ryder thought back to Ian's assertion at the park that it had been Ciara who'd demanded Jane be sent away. That he had wanted Jane to stay with them. "You said he molested her. Did he...?"

The veins in Finn's neck bulged as he unloaded the burden he'd been carrying. "Yes. Almost daily for years. She ran away a few times but he always found her. She reported him to her teachers. To the police. And every time, the investigation came back that Ciara was a disturbed child seeking attention and that there was no proof of any abuse. He even managed to get them to bury the records. It pays to be a billionaire," he spit out.

Ryder didn't have the words to convey how sorry he was. Not only for what she'd gone through, but also because he'd misjudged her. No wonder she was so cold toward Jane. He understood it completely. To bring her into the family fold would be like inviting her into a monster's lair. Hadn't Ryder worried about doing the same to Maddox?

"That's why she sent Jane away," Finn said, confirming Ryder's assumption. "To keep Ian from doing the same thing to her."

He couldn't imagine how he was going to tell Jane.

A sick thought popped in his head, but he had to ask. "Is Ian Jane's father?"

"No." Finn leaned up against the back of the elevator. "She was a pretty messed-up kid at the time. It could have been any number of guys, but she's certain Jane isn't Ian's."

Ryder's stomach curdled. "How can she stand to even have anything to do with him now? She's an adult. She's married to you. Why doesn't she cut him out of her life for good?"

Shoving his hands into his pockets, Finn looked away. "She's got her reasons. Just like I had my reasons for coming back to work at McKay."

Unbelievable.

"So neither of you are able to cut the cord from your fathers," Ryder said. "I don't get it."

Finn puffed out his chest and pointed a finger at Ryder.

"You are in no place to judge us. Ciara and I have both made sacrifices you could never understand. She's always loved Jane. But as long as Ian was free, Jane would never be safe."

They both made sacrifices? What the hell had Finn sacrificed other than his integrity when he chose to work for Keane?

"Well, now Jane's caught in the net of another monster," Ryder said. "Two people in her department have died under mysterious circumstances. Someone intentionally ran Jane off the road. And yesterday, while Jane, Maddox, and I were down the fucking street at the community center, her room-mate, Dreama, was beaten almost to death with a baseball bat inside their apartment."

Finn's eyes widened. "Jesus. And you think they're all related?"

"I know they are. That's the reason I'm here." He pulled the SD card out of his pocket. It was possible Finn was play-ing him, but he didn't think so. Not after telling Ryder about Ciara. But Ryder also got the impression that his brother was still keeping secrets. "There's a file on this card that can only be read on Jane's computer."

"What's on it?"

"I don't know. But whatever it is already got two people killed and one woman fighting for her life."

A ding sounded and the elevator door opened to a waiting Tristan. "Sorry to interrupt, but I figured you two would have time to argue later. Guess I'm a bit impatient when it comes to life and death. Let's go see what's on that card."

Tristan was right.

It was time for all the secrets to see the light of day. And they were going to start with the biggest one of all.

Evan's file.

As Finn led them down the hallway to Jane's office, Ryder looked around. He was impressed. It was too bad he wasn't seeing where Jane worked under different circumstances. It was also too bad she happened to be employed by his father.

Once they got to her office, Ryder unlocked the door and went inside. Turning on the lights, he took in the space where she spent most of her days. Despite it being an office, she'd done her best to add touches to make it a bit homier. He inhaled. It even smelled like her.

But he didn't have the time to really soak in the whole ambiance before he sat in her chair behind her desk and turned on her computer. Finn and Tristan stayed by the door like two hulking bodyguards. In a different situation, Ryder would have probably made a joke about it.

Searching for the attachment that Evan had sent Jane, Ryder opened up the file explorer and looked for a download dated the Monday after Finn's wedding. Because Jane had indicated she had deleted it, he wasn't surprised when he didn't find it. Next, he performed a scan of the entire computer for that date, but still came up empty.

Ryder tapped his fingers on the desk.

The question was, if Evan had added a backup file to the attachment, where would he have programmed it to hide on her computer?

Ryder recalled Jane telling him how Evan and Barbara had used the picture frame to hide the SD card. Could Evan have sent the antivirus program to Jane's photo folder?

He clicked open her pictures. She didn't have many, and

the ones she did have were clearly work related, so the photo of a yellow smiley face caught his attention immediately. Hadn't Jane mentioned seeing a smiley face after seeing a flash of code?

His hand hovered over the mouse. What if opening the file caused it to destruct the computer?

He had two choices.

If he picked the wrong one, he'd destroy more than the computer. He'd destroy their only chance of finding out what was on that SD card.

What would he have done if he'd been Evan?

He blew out a breath.

And didn't open the photo.

Instead, he said a silent prayer that his gut was right. "Let's see what's on this thing," Ryder said, putting the SD card into a flash drive and slipping it into the port on Jane's computer. He held his breath as he clicked on the card's sole file.

The screen went dark.

Fuck. It wasn't going to work.

He waited for the flash of code, but instead, a message popped up.

Jane,

I know you'll do the right thing. Whatever you do, don't trust McKay.

Evan

The screen filled with code.

Code he recognized.

Code Ryder had fucking written.

"Tell me what's going on, Ryder," Tristan said, now standing beside him.

"It's the code." He shook his head. "That fucking code. Evan figured it out and re-created it. It's all my fault that people are dead. It's all on me."

If it weren't for him, Evan and Barbara would be alive. Dreama wouldn't be in the hospital. And Jane...

Because of his selfishness, Jane's life was in danger.

He just had to do it, had to prove to himself and everyone else that he could solve the riddle of the autonomous code. He'd fucking known what would happen if that code fell into the wrong hands, but he'd been cocky and stupid and had developed it anyway.

Tristan paled. "Since Jane didn't steal Novateur's designs, how did it end up at McKay?"

Finn didn't say a word. Instead, he seemed to be finding his shoes entirely too fascinating.

Ryder plucked the flash drive out of the computer and, standing, returned it to his pocket. "I don't know. But I'm sure as hell gonna find out."

TWENTY-FIVE

With Maddox sleeping over her shoulder, Jane stared at the home improvement show on the small television hanging on the wall in front of her. How did they make it look so easy? She couldn't even paint a straight line much less the walls of a house. Maybe that's what made these kinds of shows so fascinating. There were so many, each one hosted by an attractive married couple. They all seemed to blend together after a while, but she couldn't manage to look away.

Someone thrust a cup of coffee in front of her.

She looked up at Isabella and accepted it. "Thank you."

Dreama's family had already come and gone. She wasn't sure, but she thought they'd said something about eating down in the cafeteria. Jane had offered to stay in case the doctor came by with some news. The last thing they'd heard, Dreama was in recovery and they were monitoring her closely in case of more clots. She hadn't woken up yet and the doctors weren't sure if she would have brain damage when she did.

Dreama had actually died on the operating table.

The doctors had worked on her for two minutes before they'd gotten her heart beating again.

It wasn't fair. Dreama didn't deserve any of this. And she feared that her friend would never be the same because of it.

Isabella sat down in the chair next to her. "You look exhausted. Why don't you go home and take a nap?"

Forcing herself to look away from the television, she blinked the blurriness out of her eyes. "Not until I know that Dreama's going to be all right."

Isabella was right. She was exhausted. But it was Jane's own fault that she'd spent most of the night making love with Ryder rather than getting the sleep that she needed. And she didn't regret a single second of it.

"If you think she's not, you obviously don't know her as well as you think you do," Isabella said, her voice full of conviction. "Dreama's strong. She's not going to let something like a blood clot kill her. My cousin will probably live to a hundred and die while riding reverse cowgirl on some hot, nubile twenty-year-old."

She didn't want the image in her head, but thanks to Isabella, it was there anyway—a wrinkled Dreama with a rope in one hand, wearing nothing but a damn smile on her face as she died in a final blaze of glory.

Jane's amusement didn't last long now that her guilt had returned with a vengeance. Isabella needed to know the truth. All of Dreama's family should know. "It's my fault she's here."

Isabella reared back. "What? Why would you think that?"

"The guy who attacked her was looking for something that I have. Or had. Ryder has it now."

"How does that make it your fault?" Isabella asked, her eyebrows raised in question. "Was it you swinging the bat? Did you tell the guy to hurt her?"

"No, of course not. But I didn't warn her."

"So you knew someone would break into the apartment."

"I should have known it was possible."

"It's always possible someone could break into an apartment," Isabella pointed out. "Why do you think Dreama had a baseball bat in her closet in the first place when she doesn't play baseball?"

Jane frowned. She'd never thought about the fact that Dreama kept a baseball bat in her closet. "Why does she feel the need to have a weapon?"

Isabella shrugged one shoulder. "I'm not sure. She's a single woman who doesn't want a gun in her home. Maybe she figured it would be a lot easier to swing a bat than to use a knife on someone."

"Her mother said..." What was it? Something about things they never mentioned. Challenges. "Did something happen to Dreama as a child? Was she hurt by someone?"

"Hurt?" Isabella pressed her lips together and lines marred her forehead. "No. Not that I'm aware of and my family talks. *A lot.* As I'm sure you noticed at Thanksgiving." She tilted her head. "Why do you ask?"

If Isabella didn't know about whatever Mrs. Agosto had been talking about, Dreama and her family must have buried it deep. It wasn't Jane's place to stir up trouble. She'd just make sure that if there came a time when Dreama needed to talk about it or anything else, she'd be there for her. Just as Dreama had been there for her.

Jane gave Isabella a small smile. "I don't remember the particulars. I'm sure I just misunderstood."

Thankfully, Isabella dropped the subject. She put a gentle hand on Jane's forearm. "Dreama will get through this. She's the fiercest person I know. I'm not sure if she told you, but a few years ago, I was attacked by an ex-boyfriend and almost died. It was Dreama who got me out of my depression and brought me back to the land of the living. If it weren't for her, I wouldn't have met Tristan or have been strong enough to fight for everything I wanted."

"I don't believe that. You and Tristan were meant to be. Somehow, someway, you would have found your way to each other."

Just as fate had brought Jane and Ryder together.

"I'd like to think so," Isabella said on a smile. It was obvious she was head over heels for Tristan. "The attack on my life changed me. There's no way that Dreama will be the same person as before, but I guarantee you that eventually, she'll heal. And she'd never blame you for what happened to her, so don't beat yourself up for it."

When Jane's phone rang, she quickly snatched it out of her purse, expecting to see Ryder's number on the screen. Instead, she recognized Ian's number.

Why was he calling her on a Saturday morning? In fact, why was he calling her at all?

She put up a finger to Isabella, letting her know she'd only be a minute, and answered. "Hello?"

Needing to stretch her legs, she moved Maddox to his car seat for him to finish his nap and stood, taking her coffee with her to the other side of the room.

"Jane. I heard about your roommate. Is there anything I can do to help?" Ian asked, concern evident in his voice.

She racked her brain as to how he'd found out. "Who told you?"

"Finn."

Of course.

"I'm good. But thank you for asking."

"I've spoken with your mother and we both would like you to come stay with us for a little while, at least until you find somewhere else to live. I can't imagine you want to go back to the apartment where your roommate was attacked."

Right. He didn't know that she and Ryder were together.

"That's awfully kind of you, but I'm sure I can—"

"You sound tired. Why don't you come over to my house and take a nap. Your mother is here and she's extremely worried about you. We both are. And we can watch Maddox for you while you sleep."

Sighing, she realized she didn't have the energy to argue. She'd watched with envy as the Lawsons and the Agosto families leaned on one another during this tragedy. "I'd really appreciate that. Thank you for offering."

After hanging up, she typed out a message to Ryder letting him know she was leaving the hospital for Ian's house.

She didn't know why her own family had chosen now to

suddenly support her, but she wouldn't bite the hand that was feeding her.

Not when she needed it so damn much.

* * *

Tristan parked the car in Keane's driveway and turned to Ryder. "Are you sure you don't want me to go in with you?"

They'd left Finn back at the offices with instructions for him to look for any evidence tying Keane to the theft of Novateur's designs or any plans for what Keane intended to do with the code. Because Ryder didn't for one second believe his father had stolen them simply to go into the restaurant automation business.

This was about something far more dangerous—Ryder's worst nightmare brought to life.

Ryder slid out of the car and placed his hand above the passenger door as he leaned in to speak to Tristan. "I'm sure. If I'm not out in fifteen or you hear anything suspicious, get the hell out of here. I don't need Isabella's wrath raining down on me if anything happens to you." With that he slammed the door and ran up to the porch.

He wasn't surprised when Keane's maid opened the door before he even knocked.

"Where is he?" Ryder asked curtly, not up for pleasantries.

If the maid was offended, she didn't show it. "He's in his office, sir. If you follow me, I can—"

He didn't wait for her to lead him politely through the

house. Instead he barreled his way inside and kept moving, knowing perfectly well where the damn office was located, even though this was the first time he'd set foot in the house in more than a decade.

A chill swept through him as he stepped over where his father had killed the woman—his *mother*—all those years ago. Today he would get retribution for her. He would make sure of it.

The house hadn't changed in all these years. A beautiful showpiece filled with priceless artwork and nothing of real value. Ryder would take a framed photo of Jane and Maddox on his wall over a Picasso any day.

When he got to the old man's office, he didn't knock before he threw open the door and went inside.

His father was at his desk, a glass of bourbon on the rocks sitting in his hand. Just like old times. "Ryder. This is a surprise," he said pleasantly. "Come in and have a seat." He gestured to the chair in front of the desk. "Can I get you a drink?"

Ryder stopped by the chair but didn't bother to sit. "This isn't a social call. I'm going to get right to the point. Jane had a break-in at her apartment. Her roommate was severely beaten."

Keane's skin turned ashen. He covered the left side of his chest with his hand. "My God. Is Jane okay?"

And the Academy Award for best actor goes to . . .

"She wasn't home at the time," Ryder said, knowing damn well the man already knew that.

"Thank goodness." On an exhale, his father's shoulders

dropped, and he reclined back in his chair. "I'm so sorry to hear about her roommate. But I don't understand what that has to do with me."

Keane's confusion seemed genuine, proving to Ryder once again that his father was the consummate liar.

It was time to cut through all the bullshit.

"Were you behind it?" Ryder asked point-blank. "Did you send one of your men after Jane?"

His father frowned. "Why would I want to hurt Jane or her roommate?"

"Two of your employees have died recently under questionable circumstances."

Keane tipped his head to the side. "I hardly think a suicide and carbon monoxide poisoning could be considered questionable."

Oh, he's good. No wonder he's gotten away with everything for so long.

"It is when the person who committed suicide had no history of depression and the other died accidentally the next day," Ryder said, ticking off his fingers. "Two separate events that in any other circumstance would seem unrelated." He leaned over the desk. "Except I don't think they are. What is the statistical probability of two people in the same department dying and the third having her apartment broken into in the same month?"

"I understand you're worried about Jane." Keane pushed back in his chair and stood. "But I won't allow you to come in here and accuse me of having people murdered. You've always viewed me as some kind of monster. I admit I use tactics that most would find reprehensible. But I have never ordered a hit on anyone. Certainly not on my own employees."

Lies. They fell from his lips like rain from the sky.

Ryder didn't bother keeping his voice down. Let the staff overhear. They should know the kind of man they were working for.

"Jane thought you walked on water until I told her the truth about you. How you had your enforcers convince others to do what you wanted."

Keane coughed into his hands, the congestion sounding thick and deep. That's what a lifetime of smoking got him. He took a sip of his bourbon. "You were always too soft. There are things you have to do in business. I was no different than other billionaires like Ian Sinclair. But I never killed anyone."

Never killed anyone?

Did he really think Ryder didn't remember?

"Jane thought you cared about her, but you were just using her, weren't you? You never cared about anyone or anything other than the deal."

"That's not true." He coughed again. "I care for Jane and Maddox. I love you and your brother. And I loved your mother."

Ryder shook with fury. "My mother? You loved my *mother*? You killed her! I saw you!"

Keane stumbled and put a hand over his chest again. "I didn't kill your mother. She died in Mexico giving birth to you."

"Lies. All lies. You think I don't remember because I was only five? I saw you kill her. She came for me and you took the gun out of her hand and shot her out there in the foyer as I looked down from upstairs."

His father hung his head and gripped the edge of the desk with both hands. "You remember that?"

That sounded like a confession to him.

Keane took a moment, seemingly having a difficult time catching his breath. Ryder supposed that could happen when confronted with one's sins. When his father looked up, there were tears in his eyes.

"I always regretted the way I handled things that night with you. I thought if I told you it was only a nightmare, you would eventually forget about it. I didn't know..." He reached out to Ryder, then suddenly thought better of it and dropped his hand to his side. "That wasn't your mother. It was your aunt Alma, your mother's older sister from Mexico." He sighed. "It's a long, complicated story."

His aunt?

"Condense it," Ryder ordered.

"Alma wasn't a well woman. She'd suffered from mental illness since she was a young girl. That's why when your grandmother got sick, Maria needed to return to Mexico and care for her. Alma just didn't have it in her to care for anyone. What I told you about your mother dying shortly after giving birth to you in Mexico was true. But I left out a piece of the story. After your mother passed, Alma refused to give you to me unless I paid her a hundred thousand dollars. Of course, I didn't hesitate. The money meant nothing to me. You were my son. I would have paid everything I had to bring you home."

Ryder felt as if he were in the middle of a soap opera.

His father's words seemed scripted and overly emotional, intended to pull on his heartstrings. "Why did you kill her?" he asked.

"It was an accident." Keane's voice was raspy. "About a month before that night, she came to the door and accused me of kidnapping you. She thought you were her son. Her mother had passed away and she'd totally lost her grip on reality. I tried to have her institutionalized but they ended up releasing her after the initial seventy-two-hour hold. When I didn't hear from her again, I'd assumed she'd returned to Mexico. I obviously had assumed wrong. The next time she returned, she brought a gun with her. I tried to reason with her, but she was determined to take you away from me. We fought over the gun and it went off. She'd been trying to shoot me, but in the scuffle, she lost control and the bullet lodged in her stomach."

Ryder closed his eyes, able to recall the image from his nightmare of the bloody woman lying on the floor. "If it was an accident, why didn't you report it to the police?"

"I was afraid they wouldn't believe me and that I'd lose you and Finn. I had the means to take care of it quietly. All I can say is that at the time, I thought I was doing what was best for my family. In the end...I lost you anyway." Keane looked beaten down and *old* as he clamped a hand on Ryder's shoulder. "I realize I wasn't a good father and that I've done things in business that I'm not proud of, but I've changed. I have been trying for years to get you to see that. Finn has forgiven me. Maybe now that you know the truth, you can too?"

"I don't know," Ryder said. "Even if Alma's death was

an accident, I'm not sure I can get over the dozens of other crimes you did commit. The night of Alma's death, you told me I belonged to you. As if I was your property. You were always my father in name only. And I'm not sure I can ever forgive you for that."

Keane winced as if Ryder had inflicted physical pain with his words. "I'm sorry, son. I wish things could be different. But do believe me when I tell you this. I didn't have anything to do with Jane's break-in or those deaths. And I don't believe it has anything to do with McKay Industries."

Ryder stared at his father.

He didn't know whether to believe him.

"If everything you say is true, then tell me, why did you order someone to steal my designs?"

Deep grooves were etched in Keane's forehead. "I have no idea what you're talking about."

"Are you telling me it was a coincidence you got into the restaurant automation business?"

"Well, no. I suppose it wasn't a coincidence." His father's cheeks reddened. "I thought... I'd hoped that one day you would decide to come work for McKay. I created our restaurant automation division for you, Ryder. But I know nothing about your stolen designs."

If he wasn't behind the theft, who was? And how did his code end up on that SD card?

"Who did the designs for you?"

Keane answered quickly. "Derek Gardner. He took credit for it all. The designs, the software, everything. I had no idea he'd stolen it from you."

Derek Gardner.

Ryder's neck prickled and his pulse increased. "Why does that name sound familiar?" It couldn't be the same man. He stuck his hand into his pocket and brought out his wallet. "I think I still have it." He flipped it open and rifled through the dozens of business cards he kept in there. "Here it is. A year ago, I met him at a conference on Mackinac Island. He wanted to talk to me about Novateur, but I blew him off. That's the same night someone made a copy of my files." His gaze fell on the name of the company Gardner had been working for. "When you hired him, had you known he worked for Sinclair?"

"Derek made no mention of ever working for Ian Sinclair. Trust me, I make a point of never hiring any of his castoffs," Keane said with disdain.

All this time, Ryder had been blaming the wrong monster.

"I thought you had Finn marry Ciara in order to consolidate the two families?"

His father shook his head. "I had nothing to do with Finn and Ciara. They didn't marry because of me, but in spite of me. When they announced their engagement, Ian and I made a deal that we would stay out of one another's way for the sake of our families. A truce of sorts."

Ryder couldn't begin to comprehend what a truce meant between two corrupt businessmen. But he didn't have the time to dissect the idea. Not when Jane was still in danger. "I think I need to pay a visit to Mr. Gardner. Can you access your work records from your computer and give me his address?"

"Of course." Keane moved swiftly, going to his desk and typing. A moment later, he wrote out an address on a sticky note and handed it to Ryder. "I'm coming with you."

"No," Ryder said firmly. "Don't confuse me coming here as some sort of an olive branch. My feelings about you haven't changed. It doesn't matter how many stories you spin, I'm still not convinced you didn't have anything to do with what's on the SD card."

His father's lips parted as if he was about to speak, but he simply nodded. Ryder stormed out of the house.

Why couldn't he shake the feeling that time was running out?

TWENTY-SIX

Jane had never been to Ian's house before. Sad but true. In the past, she'd dreamed of what it would be like inside, the warmth and the love that would fill its halls. But as she handed her coat to her grandfather and set Maddox in his carrier on the floor, she realized reality was nothing like her fantasy. No one could claim it wasn't beautiful, with the Persian rugs and crystal chandeliers. Surprisingly, it was warm and homey, despite the enormous size of the house. But it didn't feel like home to her. And she doubted it ever would.

Still, she was grateful that Ian had extended the invitation. She was so tired, she could barely stand. "I really appreciate you helping me out today," she told him as he greeted her.

He folded her into his arms and hugged her tight. "That's what your family is here for. With you and Maddox living nearby, there's no reason we can't all be a family." Still embracing her, he held her tighter and brushed his hand from the crown of her head to her neck. "You've grown into a beautiful woman, Jane," he whispered.

Something about his hug seemed...off. It wasn't his

words, but the way he said them, with reverence. It made her uncomfortable.

She pushed against him and stumbled backward. "Thank you." She picked up Maddox's carrier, hoping it might work as a barrier. "Where's Ciara?"

"Your mother wasn't feeling well," he answered casually. "One of her headaches. She took a couple pills and went to lie down."

Warning bells were ringing in her ears. In a half hour, her mother had suddenly come down with a headache? Ian had lied to her. She'd bet her entire bank account that her mother hadn't wanted her here and the invitation had come solely from Ian.

"Oh." She searched his eyes for the truth, but his eyes were blank. Unreadable. "I thought she was going to watch Maddox for me so I could nap."

He nodded. "She will. But for now, why don't you and Maddox come into the parlor and relax." He plucked the carrier from her hands and strolled away, requiring Jane to follow. "It will give us a chance to catch up."

"Sure." As if he'd given her a choice. How had she never noticed how odd Ian was? "My mother doesn't really have a headache, does she? Is she even here?"

Bringing her into the parlor, which reminded her of a Jane Austen novel, and closing the double doors, Ian smiled and slowly perused the length of her body. "You've grown into a beautiful woman, Jane."

She shivered with revulsion as her heart went into overdrive. Why was he standing in front of the doors? It was as if he was blocking her exit. "You said that already."

Perhaps coming here hadn't been the wisest decision. She should take Maddox back from Ian and leave.

Ian laughed. "I did, didn't I? I've learned you can never tell a woman she's beautiful too many times." He set Maddox down by the door. "You're built less like your mother and more like your grandmother. She had that same willowy figure, small breasts, and tiny waist."

"Excuse me?" Had he just commented on her breasts? She fought the urge to cross her arms over her chest.

"Your mother hated having large breasts," he said as if it was perfectly natural to discuss his daughter's breast size with his granddaughter. "But I always told her she should be proud of them. They were a sign of her becoming a woman. They got so swollen when she was pregnant with you." He paused to lick his lips.

There was something wrong here, something she was missing. She would almost think Ian had lost his grip on reality, but at the same time, he appeared perfectly sane. Maybe she was just seeing a side of him he'd never revealed before. Well, she didn't want to see this side. Ever.

Thank God she'd told Ryder where to find her. She'd thought she would have heard from him by now. What if Keane had done something to Ryder and Tristan, and she was stuck here, unable to help?

"Maddox looks a lot like his father," Ian said, jarring her out of her worries. "But I see me in him too. Don't you?"

She jolted as if he'd electrocuted her. He knew Ryder was Maddox's father? "I suppose. Maybe I should—"

The sound of the door's lock being engaged was quiet, but to Jane, it was deafening.

"Don't be scared," he said, stalking to her. "It's time you know the truth. I just have a phone call to make, and then you and I will finally have the chance to get better acquainted." He smiled, his teeth reminding her of a shark's. "The way we should have years ago."

* * *

Ryder slid into the passenger seat of the car and slammed the door. He plugged the address that Keane had given him into the car's GPS. "I know who was responsible for breaking into my room at the conference. Name's Derek Gardner. He wanted to meet with me, but I blew him off. At the time, he worked for one of Sinclair's companies. But shortly after the conference, he left Sinclair to work for McKay, bringing our designs with him."

"Sinclair?" Tristan drove through the open gate of Keane's property and turned onto the main road, following the GPS's directions. "What about Keane?"

"Keane claims he didn't know Gardner had stolen the designs from me or that he'd worked for Sinclair."

Tristan scowled. "Do you believe him?"

"I don't know. It's possible it's all bullshit and he's in on it with Sinclair."

"If Derek was working for Sinclair, why did he take the job at McKay?"

"I'm not sure," Ryder said. "If I had to guess, Derek

needed someone who could figure out the missing code. Other than me, there aren't many programmers of that caliber. But Evan obviously fit the bill."

"This has nothing to do with competing with Novateur, does it?"

"I don't think so," Ryder said. "Sinclair builds weapons."

If Ian Sinclair got ahold of the finished software program that would make weapons autonomous, the world would become a lot more dangerous.

"Why kill Evan?"

"Either Evan was in on it...or he really did think he was working on restaurant automation software and when he solved the code, he figured out he'd been lied to. Before he died, he protected his computer with a virus and sent the antivirus program to Jane."

"So who killed him? And why kill Evan's secretary?"

"I don't know." Ryder bounced his leg up and down. A feeling of unease passed through him. "Hopefully Gardner can fill in the blanks."

A few minutes later, Tristan pulled up to a modest single-family home with blue siding and white trim. For a guy who had previously worked for Sinclair and now McKay, Derek didn't appear to have a lot of money. After parking, they got out of the car and walked up the driveway, past a sedan with a smashed headlight.

Hadn't a car with one headlight followed him and Jane when they'd left the hospital the other night? It was possible it was a coincidence.

But it was also possible Gardner had been tailing them.

If Gardner was responsible for hurting Dreama, he was a dead man.

"Ready to get this guy to talk?" Ryder asked Tristan as he knocked on the door. "Gardner? Open up."

"Are you sure you wouldn't rather have the cops handle this?" Tristan asked from beside him.

"Fuck the cops. We don't have time for all their procedural bullshit. Desperate times call for desperate measures." He knocked again and this time rang the doorbell. "Dreama's fighting for her life in the hospital and two people in Jane's department are dead and I'm not about to let Jane become the third." *Fuck it.* The guy obviously wasn't going to answer his door.

Gardner had probably broken into Jane's.

It was only fair that Ryder return the favor.

He put his hand on the doorknob, preparing to bust it if he had to, but surprise, surprise...it was unlocked. He turned it and pushed the door open.

A stench of shit, piss, and rotten meat hit his nostrils.

He and Tristan both covered their mouths and noses with their hands and proceeded to walk through the house. Everything seemed neat and orderly. Other than the strong foul stench, there were no signs that anything could be wrong.

But Ryder's gut was churning.

The smell got stronger as they neared the back of the house.

"What the hell is that stink?" Tristan asked through his hands.

They stepped into what appeared to be Gardner's family

room. There, slumped over on the couch, was the man Ryder had met up on Mackinac Island. But for the missing part of his head, which was splattered all around him, and the blood on his abdomen, he looked the same as he had the year before.

"I'm no doctor," Ryder said, "but I'd bet anything the stench is coming from Gardner's dead body."

Guess they weren't going to get any information out of him.

With the smell overpowering them, they immediately went outside for fresh air. There was nothing they could do for Gardner at that point.

Had Keane ordered a hit to keep Gardner from talking, knowing Ryder was on his way to Gardner's home? Or had someone else killed Gardner?

Ryder wasn't certain, but he did know that whoever had done it was after his software.

His stomach churned and not just because of the dead body.

Of the dozens of applications for his software, there was only one worth billions of dollars.

Weapons.

Gardner had worked for Sinclair Corp, an arms manufacturer. What if he'd continued working for it while he was employed at McKay?

"I think it's time we called the cops," he said to Tristan as they got into the car. He pulled his iPhone from his pocket and saw he'd missed a message from Jane.

No, no, no.

His heart nearly exploded as he read the text.

"Jane." He immediately dialed her cell. "Come on," he said frantically after two rings. "Pick up."

Tristan hit the gas. "What's wrong?" *Please, tell me you're not at Sinclair's yet. Tell me I got to you in time.*

"Ryder." Her voice was panicked, but he had to warn her before it was too late.

"Jane, you have to listen to me. Don't go to Ian's. It's a trap. He's behind everything."

"So good of you to call," said Sinclair. "It appears we both have something the other wants. How about we make a trade."

TWENTY-SEVEN

Jane sat on the couch and tried to calm a crying Maddox. For the last twenty minutes, her red-faced son had been kicking out his legs and punching his fists, almost as if he knew they were in danger. It was likely something minor like gas or cutting a tooth, but her best efforts refused to soothe him. He wouldn't take a bottle, his diaper was clean and dry, and she couldn't get him to burp. She was at her wit's end.

And so was Ian.

"Make him stop fussing," he demanded, bits of spittle flying from his mouth. "Or I'll do it for you."

She didn't doubt his words.

Or the gun in his hand.

"I'm trying," she said calmly. "I don't know what's wrong with him."

All these years she'd dreamed of having a relationship with Ian. And apparently she wasn't the only one. Although he hadn't come right out and said it, she'd read between the lines.

The man was a pedophile.

He spoke of Ciara like she was his lover rather than his daughter. First, talking about her breasts and later referring to their relationship as "special." There was nothing special about molesting a child. He'd been wistful when he'd lamented that he'd never gotten the chance to have the same special relationship with Jane.

No wonder Ciara had sent her away.

She'd done it to protect her.

But where was she now? Had Ian done something to harm her or was she truly upstairs sleeping?

She had to get away from him before Ryder arrived.

Because despite what Ian had said on the phone to him earlier, he had no intention of abiding by the terms of the exchange: the SD card for Jane and Maddox. Ian had made it clear to her he would never let her or Maddox go. Once Ryder delivered the software, Ian would kill him. "You don't have to do this. Let me and Maddox go. We're your family," she pleaded.

He brandished the gun at her. "Right now you're bait. You're not going anywhere until I get my fish."

She closed her eyes, refusing to let Ian see her cry. There had to be a way to get through to him. She couldn't allow Ryder to walk into a trap.

Ian hadn't revealed what he planned to do with whatever was on that SD card. She still didn't even know what was on it or whether Ryder had been able to open the file using her computer. But whatever it was, Ian was intent on getting it, no matter who he had to hurt.

Including her and Maddox.

The doors to the parlor flew open and Ciara strolled inside. As usual, her hair was perfectly coifed and her clothes didn't have a single wrinkle. If Jane had to guess, she hadn't been napping.

Her gaze bounced between Ian and Ciara. Was it possible they were working together? Ciara didn't seem fazed by the gun in Ian's hands or the fact that it was pointed at Jane and Maddox.

Jane's stomach sank to the floor. "Hello, Mother. I take it your headache is gone."

Ciara ignored her as usual and spoke directly to Ian. "Is Ryder on his way with it?"

"He should be here momentarily. Is everything ready upstairs?"

She nodded as she smiled up at him. "Of course. I always do what you tell me, don't I?"

To think Jane had felt sorry for her mother. It didn't matter what she'd gone through at the hands of her father; she had choices now and she was making the wrong ones. Didn't Jane and Maddox mean anything to her?

"How could you do this? To me? Your grandson? Your husband?" Jane asked.

Having cried himself out, Maddox finally gave one final sob as his eyes closed and he thankfully fell asleep. Ciara's gaze flickered over to them and fixed on Maddox. Automatically, Jane held him closer to her chest.

"Finn was nothing more than a way to spy on McKay Industries. He means nothing to me. And neither do you. No one matters to me but Father." Ciara turned her attention back to Ian as if to reassure him of it.

The dynamics between Ciara and Ian caused bile to rise in Jane's throat.

Ciara hadn't sent her away to protect her.

She'd probably done it because she didn't want to lose any of the attention Ian lavished on her.

Her mother looked down at the buzzing cell phone in her hands. "Ryder just went through the gate. I'll go be a good hostess and let him in."

"Make sure he followed directions and came alone," Ian instructed as she breezily strode out of the room. Shaking, Jane prayed that Ryder had some kind of plan to get them out of here.

But apparently, God hadn't listened.

Because not a minute passed before Ciara marched Ryder into the room with a gun to his back.

Jane jumped to her feet and raced to him. He took her into his arms, careful not to smoosh Maddox between them.

"Are you okay?" His hands were on her back and in her hair. "He didn't touch you, did he?"

"No." She swallowed and stepped out of his embrace. "I'm fine."

"Okay. So I'm here. Now you can let Jane and Maddox go," Ryder said to Ian.

"Did you bring the SD card with you?" Ian asked.

She looked at Ian, wanting, *needing*, to know what was so important that her own family was willing to kill her for it. "What's on the card that makes it so valuable?"

"The program that will make weapons autonomous," Ryder said. His eyes narrowed on Ian. "So who are you planning on selling it to?"

"I haven't decided yet," Ian said, his gun remaining aimed at Jane. "ISIS would love to get their hands on it, but I doubt they could afford it. I'm sure North Korea would pay quite generously for the technology, as would the Russians. Maybe I'll sell it to all of them. Who's to say I can't sell the code to anyone willing to pay the right price?"

"Why didn't you just kidnap me as soon as you realized there was a piece of code missing from the software?" Ryder asked Ian. "Why kill people rather than just forcing my hand right from the start?"

"What?" Ciara's face drained of all color. "You did what?" With her gun still on Ryder, she stepped out from her place behind him.

Seemed someone had been kept in the dark.

"Necessary casualties, my dear," Ian said dismissively to Ciara. "I didn't want you to worry. I know how little things can set off your depression." Switching his attention to Ryder, he shrugged. "There aren't many people who have enough resources to destroy me, but Keane is one of them. That made you off-limits. We even made a pact at the wedding that for the sake of Finn and Ciara, we'd consider each other's family as our own."

Considering how Ian treated his own family, that wasn't saying much.

"When Keane told me he was going to start a restaurant automation business," Ian continued, "I sent Derek to him.

It was a win-win. Keane got designs for his company—unknowingly yours—and I got access to a programmer who could fix the software's missing code."

Ryder clenched his fists. If he didn't have a gun pointed at him, Jane was certain those fists would be flying. "Evan's suicide? Barbara's carbon monoxide poisoning? Jane's car accident? Dreama's attack? You were behind all of it?"

Ian shrugged. "It was unfortunate that Evan—and possibly Barbara, although I never confirmed it—figured out what the software could be used for. I had to make sure they didn't tell Keane before I got my hands on it. But Gardner screwed up. The files Evan had created disappeared. I wasn't pleased when Gardner told me about running Jane off the road. He'd become desperate and desperation breeds carelessness. After he failed to obtain the SD card for me, he was no longer useful."

How could Ian be so callous? There wasn't a doubt in her mind that Derek would have died even if he had succeeded in his mission.

Jane's stomach churned.

They weren't getting out of here.

Her own grandfather was going to kill her.

Ian looked at his watch. "I do wish I had been able to keep my word to Keane, but I'm afraid that circumstances have left me with no choice. The bidding goes live in two hours and my friends around the world would be rather...pissed...if I failed to deliver what I promised."

Wait. What was that?

It was subtle, just a quick glance at the window and a slight nod, but Jane caught it.

Had Ciara just sent some kind of signal to someone outside?

"And you're okay with knowing the code will be used by our enemies in weapons against us?" Ryder asked, still deep in conversation with Ian.

Ian bared his teeth in a sneer. "Not my problem. Let our government figure it out. Ciara and I will be retired on our own private island in the middle of the Pacific."

"Yeah, until the autonomous weapons begin World War Three and your island is wiped away by a fucking tsunami caused by a bomb," Ryder said.

"We all have to go someday," Ian said on a sigh. "At least I'll die in luxury."

"You already have more money than most people will ever see in their lifetime," Jane said. "Don't you care that innocent people like me and Maddox might die because of your greed?"

Ian's eyes glazed over, giving her the impression that although he was staring at her, he wasn't really seeing her. "It's a shame you didn't get the chance to grow up with me, Jane. Then you'd see that no one is innocent. Life is just one big game and the person who wins it is the one who controls all the power. The code that Ryder wrote is the source of that power." He looked at Ryder. "Are you really willing to let Jane and Maddox die over it?"

"How do I know you won't kill them and me anyway once you have the software?" Ryder asked.

"I would never hurt my family," Ian said.

All evidence to the contrary.

Jane grabbed Ryder by the arm. "Don't do it."

Ryder removed her hand from his arm and slid his own into his pocket. He pulled out the SD card and held it in his palm.

She couldn't hold in her tears any longer. Didn't care about being strong. Didn't care who saw them. Ryder had just signed his death warrant.

Ian jerked his head toward the door. "Ciara, put Maddox in the nursery upstairs."

What the fuck?

Jane quickly weighed her options. She didn't want to hand over Maddox willingly. But Ciara and Ian had guns. She couldn't take the chance that Maddox could get hurt if she refused. "Nursery? You were planning this?" Jane said accusingly as Ciara took her son out of her arms without even looking at her.

"Ciara will raise Maddox as her own child." Ian smiled at Ciara like no father should ever smile at his daughter. "As our child."

There were so many things wrong with that statement Jane barely knew where to begin.

Without Maddox, Jane's body shook uncontrollably. Her heart was beating so fast, she was sure it was about to burst. What kind of life would Maddox have with these two? Would they tell him about her or would he grow up never knowing he had a mother who'd died for him?

Instead of leaving the room with Maddox, Ciara quickly deposited him into the car seat and shoved him under a desk. Jane's pulse pounded in her ears as she realized something was about to happen.

A red laser coming through the window caught her eye.

She wasn't the only one who noticed.

Ian turned toward the light a second before the window's glass exploded and a splotch of crimson spread out from Ian's left shoulder. He raised his gun and pointed it straight at Jane's head.

She saw her life flash before her eyes. The faces of the people she loved the most.

Ryder shoved her and she tumbled sideways. Ciara jumped in front of her. A gun went off, the noise louder than she'd ever imagined a gun would sound, and the smell of sulfur reached her nose. She waited for the pain to bloom, the pain that came from being shot, but as her shoulder bounced off the carpet, there was no pain other than from the soreness of falling.

A body lay on top of her.

And another in front of her.

Her eyes took it in and yet she couldn't process it.

She closed her eyes and opened them again.

There, on her side, was Ciara.

Her *mother*.

She wasn't moving and there was blood, so much blood, staining her back.

The sound of multiple footsteps filled her ears as more gunshots rang out. Ryder's weight pressed down on her, preventing her from going to her mother. She closed her eyes as she waited for it all to be over. There were voices. Lots of them. Men and women. One of them sounded like Keane's. She'd never felt so helpless until the moment she remembered Maddox was still in the room.

"Maddox!" She fought against Ryder, rolling back and forth in an attempt to get him off of her so she could get to her son. "Let me go! We have to get Maddox."

"Stay down," Ryder ordered. "I'll get him."

And then the weight was gone.

"FBI! Don't move!"

"Ciara!"

Jane didn't stay down. She couldn't. Not when the people she loved were in danger. She pushed herself to her feet.

On his knees, Finn was by Ciara, kissing her forehead and crying. "No. Damn it. You are not leaving me. Wake up, baby."

A group of men dressed in all black stood by the door—several of whom she recognized from McKay Industries—with their guns trained on Ian. There were also a handful of men and women wearing FBI vests, some of whom had their guns pointed at Ian and others with their guns on Keane.

Keane and Ian were at a standoff, each with their guns aimed at the other's heads.

But none of it was important to Jane. Her eyes fell upon Ryder as he stormed across the room toward her with Maddox cradled in his arms.

"Put your guns down on the ground and put your hands on your head," shouted an FBI agent.

There was a long pause before Keane complied. Soon after, Ian gave up as well.

It was over.

Ryder slammed into her, this time not to protect her, but to claim her, his mouth stealing the air from her lungs. And

for a moment she gave in, forgetting the chaos and blood-
shed all around them. But Finn crying her mother's name
cut through her sweet reunion with Ryder and brought her
crashing back to reality.

She looked over to her mother.

Her eyes were open. Fixed and unblinking. Blood trickled from her nose and mouth.

She knew immediately her mother was dead.

She'd placed Maddox in the safest spot in the room and
then had taken the bullet meant for Jane.

She'd saved both their lives.

And now she was gone.

In a little more than a week, everything Jane thought she
knew had changed.

People like Keane, Derek, and Ian had fooled her into be-
lieving they were trustworthy, while the mother who she'd
believed hated her had actually been protecting her since birth.

Maybe if Jane had been less naïve, things might have
gone differently. Evan and Barbara would be alive, and
Dreama wouldn't be fighting for her life.

She loved Ryder with all her heart.

But how could she trust her judgment when she'd been
so wrong about everyone else?

* * *

Ryder had never been so relieved.

If he'd had his way, he would've gone off half cocked and
walked straight into Ian's trap.

Bring the SD card.

No police.

Tell no one.

Yada, yada, yada. Typical psycho kidnapper language.

And Ryder had been so filled with rage and fear, he would've followed Ian's directions to a T. But once Tristan had calmed him down and reasoned with him, he'd called Keane for reinforcements instead.

In the end, his father had come through for him, showing up at Sinclair's house with his old trusted enforcers, many of whom now sat on the board of McKay Industries.

Oh yeah, and the FBI, although he had no idea how they'd gotten involved.

There were a few minutes there when he thought they might not make it out alive.

But they had . . . at least most of them.

Finn was kneeling by Ciara, tears streaming down his face. He'd never seen his brother so wrecked. Hadn't even thought it was possible. He'd always seemed so strong and in control.

He didn't seem that way now.

The man in front of him was in mourning. Broken.

Ryder would have been the same if the woman lying there had been Jane.

He should have never doubted his brother's feelings for Ciara. It was obvious to him now that he'd loved her.

Hands together, he and Jane walked over to his brother.

Jane put a hand on Finn's shoulder. "I'm sorry."

His brother's eyes were haunted. "It's all my fault. I should've never talked her into it."

"Talked her into what?" Ryder asked.

"Taking down our fathers. Working as informants for the FBI. All of it. I swear, Ciara and I knew nothing about your software. I called them after you came by McKay and got them into position here at the house. Keane followed me over here to take matters into his own hands...as he prefers to do. We've got enough evidence on both Ian and Keane to lock them up for the rest of their lives."

Ryder rubbed his temple. "That's why you were working at McKay?"

Finn nodded. "Keane isn't all bad, you know. I found plenty of evidence of financial crimes, but from what I've pieced together, he stopped his other criminal activities right about the time you left for college."

"And Ciara? Were the two of you really together or was it just for show?"

"I loved her." Finn hung his head. "It was real. More real than anything else in my life. I should've never approached her at that club two years ago. I should've just walked away. Maybe then she'd still be alive." He pushed off the floor and stood. "The men in our family are cursed." He let out a pained chuckle. "I wish you two the best of luck. You're going to need it. I've got to go speak to my supervisor and arrange for Ciara..."

Tears gone, he straightened and threw back his shoulders as if he hadn't just lost his wife. He was all business now as he marched out of the parlor.

Ryder curled his hand around Jane's waist and pulled her to his side. "I'm sorry about your mom."

Jane nodded blankly. "Me too."

A commotion on the other side of the room snagged Ryder's attention.

"I think he's having a heart attack!" someone yelled.

Clutching his chest, Keane fell forward onto the floor.

"Keane!" Ryder pushed his way through the throng of people to get to his father. He kneeled down beside him. "Find Finn," he told one of the agents.

His father's skin was gray and sweaty and his lips were white. He grimaced. "I need to tell you something before I die."

"You're not dying," he said, taking Keane's withered hand in his. "The FBI's worked too hard to see you behind bars to let you go ahead and die on them now."

"I am dying. This isn't my first rodeo, kid. Doctor said I didn't have much time before my heart gave out. Guess tonight was a little more action than I'm used to these days."

No.

Ryder was supposed to have more time. Time to learn to forgive his father and to let go of all the anger he'd been holding inside of him all these years.

"Maddox is your grandson," Ryder said, choking back the emotion.

Keane gave a little smile. "I know. I've always known." He coughed. "I'm glad you and Jane found your way to each other. All I wanted was for you to find happiness." His eyes closed as his body jerked. "I need you and Finn to do something for me when I'm gone."

"Anything."

"I need you to find your brother," Keane said so quietly, Ryder almost couldn't hear him.

"Finn? They're going to get him, so just hold on."

His head rolled back and forth. "Not Finn. Your other brother. Find him." His father gasped. "Give him...his share and...tell him I looked for him..." His eyes closed and he grew still, his chest not moving.

The medics arrived and tore Ryder away, but he knew they were already too late.

His father was gone.

But he'd left Ryder a parting gift.

A fucking brother.

He could not deal with that shit.

Besides, who knew if Keane's words were just a delusion brought on by lack of oxygen?

Suddenly, the adrenaline in his body dropped and he was exhausted. All he wanted to do was go home and slide under the covers with Jane and hold her all night long knowing nothing was in their way anymore.

He scanned the room, but he didn't see her.

Where had she gone?

He found Jane feeding Maddox on the bottom step of the staircase. She didn't look up as he approached.

"Let's get out of here and go home," he said, offering his hand to her. "I need to hold you."

She still wouldn't look at him. "I can't do this."

"This?"

"Us."

She wasn't making sense. She was in shock.

"But it's over. We're not in danger anymore. There's nothing standing in the way of us being together."

"I know. It's just... with everything that's happened... it's too much." Her hands were shaking. "I can't deal with it all right now. I need some time."

"Fuck time," he roared, causing Jane to jolt.

Hell, he didn't want to scare her. But right now she was scaring *him*.

He lowered his voice and crouched down to speak to her face-to-face. "Please don't leave me. Just come home with me tonight and we'll talk about this in the morning."

"I'm sorry," was all she said.

He leaned forward, trying to get her to look at him. "What happened to wanting a stable environment for Maddox?"

"I'm doing this for Maddox." Finally, she met his eyes. They belonged to another woman. Not his Jane. Usually full of light and mirth, they were now cold and lifeless. "Maddox will always be your son. But right now, I can't be with you. It's too difficult."

Too difficult.

He'd offered her everything and she was throwing it back in his face because it was *too difficult*. This wasn't the woman he'd grown to know. There had to be something he was missing. "You're in shock. You don't know what you're saying."

She turned her head and stared off into the distance. "I'm not in shock. I'm doing what's best."

"What's best?" he repeated.

What had changed? How could she suddenly decide that he wasn't what was best for her and Maddox?

He grabbed her face between his hands and forced her to look at him. "I love you, Jane." Other than sucking in a breath, she gave no sign that she heard him. Or even cared. "I've been waiting for the right time to say it, but do you know what I learned tonight? There's no such thing as the right time. Every second we have on this earth is precious and should never be wasted." When she didn't respond, he let go of her and stood. "But you know what else I learned?" He gave himself a long moment to soak up the image of Jane and Maddox, knowing it might be the last time he got the chance. "Love sucks."

She didn't say a word as he turned and walked away.

And that alone said it all.

TWENTY-EIGHT

Whoever said time heals all wounds was an idiot.

It had been a month since Jane had seen or heard from Ryder.

And she missed him *more* with every day that passed.

Not less.

She'd stumbled through the first few days like a zombie, going through the motions, but completely numb inside. If it weren't for having to care for Maddox, she would've gotten into bed and stayed there. Instead, she packed up her apartment and made plans for a new life for them, one that didn't include Ryder.

She'd learned her lesson the hard way. It was much better to rely on herself than on others. That way she'd never be disappointed.

Pushing Ryder away had been for the best.

So why did her heart hurt so damned much? Why did she wake up in the middle of the night crying for him?

Like everything else, the numbness didn't last. As she

and Maddox had boarded their plane for Florida, she'd been overcome with grief and regret. She was back in Michigan now and those feelings had only intensified.

She'd dropped Maddox off at the daycare center so that she could go visit Dreama in the hospital. In the last month, Jane had only spoken with her once on the phone. She was slowly recovering, but it would be a long process.

Jane ignored the nervous knots in her belly as she walked down the hallway of the hospital to Dreama's room. Because of Ian, Dreama would never give birth to a child. Now that Dreama knew the truth about why she'd been attacked, would she blame Jane?

Her fingers tightened around the plastic handle of the suitcase. She took a deep breath and entered the room.

Dreama was sitting up in bed watching a reality television show about some housewives. Both her arms and legs were in full casts. The bruising on her face had gone from purple to yellow and the swelling was gone. She smiled at Jane, but it wasn't the same smile Jane had come to know. It was less vibrant. Less enthusiastic. Less Dreama.

"Hey, Chickie. Welcome back to Michigan. With this weather, bet you're wondering why you didn't stay in Florida."

That's what their friendship had come to? Small talk about the weather?

Setting the suitcase in the corner of the room, Jane didn't respond. "I brought you some of your things. Some of your favorite pajamas. Your stuffed bear." She turned to Dreama and tried not to blush. "And some of your other toys that you probably wouldn't want your mom to have. Your parents have the rest of your things at their house."

Packing up Dreama's sex toys had been eye opening. How many vibrators and dildos did one woman need?

"Thanks," Dreama said simply. The old Dreama would've made a joke about it. "How are you holding up?"

Jane didn't know whether to laugh or cry. Dreama had spent the last month in the hospital, was facing months of physical therapy, and she was worried about Jane?

Jane pulled the chair next to Dreama's bedside and sat. "I'm fine. Don't worry about me."

Dreama raised a brow. "You've never been a liar, so don't start now. Just because I'm in this hospital bed doesn't mean I'm not capable of being your friend. I know you, Jane. You're not fine."

Her throat tightened. "No. I'm not fine. I'm a mess."

"You didn't say much on the phone when we talked, but I got the rundown from Tristan about everything that happened and who was responsible for putting me in here."

Jane's eyes filled with tears. "I'm so sorry—"

"Stop," Dreama said firmly. "It wasn't your fault and I don't blame you. Derek Gardner is dead and Ian Sinclair will spend the rest of his life behind bars. The guilty have been punished, and you're not one of them, so stop taking on the sins of others."

She gave Dreama a half-hearted smile. "I'll try."

Dreama didn't pull any punches. "Tristan told me your mother saved your life."

"I miss her." Jane couldn't believe how much. "Which is

weird, right? Because I never really knew her at all, did I? Now she's gone. She never really hugged me. Did you know that? My mother took a bullet for me, but she never gave me a hug. And I can't even visit her grave because she was cremated." She shook her head. "I was so wrong about her. About so many things."

And people.

"Just because Ciara's not buried in some cemetery doesn't mean you can't talk to her," Dreama said. "But I have to be honest. Once you became an adult, she could have established a relationship with you. Don't turn her into a martyr. Ciara had flaws just like everyone else. We all have pieces inside of us that we keep hidden. So, yes, you were wrong about her. But that's on her, not you."

Jane's throat tightened. Unable to speak, she simply nodded.

"How was your trip home to Florida?" Dreama asked, thankfully changing the subject.

"It was nice. My aunt and uncle were thrilled to finally meet Maddox. And it was good to get some sunshine. I even took Maddox swimming." She'd considered moving back. Tucking her tail between her legs and starting over again. Finding a new job. A new place to live. New friends. Then she realized she'd only be more miserable. "But it's not my home. It hasn't been for a long time." She loved her aunt and uncle, but she'd never felt as if she belonged in their house. "I'm going to miss our home. I'm going to miss living with you."

"Aw, Chickie, I'm going to miss living with you too. But

that apartment was never your home. It was just a place for you to live until you found your real home."

Jane's heart beat a little faster. "And where's that?"

"Not where. Who." Dreama turned off the television with a press of her finger on the remote. The room grew quiet. "Isabella told me you broke up with Ryder."

"It was for the best," she said automatically. How many times had she said those words this past month? "We would have never worked out in the long run."

"Huh. I never thought of you as a coward."

"What? I'm not a coward."

Dreama eyes flashed with annoyance. "Then stop acting like one."

If only it was that easy.

"What if I'm wrong about him?" Jane asked, her voice as weak as she felt inside. "Like I was about Keane. And Ian. And my mom. I'm a terrible judge of character."

Dreama huffed. "I take offense to that."

"I obviously didn't mean you."

"Well, why not?" Dreama's lips were tilted up. "Come on. If you were wrong about them, you must be wrong about me."

"No. That's not true. You're the kindest, most generous person I've ever known."

A full smile bloomed. "Thank you. So, if you were right about me, why couldn't you have been right about Ryder?"

Inside, she knew Dreama was right.

About everything.

Jane had been a coward.

But it didn't matter.

"He didn't fight for me," Jane whispered.

"What?" Dreama asked.

"I might have pushed him away, but he let me." The truth of that hurt more than she could say. "That's how I know I made the right decision. After that first night, he never even tried to change my mind."

* * *

Ryder swatted at whatever was hitting his face.

Water.

Was it raining in his house or had he fallen asleep outside? Last he remembered, he'd taken refuge on the couch. For some reason, it was the only part of the house that didn't make him automatically think of Jane.

He opened one eye. That's all he could manage. Isabella was standing over him with a spray bottle in her hand.

"It smells in here." She waved her hand in front of her face. "When was the last time you showered?"

"What day is it?" he asked, his voice raspy from non-use.

And bourbon.

Lots and lots of bourbon.

"Tuesday."

He threw his arm over his eyes to keep the sun out. Damn woman must have pulled back all the curtains. "What month?"

"Jesus, Ryder. You look like shit."

Oh good. Tristan was there as well. He should've never

given the bastard a key to his house. Ryder flipped to his side on the couch and spoke into the cushions, so the sound of his voice wouldn't reverberate in his head so much. "If I cared, I'd really appreciate your opinion. But I don't. Now get out."

A soft hand rolled him over onto his back.

"Can't," said Isabella. "We're all here for an intervention."

"All?"

"Hello, Ryder," Isaac said from across the room.

Hail, hail. The gang's all here.

"Isaac." Ryder was in no shape to deal with this at the moment, but at the same time, he wasn't in shape to fight them either. He was fucked. "What are you doing here?"

"You haven't been to work in a month and haven't returned any phone calls," Isaac said.

"I'm fine," Ryder said.

He almost believed his own words.

Except he hadn't been fine since Jane had broken up with him. The copious amounts of alcohol he'd drunk this past month had done little more than pickle his liver. Every day—hell, every second—he spent without Jane and Maddox was pure torture.

Even learning that Ian had pled guilty and would be serving life in prison hadn't helped. Charged with federal and state crimes, he'd landed under the jurisdiction of the federal court, which, despite the crimes having occurred in Michigan, allowed for the death penalty. In exchange for a life in prison, he'd listed out his numerous crimes. He'd admitted to ordering Gardner to get rid of all loose ends, including Evan and Barbara.

Gardner had also been responsible for Dreama's beating, although Ian swore he'd had nothing to do with that. Ryder didn't believe him. Why else had Ian been at the community center but to ensure Jane didn't return home too early? Too bad Gardner hadn't anticipated becoming a loose end himself on the other side of Sinclair's gun.

Because Ryder would have loved to have had the chance to kill him.

Novateur sold the patent for the autonomous software to the U.S. Army for a mere dollar. He hoped to God they used it wisely. But it wasn't his burden anymore.

"You're not fine," Isabella said sweetly. If she hadn't been spraying him with water, he almost wouldn't mind her being there. "It's ten in the morning and you're already drunk."

Ryder rolled back over onto his side, completely done with their conversation. Nothing they could say or do would help, so what was the point? "I'll have you know, I am not drunk. I have a serious case of the *fuck you*s."

The next thing he knew, he was hoisted off the couch and dragged by Tristan and Isaac toward the bathroom. "What the fuck? What are you doing? Let me go!"

They shoved him into the disaster area formerly known as his bathroom and, from the hallway, blocked the door.

"Take a shower," Tristan ordered. "Brush your teeth. Put on some damned deodorant. Then put on some clean clothes and meet us in the kitchen. You've got fifteen minutes."

"And if I don't?" he challenged.

Isaac glared at him. "I have some contacts at the hospital. Maybe a seventy-two-hour psychiatric hold might do the trick."

Ryder didn't doubt he'd do it. "Assholes," he muttered, slamming the door in their smug faces.

When he caught his reflection in the mirror, he didn't recognize the wreck staring back at him. His brown hair was a shaggy, tangled mess and his eyes completely blood-shot. He had a full beard, and not one of those well-kempt ones. He looked like someone who lived out in the middle of the woods, spending his days writing a manifesto.

This wasn't him.

No matter how much his heart ached over his loss, he was still Maddox's father. He needed to be a role model for him. Whether he was in his life or not.

It took Ryder more than fifteen minutes to return to the land of the living, but thankfully, no one in the house both-ered him. After an hour of scrubbing, shaving, trimming, and brushing, he went to his bedroom and changed into some clothes. Clean ones.

The smell of bacon taunted him into the kitchen.

His three friends sat around the table, patiently waiting for him. In front of the one free chair was a pile of bacon and a bagel topped with a thick layer of cream cheese.

"Here." Isabella patted the seat and gestured with her chin toward his plate. "Eat."

He sat and picked up a piece of bacon. "Where did this come from?"

Isabella's brows dipped together. "The freezer. When was the last time you ate?"

"Other than pizza and wings?" Ryder had a standing order at the corner chain pizza place. Every night, the same kid delivered to the house a small sausage and mushroom pizza and an order of wings.

Isaac harrumphed. "More like vodka and bourbon."

Ryder ignored him, too busy shoveling the bacon into his mouth.

"Better?" Isabella asked softly.

He nodded. "Thank you."

Isabella leaned forward and inspected him closely. "I was at the hospital earlier visiting Dreama and ran into Jane."

He choked on his bite of bagel. After taking a sip of water, he responded. "Oh yeah?"

"Yeah." Isabella pursed her mouth. "She mentioned something about you being a stubborn prick."

His jaw dropped. "She said that? She's the one who told me she needed time."

"Actually she said she hadn't seen you in a month, and I just read between the lines," Isabella quipped.

Tristan chimed in. "Why the hell are you lying around the house drunk off your ass instead of going after her?"

They were blaming *him* for ruining their relationship? He'd done everything to show her he was in it for the long haul and she'd rejected him.

"I was just giving her the space she asked for." Ryder pushed his plate away, no longer hungry. "Besides, maybe she was right and they're better off without me."

He'd had nothing but time to think about everything that had happened with his father and Finn.

Seeming to be having a silent conversation, his three friends shot glances at each other.

Isaac interlaced the fingers of both hands and sat forward in his chair. "Why do you believe that, Ryder? Is this because of your father?"

Oh great. Apparently, it was time for him to be psychoanalyzed, with Isaac playing the role of Sigmund Freud.

"It's because it's true. The McKay men are cursed. My father lost my mother when she died in childbirth, Finn lost Ciara to a bullet, and I lost Jane because . . . hell, I still don't even know. If she's not willing to take the risk, then why should I?"

"You're letting her go because you're *scared*," Isaac said as if it was obvious. "You and Jane both are. It's easier for you both to end things now than to live every day knowing that something might take you from one another in the blink of an eye. But when we love someone, we take that risk."

He narrowed his eyes at Isaac. "You saying I don't love them?"

"Do you?"

"Fuck yes, I love them." He stood and paced the length of the kitchen. "It's killing me to be apart from them. *I* was willing to take the risk. *She's* the one who ended it."

Isaac stood and strode over to him. "Jane is a strong woman who has never in her life had a single person fight for her." Grabbing Ryder by the arms, Isaac shook him. "Fight for her, Ryder. Show her that there's nothing she can do that will ever cause you to leave."

"You should know, she quit her job at McKay," Isabella said. "With Dreama in rehab for the next several months, she decided to move back to Florida."

She was leaving? "Shit. When?" he asked.

Isabella played with the ends of her hair, winding it around her fingers. "I got the feeling the move was imminent. Jane mentioned something about her car being all packed."

"I have to stop her," Ryder said, looking at his friends for help. "I can't let them go."

Tristan smiled up at him and said the obvious. "Then what are you waiting for?"

TWENTY-NINE

Sitting on the floor of her living room folding laundry, Jane tried not to look at her surroundings. She hated her new one-bedroom apartment. She hated the brown shag carpet. She hated the yellowish painted walls. She hated the outdated avocado-colored appliances.

But it was home.

For now.

Jane snapped her head up at the sound of a knock on her door. She got off the floor and went to it. "Coming." Before opening the door, she peered through the peephole.

The image was blurry, but there was no mistaking the person on the other side of her door. Her heart simultaneously ached and jumped for joy.

What was Ryder doing here?

She didn't allow her hopes to get up. Maybe he was there solely to visit Maddox. After all, he knew she would never deny him the right to see his son.

She smoothed her hand over her frizzy hair, then opened the door.

The first thing she noticed was his hair had gotten longer. She liked it.

A lot.

But he'd also lost weight. His cheekbones were more pronounced and his blue sweater was big on him.

That she didn't like.

As she took in the rest of him, she almost melted right there on the spot. He was wearing the sweater he'd worn the night they'd met.

Was it a coincidence?

"Hi, Jane." There was apprehension in his eyes. "Can I come in?"

Oh. Right. How long had she been staring at him? She took a step backward to give him the space to move inside. "Of course."

There wasn't much to her apartment. Once he came inside, they were already in her living room. She didn't watch TV and most of the furniture from the other apartment had been Dreama's, so her living room was empty. "I'd offer you a seat, but..."

"That's fine," he said softly. "I don't need a chair for what I'm here for."

She inhaled his scent, taking it deep into her lungs. God, she'd missed it. Missed *him*.

There had been so many nights she'd dreamed of him and had woken up throbbing and wet. But she hadn't touched herself or relieved the ache pulsing inside of her. Nothing would satisfy her but Ryder.

He stared at her with such intensity, she had to drop her gaze.

"Oh. Um . . ." She tugged on the bottom of her sweatshirt as her heart thumped erratically. "Maddox is sleeping."

"That's okay." He stalked toward her, pushing her back against the wall. "Because what, or rather, who I'm here for . . . is you."

"Me?" she said breathlessly.

"I've given you space and now I'm taking it back. I know being with me comes with a risk, but I'm not going to let you drive me away. My life isn't complete without you and Maddox. I love you, Jane."

Her body heated as he pressed against her, and for the first time in a month, she felt alive.

He was here.

Fighting for her.

And it was time for her to fight for him. "I love you too. I'm sorry I pushed you away. Ryd—"

Sealing his lips over hers, he stole the words out of her mouth. Which was fine because the second he'd kissed her, her mind had gone blank. It was as if all the words they'd been holding inside tumbled out through their kiss, making speech unnecessary.

He tugged her sweatshirt over her head and as he removed his sweater, she yanked off both her panties and sweatpants. It only took a moment more before they were both completely naked.

When he lifted her off the ground, she wrapped her legs around him and guided his cock inside of her. "Fuck me, Ryder."

"God, I've missed you," he said reverently. "And being

inside you. You feel so good around me." He suddenly stilled. "Shit, I forgot the condom."

"We don't need one. I'm on the birth control shot now."

Pinning her to the wall, he stretched her wide with his cock as he drove himself fully inside her. "Thank the fucking stars because it would have been torture to pull out."

She held on for dear life, digging her fingernails into his shoulder blades. He slammed himself into her over and over until they both groaned as they climaxed together.

He collapsed onto the carpet, bringing her down with him, and pulled her onto his lap. She put her ear over his heart and listened to his racing heart. "I didn't push you away because of anything you did. I pushed you away because I doubted myself. Loving you is easy and I haven't had much easy in my life. I was afraid to trust it."

He tipped up her chin. "You love me?"

How could she not?

"From the minute you propositioned me up on Mackinac," she admitted.

His brows wrinkled. "That's not what I remember. I seem to recall you were the one who propositioned me."

"What?" She sat up straight. "No, I didn't."

He smiled. "You specifically said 'fuck me.'"

She rolled her eyes. "I was talking to myself. You'd just pointed out that my shirt was misbuttoned."

"We'll have to agree to disagree."

She giggled. *Giggled.* "You're incorrigible."

His hand curled around the back of her neck. "And you love me."

"And I love you."

He nodded once. "Good. Because I love you too." The smile fell from his face. "But I have to tell you something even more important."

She steeled herself for bad news. "What is it?"

"This apartment is hideous," he said, shuddering in revulsion. "I don't even know how you can stand to look at it. But I have a solution." He swept his thumb over her bottom lip. "Move in with me. You and Maddox. Don't move to Florida."

"Florida?" How had he gotten the impression she was moving to Florida? "What are you talking about?"

"Isabella told me you were moving back there. She said you'd packed your car already."

"My car was packed," she explained, "because I was moving to this apartment. Isabella played you."

That little matchmaker.

Ryder snatched her wrist and tumbled her onto her back. Apparently ready for round two, he slid his cock inside her. "Well, there's only one person I want to play with...and that's you."

EPILOGUE

Looking into the backyard, Jane dried off the platter and placed it on the kitchen counter. Laughter and squeals of her littlest guests floated in through the open window. She couldn't have asked for a more perfect day. Despite the news reports, the rain had held off and instead they'd gotten a hot, sunny day perfect for playing on the swing set and cooling off in a kiddie pool. Their newly adopted pug sat at her feet, looking up at her with pleading puppy eyes.

"Sorry, Otis. No going outside until we finish dessert," she told him as if he could actually understand her. With thirty guests in the yard, five of them under the age of three, she didn't want the dog snatching hot dogs and burgers out of the little fingers that held them. He'd gotten plenty of human food already that day since Maddox decided to share his breakfast with his furry best friend.

She and Maddox had moved into Ryder's house the day that she and Ryder had reconciled. Although she'd loved his décor, she'd added her own personal touches to make the house a home. A few throw cushions here and there. Framed photos of Maddox. Pictures from their wedding, a small affair that had been attended by their closest friends and ring bearer Maddox, dressed in a tiny tuxedo. And lots and lots of toys.

She grabbed the matches and stuck them in the pocket of her shorts, then slid the birthday cake onto the platter. Isabella had designed the cake in the shape of a bright yellow dump truck with crushed sandwich cookies as the dirt. Maddox loved them so much that *truck* was his first word. Much to the delight of his father and to her absolute horror, Maddox pronounced it as "fuck."

The patio door swung open and a sopping wet Ryder slogged inside with a towel around his shoulders and dripped water onto the hardwood floor. "Ready for the cake?"

In response, Otis hopped to his feet and wagged his tail. Ryder opened the screen door and let their dog run outside to go play with their guests.

"What happened to you?" she asked, giggling at the sight of her drenched husband.

"I tripped over a ball and fell in the pool," he mumbled sheepishly. At her increased laughter, he stalked to her, his evil intentions clear in his eyes. "*Ha-ha.* Seems only fair that I not be the only one wet."

Shrieking, she tried to run, but he caught her by her waist and yanked her to him before she could get away. He wrapped his arms around her from behind, but the joke was on him because even as the cold water soaked the back of her clothes, her body heated in his embrace, just as it always did. And when he rubbed his hardened cock against her ass, she knew she wasn't the only one aroused.

He lifted her ponytail out of the way and sucked on her neck. "Are you wet, Jane?"

Her eyes closed on a quiet moan. "You know I am," she whispered. Even more than normal these days thanks to her secret.

Ryder walked her forward until she was trapped between the sink and his hard body. He reached around her waist and unbuttoned her shorts.

"What are you doing?" She glanced nervously at the door even while her core clenched in anticipation. "The kids are busy playing, but what if one of our friends walks in and catches us?"

"Let me worry about that. I need to feel you come on my fingers." He slipped a hand down her shorts and underneath her panties and slid his fingers through her folds. "You're even wetter than me, aren't you, filthy girl? God, you're soaked."

It was so wrong. They should at least go into the bedroom or use the now smaller playroom, the space reserved for just the two of them hidden behind Maddox's playroom filled with children's toys. But knowing they could get caught just added an extra layer of deliciousness. She pushed her ass against him in invitation. "Please."

"Please what?" he muttered into her neck. He bit her lightly. "You know I like you to ask me for what you want."

She still wasn't an expert in dirty talk—in fact, she tended to blush from head to toe whenever she did it— but she was vastly improving as she grew more comfortable with her sexuality and with her husband.

"Touch my clit," she ordered. "Put your fingers inside me and fuck me. Make me come."

"My pleasure." He shoved at least two fingers inside her, while his thumb rubbed circles over her swollen clitoris.

She was so fucking horny all the time. It was like this before, but back then, she'd only had her own fingers to soothe the ache.

She much preferred to come by her husband's hand.

Or mouth.

Or cock.

Or occasionally, just his words.

Hell, these days, all he practically had to do is look at her and she convulsed with an orgasm.

The storm inside her built quickly. Everything tightened, from her fingers wrapped around the counter to her toes in her sandals. Stars exploded behind her eyelids as waves of hot liquid bliss poured through her sex, then shot outward toward her limbs.

Rocked by powerful aftershocks, she hung her head forward. She was temporarily sated and much more relaxed now. Ready to rejoin the party. But yanking down her shorts to her thighs, her husband obviously had other ideas.

He lined himself up to her soaked opening and pushed his way in on one not-so-gentle thrust. Standing this way, bent forward at the counter with her legs close together, she could feel every inch of him inside of her.

"My turn," he said into her ear. "You just stand there like a good girl and let me love you." He drove himself into her and took her hard, no longer seeking her pleasure but his own.

That didn't matter to her body, though. Every thrust sent her climbing higher toward another release. "I'm going to come again."

His teeth sank into her earlobe. "If you come, I'll have to punish you later."

She was the worst submissive ever.

Or maybe the best.

Guess it depended on how you looked at it.

Because the words only managed to act like fuel to a flame. She didn't just come. She detonated. Her inner walls clamped down on his cock, over and over in waves so pleasurable, Ryder had to cover her mouth with his hand to keep her from alerting all their guests with her screams.

Two more thrusts and Ryder groaned into the back of her neck. She could feel his cock twitching inside of her with each powerful spurt of come.

Mindful of their company, he didn't pause before withdrawing from her body and zipping them both up. He flipped her around and gave her a passionate kiss. "Don't think I'm going to forget you're due a punishment."

She smiled up at him. "Oh no. Not a spanking," she said sarcastically.

"You know, it's not a punishment if you enjoy it."

She shrugged. "Okay. I'll just pretend the next time you bend me over my desk and spank me that I don't like it."

After resigning from her job at McKay, she took over Novateur's sales and marketing duties from Ryder so that he could remain focused on software and hardware design. She loved that she was not only able to work with her husband, but she could also bring Maddox into work with them now and then.

At some point, Tristan and Isabella would move back to the city after she graduated and he'd likely return to his position as head of sales, but for now, she was happy with this arrangement.

Besides, at the rate Novateur was growing, even without manufacturing completely autonomous kitchens, they were headed toward needing all the employees they could manage. It wouldn't surprise her if they had to hire additional people soon to keep up with the business.

She enjoyed it being just the two of them, she and Ryder, working together. They tended to keep long hours during the week, but thankfully they'd hired a nanny who Maddox adored. When they came home each day, they'd devote a few hours to their son, and then when he fell asleep for the night, she and Ryder would connect not as coworkers, but as lovers and husband and wife, down in the playroom or in their bedroom.

Their scenes always began with a spanking. It didn't matter if Ryder used his hand, a paddle, a crop, or something more imaginative, but the second he made contact with her ass, all the stress melted away.

She didn't know why it helped, but it did.

Guess she was just wired that way.

She'd stopped questioning it.

She reached up and placed a hand on her husband's cheek. "Did you get in touch with Finn?"

Ryder's lips turned up in a small smile, but she didn't

miss the sadness lingering behind it. "He sends his love. Hopes Maddox enjoys his gift."

They hadn't seen him since the night Ciara had died.

But he did check in once a month. He wouldn't tell them where he was, but they'd received a Christmas card from him with a postmark from Maryland.

She hoped wherever he was, he found the kind of peace that she and Ryder had found.

Jane threw her arms around Ryder's waist and smiled up at him. "What one-year-old wouldn't enjoy his very own train to ride on?"

Between the Lancasters, Lawsons, and Agostos, Maddox would never want for anything. She and Ryder might not have much of a biological family, but they had created their own. And once Dreama beat her depression and returned to the land of the living, she would take her rightful place as Maddox's aunt.

"Did Finn say when he's coming home?" she asked.

"No. Still won't even tell me where he is." He sighed and frustration radiated off him. "It's been months and all I get is a phone call every now and then. I'm this close to hiring Wyatt to find him for me so I can go drag him back here."

They'd met Wyatt Agosto, Dreama's cousin, while visiting Dreama in the hospital. He was young, around Jane's age, and had just opened his own private detective agency. Ryder took an instant liking to him and had hired him to find out if there was any credibility to Keane's assertion that he had another son somewhere out there.

For now, they were keeping the information to themselves.

Not even Finn knew.

Jane stroked Ryder's arm. "After everything that happened, he's going through a rough time."

"That's why he needs his family. Hell, you lost your mother. Finn and I lost our father. He's not the only one who's grieving."

"But it's different. We have each other to rely on." She rested her head on his chest. "I can't imagine what it would be like if I ever lost you."

He kissed the top of her head. "You don't have to. I'm not going anywhere and neither are you. You, me, Maddox... we're a family."

She tilted her head up and smiled. "Now is probably a good time to tell you that in seven months, our family is going to be one bigger."

His eyes popped wide. "You're pregnant?"

"About eight weeks. I wasn't sure, so I took a test just before the guests arrived. I was going to wait—"

He dropped to his knees and pressed a gentle kiss to her lower abdomen. When he looked up at her, his eyes appeared a bit misty. Not that he'd ever admit to it. "Whatever you need this time, I'm here for you. I promise you, you'll never be alone again."

The screen door leading to the backyard slammed against the wall and Isabella appeared in the kitchen. "Hey, Jane..." Seeing Ryder on his knees, she turned as red as her hair. "Oops, sorry to interrupt. I just wanted to let you know Tristan and I managed to get Maddox in the high chair, so he's ready for his cake."

"Oh, you didn't..." She gestured to Ryder, who was laughing his ass off. "I mean we weren't..." She smiled at her friend. "We'll be right there."

As Isabella went back outside, Ryder's cell rang, which was odd since everyone who mattered, other than Finn, was currently in their yard. She was even more surprised when he answered it.

While he listened to whoever was on the other end, Jane grabbed everything else they needed to take outside. Ryder didn't say much and the call lasted less than a minute.

He stared at her in shock. "That was Wyatt. He's got a lead. My father was telling the truth." Running his fingers through his hair, he blew out a breath. "I have another brother."

"Wyatt found him?"

"No. Apparently, he was adopted. Wyatt hasn't been able to trace him yet, but he's confident he will." He shook his head. "I can't believe it."

Once he got over his shock, he'd see this was a good thing. Both of them had spent their lives without a family. They understood what a precious gift it was.

She covered her belly with her hand. "Looks like our family will be growing in more ways than one. How 'bout we go sing happy birthday to our son and watch him eat cake for the first time?"

Ryder leaned forward and kissed her tenderly.

On this day a year ago, her life had changed irrevocably for the better.

She couldn't wait to see what the next year had in store for them.

About the Author

A sucker for a happy ending, Shelly Bell writes sensual romance and erotic thrillers. She began writing upon the insistence of her husband, who dragged her to the store and bought her a laptop. When she's not working her day job, taking care of her family, or writing, you'll find her reading the latest romance.

Learn more at:
ShellyBellBooks.com
Twitter @ShellyBell987
Facebook.com/ShellyBellBooks

Don't miss the thrilling, suspenseful
next installment of
Shelly Bell's Forbidden Lovers series!

For His Pleasure

Available Winter 2018